Pluto in Furs

Edited by Scott Dwyer

Pluto In Furs: Tales of Diseased Desires and Seductive Horrors

Copyright ©2019 by Scott Dwyer
Cover Art by Matthew Revert
Formatting by Justin A. Burnett
A Plutonian Press Publication
www.theplutonian.com
ISBN 9781074611736

Table of Contents

An Abysmal Masochism

Scott Dwyer

The erotic and the horrific. Both are intimately tied to the body. Both thrive in the shadows and the dark. Both transcend the banal and the everyday, but rarely are they seen as related when it comes to literature. It is much more comfortable to keep them in their separate domains. But if we are honest, the two most fetishistic literary genres are horror and erotica, trafficking with private obsessions and secret desires. Certainly, they are the most misunderstood of literary genres, judged by their lowest common denominators and seen as cheap thrill entertainments. To most, some flashes of breasts and the repeating of the word "fuck" is the definition of erotica. Whereas in horror, to most, a monster jumping out to say "boo," only to be defeated by a hero, restoring normalcy with a cross or a sword, is the pleasure sought within. But there are those who desire more from their fiction. Where some see maybe horror, maybe erotica, as a relaxing night of reading, others seek transcendence; they seek a deep delve into the stuff of the flesh and its tenebrous existence.

On their own, what do these genres entail? Erotica is the literature of desire. Erotica concerns itself with the tease and the push. The not giving you quite what you want and making you wait for it, then giving you more than you were expecting. It sees the sexual drive as the hidden motivator of everything outside it, an invisible force that manipulates all living things. By proxy, it is also troubled subconsciously by the death of the flesh, and the urge of the sexual drive to overcome death. It shows the flesh in infinite combinations, all the infinite variations of partners and perversions. Horror, on the other hand, concerns itself with the aberrations and the abominations of existence. Horror makes us question all things and then shows us that life is even more nightmarish than we thought. It shows us existence as slow rot, identity as strange hallucination, the world as a mass graveyard. Horror does not care about the everyday failures and brutalities of life. Horror is concerned with twisting what you see as existence in ever new and even more nightmarish ways. Both genres represent an escape from the trivialities of life: in the case of erotica, a sense of unending desire, in the case of horror, a sense of inescapable dread. Erotica and horror are twins; one is the poetry of the life urge, one is the poetry of the death urge.

So then, what is erotic horror? Taken together, the erotic and the horrific are strange bedfellows. To answer this question, we need to look at why some people are drawn to the horror genre, and what it is they seek within. First off, erotic horror is horror without the need to conceal its intent. While it can be, it is not mainly a device for things like social commentary, philosophical musings, or cheap roller coaster ride thrills. Erotic horror is a purpose in and of itself, and for those who find meaning and satisfaction in it. But why not just call it "horror," why add the "erotic" into this? Because of the stimulating effect horror has on its most obsessive readers. Is erotic horror meant to be sexual stimulating? No, erotic horror does not seek to stimulate a sexual response, at least not fully. When horror is functioning at its highest level, at the peaks of the nightmarish and the unnerving, it produces an almost orgasmic response in the reader. In erotic horror, all the frightening things in life: death, the dark, the inhuman, are made beautiful, a dark poetry that elicits an orgasmic rapture. But only a rapture in a nihilistic way, only an orgasmic response in a nonsexual way. So, to be clear: why erotic horror? It is the mix of desire for terrible insights, in the obsessive perverting over and over again of the human form, and the pleasure derived from nightmare. In erotic horror, night becomes blinding and death becomes a banquet of delights.

To end, let us look at some precursors to what we would consider modern erotic horror. First the myth of Hades and Persephone. Classically told, Persephone was a goddess of spring who was captured by the lord of the underworld, Hades, also known as Pluto, to be his bride. Her beauty was so exquisite it caught the god of the dead's attention and he came up from his subterranean realm and took her from her sunlit world of innocence and abducted her to his kingdom of darkness. At least this is how the story has reached us thousands of year later, but, like all tales, each time the story is retold, it becomes safer, staler. What if we look at the myth afresh? Maybe the myth of Persephone was one of the original tales of erotic horror? Maybe Persephone was not an unwilling victim, but a willful debutante? What if Persephone longed for dark pleasures, wanted to see what terrible hands awaited to caress her in the chthonic lands? To see what ebon landscapes and what lurid bodies writhed and wailed in the darkness? Who better to represent both the burgeoning eroticism and black rot of life? Persephone is both the goddess of flowers and the queen of the dead, and maybe her kingdom of rotting bones intertwined with black flowers is where those seeking the erotic and the horrific shall find their home.

Now let us look at Sacher-Masoch, the author of the classic erotic novel *Venus In Furs*. Sa-cher-Masoch was a man who lived his life in pursuit of a woman who would enrapture and seduce him to the point of absolute worship. His highest ideal was in devoting his life to a woman who would ravage him with her cruelty and her sexuality. His novel *Venus in Furs* is this delirious and poetic novel of whips and humiliations, goddesses in furs and boots. Women scared and awed Sacher-Masoch, and he spent his life worshipping them and paying them devotion with his writing. The word masochism is derived from his name, a word that expresses the desire to derive pleasure from what harms you. And I think this masochism can also be found in horror. Taking what is frightening and inhuman and making a poetry of it, of making it unreal and worshipping it. Maybe the horror genre should be more properly considered a genre of a kind of dark devotion, its readers longing for and seeking abysmal sights that will ravish them to the core of their being. May we all descend into an abysmal masochism.

The Tangible Universe

Jeffrey Thomas

With his fingertips Gerber felt at the hard carbuncle that had formed in his left underarm, palpated it as if it were a misplaced testicle or a miniature breast, and said under his breath to the mirror, "Oh no."

It must be happening again. It had started a little differently the last time, though; it appeared this time it was skipping the rash stage.

In his estimation, the infection had begun the first time like this:

He had been noticing, after showering each day before work, that he was losing a distressing amount of hair, and he'd naturally thought it was from his head...until finally he'd noticed his underarm hair had radically thinned out. He was in his fifties now, and knew that as men aged their testosterone level decreased, which could lead to the loss of body hair. This in itself didn't bother him; in fact, he hoped this change would also decrease the constant background grumblings of his libido. After all, being in his fifties, it was harder and harder to feed that insistent beast. Not to mention that, having indulged the beast religiously for the past thirty-plus years in such a wide variety of ways – to the point where he had forsaken marriage for its sake – the thing had become easily dissatisfied...howled for ever more diverse flavors to stimulate its appetite.

One morning Gerber ran out of his preferred deodorant, one which like his hand soap and shaving cream was designed for sensitive skin. In one of the drawers of a chest in his bathroom he discovered a deodorant left by a former lover – a married woman a few years older than himself, into shibari – whom he'd met on a sex hookup website and seen for several months. The deodorant's scent was strong but not unpleasant, so he rubbed it on. Almost instantly he felt the skin of his left underarm burning. In no time, a painful and itchy red rash developed there. Gerber guessed that an inflammation had begun in the follicles from which he had shed his underarm hair, an inflammation that became an infection.

For just as quickly, on the heels of the rash came an outbreak of what at first seemed like pimples or insect bites, but which soon swelled into nodules, like eggs laid under his skin, the largest of them in fact the size of a quail's egg.

When this profusion of boils ended up bursting – now resembling makeup effects from some bad horror film – pus and blood would run down his side from the open abscesses so that he had to tape gauze over them and wear dark shirts to work. At this point, he went to see his primary care physician.

It was methicillin-resistant Staphylococcus aureus – MRSA – and his doctor prescribed antibiotics. Fortunately, these proved effective and the infection cleared up soon enough, rather surprisingly leaving no scars he could discern. Still, he'd been told that another outbreak was always possible.

So now, apparently, here it was.

He debated making an appointment again with his doctor, but decided to wait just a little longer to see how it played out. He didn't relish another visit to her. His doctor was a woman and he'd been meaning to find a new PCP, though he'd been seeing her for years and she knew his history well. His history of STDs all too well. Her thinly disguised jokes about his habits grated on him, though in her examination room he would chuckle along with her. It was bad enough she'd see the ever-growing white sphere of his belly and ask if he were pregnant, without her joking – when he admitted he'd just returned from another vacation to Thailand – if he'd brought back another *souvenir* this time.

Ha ha ha, Gerber thought. *I'm glad you're so easily satisfied by sticking your finger up rectums to*

check the prostates of sad old guys like me. Some of us,
though, require more.

He'd learned of the establishment through a thread
on the web site Reddit. He preferred investigating
places that were less publicly advertised, but then
this particular thread on the popular site had
thankfully not garnered much attention. Probably
that was due to the topic's vague subject heading:
A Curious Little Museum of Anomalous Growths.

It had been just the kind of heading that
would pique his interest. Gerber trawled more web
sites than this in search of such enticements.

On his various computers, over the years, he
had saved countless images of humans who were
beyond the norm; who stood out, who shone, like a
column of black light in the prosaic daytime. Humans not more highly evolved, nor devolved
(though he fantasized about fucking the poor ape-
like Julia Pastrana), but *other* evolved. Dead-ended
in their one-person race. He had pursued and
courted numerous such entities over the years, and
in his diligence had been rewarded by meeting
with a fraction of them; had fucked or been fucked
by them.

Several amputees. (One of them, a boy of
eighteen, had penetrated him anally with the
stump of his arm.) A beautiful young Indonesian

woman covered from scalp to sole in large, hairy black moles. A wheelchair-bound young woman with long blond hair and hardened porcelain-like skin, who suffered systemic scleroderma. A Pakistani woman whose face had been burned with acid, leaving her with only one eye. Of course, several gorgeous Thai transgendered women. One of them had given him her penis, in a little satin-lined box, and he'd sworn he'd take it home with him but he'd been afraid of it being discovered by customs on his return flight so he'd regretfully disposed of it in a common trash receptacle (*No, doctor, had to get rid of that souvenir*), though he'd just sent her and her family $200 as an early Christmas gift and he hoped to visit her again someday soon.

He eventually tracked down a phone number for the *Curious Little Museum of Anomalous Growths* and called...spoke with a man who sounded just like one of his revoltingly boring coworkers who played country music in their work areas and talked incessantly about sports and cars. "Sure, buddy!" this man said to him. "You can come down anytime...Christ, we're close, we're neighbors. I'm surprised you never found us before this."

"Can I come tonight...after I get out of work? Say, five-thirty? Is that too late?"

"Oh hell no, buddy. We can arrange a showing any time, as long as we know ahead. Around the clock...we're here for *you*."

10

The place *was* close; he swore he'd been by it a few times in his travels, could almost recall wondering in the past what it was. An abandoned shed or garage, maybe? Part of what made it seem memorable was that the structure, snugged up right by the side of this woodsy back road, lay crouched in a depressed area so that its mossy roof was almost level with the guardrail.

Gerber nosed his car off a little side road, descended an unpaved ramp until he found himself on level with the longish little building, with its spotty gray shingles and pale green vinyl siding. There was no parking lot; he simply pulled up in front of the shed-or-garage, his the only vehicle but for one. When he got out of his car, he heard another car whoosh past on the road above. He felt like he had passed through a veil, into another realm, from which he could see but not be seen.

He rapped on the little building's door, and soon enough it opened. In the threshold stood a man even more barrel-bellied and balding than himself, who grinned and chirped, "Heyyy – you Ken?"

That was the false name Gerber had given. "Yes," he said, smiling a smile that twitched in its stapled-up corners.

"Good to meet you man, good to meet you. I'm Burl." This Burl person pumped his hand. "So, hey, nice mild night for the season, huh? You got your Christmas shopping done? It's coming right up!"

"Yes," Gerber said, who in his life had only that transgendered beauty in Thailand, who had gifted him, reverently, with her penis. One night he had chatted, via webcam, with her and her brother and the brother's cute children. That had been nice. He had felt a weird, alien warmth that night.

"Okay," Burl said to him, "so...that'll be five hundred dollars, even. Or, odd, as it were...ha. It's a great deal, given how unique our exhibit is. That gives you fifteen minutes of anything you want, uninterrupted. Though, uh, no over-the-top rough-ness, of course. In fact, I'll give you one hundred percent privacy and stay outside here smoking cig-arettes and looking at naughty stuff on my phone."

Gerber was curious what constituted "naughty" for Burl, but not enough to ask. He dug from his wallet five hundred-dollar bills he'd with-drawn from his bank today for this purpose, the bills so crisp and fake-seeming they reminded him of the "hell money" some Chinese burned as offer-ings to the dead. Maintaining his affixed smile, he handed these to Burl and said, "Merry Christmas."

When he entered the little building, left alone by the too-gregarious ticket taker or barker or proprietor or whatever he was, Gerber was reminded of the red light district of Amsterdam. Which – given that he had no wife or children to answer to – he had visited on one of his many vacations from the company he'd long worked for.

The light inside the shed-or-garage was subdued. The smell, boxed within, was less subdued. Another person would be repulsed, he supposed...but already he was enticed. This complex, intense miasma of exposed and inadequately washed flesh was *real*, not something one could experience through smart phone or PC.

The shed's interior was one longish room. There were no windows displaying human wares, as in Amsterdam, but there were holes.

Holes in one long wall of plywood, which had been painted black. Adhered to this black wall, and glowing in the purple radiance of evenly-spaced backlight bulbs overhead, were constellations of stars that filled the gulf of space between the openings in the plywood. Stuck to the black paint: countless small gold stars such as a child might be rewarded with at school for good behavior, but mixed in with bigger glittery stars, and even holographic star stickers.

Thus, the orbs of flesh that pressed out through the various-sized circular holes in the plywood – the owners of these orbs hidden on the other side of the wall – were like planets, worlds of raw flesh, that hung suspended in the cosmos. A universe of organic spheres.

Oh, Gerber thought, standing at the start of

this ghost train corridor...this miniature solar system. *Ohhh.* He was overwhelmed.

Where to begin, but with the first in the series of planets? Like some awestruck astronaut-explorer, he floated to it. Reverently, as if he were in some secret temple, visiting the first of a series of carven saints or similarly holy entities ensconced in niches in a wall.

Such a grand tumor! It was *huge!* But what was it? Gerber guessed an immense ovarian cyst. So smooth, like the pregnant belly of a giant fertility goddess. He reached out with quivering hands, placed them upon it, suppressed a sigh. He ran them over the vast sphere. *So smooth,* though marked with veins like great rivers meandering across this mysterious unnamed world. Did he detect an answering quiver through the majestic orb?

Oh, and the next one! How could he linger long at only one of these worlds?

This world had a face, like the man in the moon. Neurofibromatosis, Gerber guessed, and from the pigmentation and facial characteristics – however catastrophically deformed – he judged the face's owner to be an African American boy. If the boy's eyes were open, and watching him in turn, Gerber couldn't even tell for the grossly swollen aspect of the flesh. Again he put out his hands, felt at that grotesquely large face that was thrust out through one of the holes in the plywood firmament. His thumb, passing over a twisted balloon-bloated lower lip, smeared saliva. The mask-like giant face, as if familiar with this process and resigned to it, didn't even flinch at his probing fingers. Gerber was tempted to speak to the face, but no...*no*...that wouldn't be good. Despite the fiery explosions in childish space opera movies, there was no sound in space.

On to the next planet of meat.

Gerber couldn't be sure without seeing the body it was attached to, but he guessed – judging from photos he had found online and saved in his picture folders – that the third growth suspended in the void was a titanic set of testicles in their impossibly stretched pouch, afflicted with elephantiasis of the scrotum. He smiled in appreciation, ran his hands over the wrinkled leathery mass, like some gigantic walnut, but was again quickly drawn to the next exhibit.

A leg, this time, also monstrously bloated through what he assumed was elephantiasis. You could only tell what it was from the toes poking out through the end of the distended mass, with its taut rolls of heaped tissue. Reminding himself that he had paid five hundred hard-earned dollars for this experience, he bent down and sucked at one of those horny-nailed toes, then another. If the owner of that leg, on the other side of the plywood veil, moaned in pleasure or groaned in revulsion, Gerber couldn't hear it. For which he was grateful. Though he wanted this encounter to be *real* – not just photos on the net, surely not just a set of Photoshop illusions – he was thankful that he felt alone here. That there was no human interaction beyond his communion with the flesh.

Now, in moving on to the fifth hole, he had grown fully hard in his khaki trousers.

The openings were each a different size, each cut to accommodate its particular flesh planet. Were the holes widened accordingly, Gerber wondered, incrementally, as these growths increased in size over time? Surely, none of the growths *decreased*.

This next bulge, as big as a head in itself, was covered thickly in black hair. A monstrous boil or ulcer of the head? A brain tumor? Gerber gently, tenderly combed the greasy hair with his fingers. Did the beings behind the star-sprinkled blackness derive as much comfort from the contact as he did? At least, *something* gratifying beyond the money they no doubt shared?

There was a sixth and final world, near the end wall of the chamber.

What next? he wondered eagerly, as he prepared to turn away from the oily-haired mass he'd been massaging. A vivid red prolapsed rectum? A malignant, fungating phyllodes tumor, with open necrotic lesions that he might explore with tongue, with digits, with more?

But this last growth Gerber couldn't identify. At least, not what part of the body it might be attached to. Certainly, most of the profound smell in the room found its source here, and it was certainly large – second only to that ovarian cyst. It was a dark grayish-brown, though he didn't know if that was the normal pigmentation of the host, and gave the appearance of an immense brain. It wasn't a brain, of course, but the mass was deeply grooved with twisty convolutions that suggested the folds of the cerebral cortex.

Gerber rested his hands upon it delicately, almost tenderly, as if afraid to awaken someone slumbering. He slid his palms along it, teased his fingers into those dark fissures.

He could stand the tension no longer, and he knew his time here was limited. He undid his pants...freed himself.

Those dark fissures...

He wished he had been able to take photos of the exhibits with his phone, but he'd understood up front that this was forbidden. Burl hadn't asked to confiscate his device, however. Had Burl monitored his actions through his own phone, while pretending to look at "naughty" things, there being hidden security cameras in the shed?

Anyway, Gerber couldn't get the experience out of his head. It had spoken to him, resonated with him. At work the next day he had to go into the men's room at one point to pleasure himself for relief.

He had hoped to save enough money for another vacation; with the start of the new year he'd have four fresh weeks of vacation time. But, now he knew he must go visit the *Curious Little Museum of*

Anomalous Growths again soon. Maybe even as soon as tonight. He was almost sorry he'd already sent that $200 to his recent lover in Thailand.

What kept coming back to him, that day at work, was the beautiful *contrast* of the display. This made it, for him, an affecting work of art. The imagery of space – the cosmic and eternal – contrasting with the material orbs, fleshly rather than heavenly bodies, formed of transitory cells. Each a sad, flawed, ephemeral microcosm in the great macrocosm. Cut off not just from him but from each other, separate, incomplete; such a melancholy, lovely representation of human existence. Of its fundamental aloneness.

On his work PC, he logged into his online banking and saw that he had $1,437.57 in his checking account.

"You know," Burl told him, accepting the five one-hundred-dollar bills, "for a thousand you could do thirty minutes. Just sayin'."

"This will do for tonight," Gerber replied.

It was colder than the night before, more seasonable for mid-December. When Gerber had pulled up, Burl had been sitting inside his car with the engine running, the red glow of his taillights painting the trunks of nearby trees and turning his car's exhaust into churning red clouds, like blood billowing underwater. Burl unlocked the door to the green shed, waved for Gerber to go on and enter, then retreated to his heated vehicle.

It was chilly inside the shed, too, but Gerber heard a few space heaters running, unseen, doubtlessly on the other side of the black-painted plywood wall.

Things progressed much as they had the night before, as Gerber moved from one exhibit to the next, lingering just long enough to admire each with his gaze and touch. Again, by the time he reached the final world in this human solar system, he was ready to burst. He briefly considered going back to the huge, sagging rubbery face of the youth with neurofibromatosis, but he was just too beguiled by the weird alien quality of that last, unidentified, brain-like mass. He let his pants slither down his legs, took hold of its sides in both hands, and nestled into one of its coiled folds.

As he did so, he felt the mass give a small but unmistakable jolt, and did he hear a muffled moan behind the plywood wall, over the hum of the space heaters? It caused him to imagine someone groaning while in the midst of a fever, or troubling dream.

When Gerber emerged, Burl was standing there smoking a cigarette, and pocketed his phone quickly. "You went a few minutes over, there, Ken, but I'll let it pass. Christmas and all."

"Thank you," Gerber said. "Sorry about that."

"I forgot to warn you to be a little gentle with

Lola. She hasn't been doing well."

"Lola?"

"The last one."

"Oh." Her suspected more than ever that Burl monitored the proceedings within the *Curious Little Museum of Anomalous Growths* via his phone. Or was that how he satisfied *his* appetite? Gerber asked, "Um, so what's the deal with her?"

"Sorry, Ken...can't give away personal information about these...about the exhibits. I shouldn't even have said that name."

"I understand," Gerber said.

"Anyway, goodnight. Hope to see you again!"

Gerber nodded, continued past him toward his car. He was certain Burl would.

Gerber felt that the best pleasures bring torment, like a ghastly half-developed twin conjoined to a beautiful host. It was all about the contrast.

At work the next day, at home the next night, he couldn't get the museum out of his thoughts. He saw everything else around him through the superimposed image of the shed, as seen from the exterior, and especially through images of its interior, as if trying to view his life through transparent photographic slides.

The museum tantalized him, called to him, a

deformed siren basking on rocks while rotting in the sun. Still, he resisted its call the next night after his second visit. His money was dwindling and he was paid on a biweekly basis; he wouldn't get a paycheck again until Friday after this.

He lay in bed, unable to sleep until after he'd relieved himself manually while paging through one of his favorite books, a heavily illustrated hardcover edition of Gould and Pyle's 1896 classic *Anomalies and Curiosities of Medicine*.

The next day at work, his fixation was unabated. It was this idea of *contrast* that was working at him. Maybe Burl had set it in motion by saying the name of the person who, from beyond the barrier, presented herself as the ultimate world in the astronomical display. He had her name, her sex. He found himself wondering more and more about this person. How old was she? What race was she? If her health was failing, what was the cause of her affliction? She was no longer merely some anonymous blob of tissue.

In a way, at first he had resented this. It impinged on the mystery, compromised the artwork's vision. Instead of the growths being unwanted attachments to human beings, the human beings were for him unwanted attachments to the growths.

But the more he turned her name over and over in his mind...*Lola, Lola*...like a rock polished in a tumbler, and the more he tried to envision her, the more strongly he felt that what made such growths so striking was the contrast between them and the bodies that bore them. For really, what was the delicious frisson of a tumor without a host? Yes, he still very much appreciated the artistic presentation of the exhibits in the *Curious Little Museum of Anomalous Growths*, the contrast between the transitory and the eternal, the material and the void, the microcosm and macrocosm. But now what he ached to have revealed to him was the human bodies that offset these grotesque anomalies. For instance, he recalled the lovely porcelain skin of his lover, of some years back, with systemic scleroderma. And aside from the hairy black melanocytic nevi that had been sprinkled all across the face and body of his young Indonesian lover – like a photographic negative of stars in space – that face and body had been very beautiful in form.

He began to imagine Lola as beautiful, as well. He now wanted to see her huge, dark, brain-like growth not contrasted against the plywood's false universe, but contrasted against her own body. Yin no longer divided from yang.

He checked his bank balance. After having bought gas and for two days coffee on his way to work, he only had $920.51. Not enough for a half hour...but enough for another fifteen minutes, with over $400 to last him until his next paycheck. Though, he'd need his next paycheck for January's rent, but he couldn't worry about that right now.

The question, he knew, was whether he could coax Burl into letting him view the subjects who hid behind the plywood. Whether he could get

Burl to have them come out into the hallway...exposing to him their full, naked forms. Like a pantheon of disfigured gods in manifestation against that glittering starfield.

He phoned Burl...arranged for another fifteen minutes that night. He couldn't find a way to frame his request, however. He'd have to think of a way in the hours that remained between now and then.

Over the phone Burl wasn't his usual affable self – he sounded subdued, distracted – but he murmured to Gerber, "Okay, Ken, see you tonight, then."

A light snow was falling, like dead skin cells shed from the void yawning overhead. Gerber got out of his car, crunched across the cold ground to where Burl stood in front of the long green shed, a cigarette in one hand and a plastic bottle of cheap vodka in the other.

"Oh, hey, brother!" Burl said, in an imitation of his usual self. Up close, though it was dark, Gerber saw tears glistening on the man's ruddy cheeks. "Celebrating the New Year a little early, I guess. You want a swig?" He proffered the bottle.

"No thanks, I don't drink."

"Ah, the man's a saint! *A saint!*" Burl joked. "I should take after you."

"Is everything all right?" Gerber didn't really want to know, but if he meant to ask a favor of the man...

"Oh God," Burl slurred. His lower lip quivered like a child's. "Lola passed last night."

"Lola..."

Burl placed a hand on his arm, the hand that held the cigarette. "It's not your fault, man. You had nothing to do with it. She was on her way already."

"Oh my God," Gerber said, at a loss. Not knowing if he felt mournful himself, or only sympathy for the other man. "I'm so sorry." He wanted to ask what Lola had been to Burl, but again, didn't truly want to know. He only knew what his fantasy of Lola, a fantasy conjoined to her real-world mass of flesh, had begun to be for him.

"But go on in, go on," Burl urged him. "I don't mean to hold you up. The show must go on, right?" He gave a brave smile.

Gerber produced his five hundred dollars, handed them over. He began to open his mouth to ask Burl his special request, but Burl was already turning away, sobs no longer contained, shoulders shaking, headed with his vodka toward his car. And anyway, Gerber was still digesting the news about Lola. Did this change things for him?

The show must go on, Burl had said. Gerber turned toward the shed and found Burl had already unlocked its door.

The miniature universe, foreshortened, like a wormhole enticing him to enter it. He walked into it, slowly. Past the moon-like ovarian cyst, this time without pausing to touch it. Past the heavy mask-like face, maybe watching him. Past the impressive boulder of testicles. Past the leg, like a monstrous swollen grub. Past the hairy mass like the head of a faceless crowning baby. On to...

Where the brain-like mass had bulged out into the hallway, there was only a large, perfectly circular hole cut into the plywood.

Gerber didn't know if Burl was presently watching him through security cameras; he didn't care. He withdrew his phone, turned on its flashlight feature, stepped close and shone its beam through the hole, into the beyond.

He had wondered if behind the plywood there was another long single room, where the museum's subjects all stood (or were seated, or propped?) within view of each other, for company. Instead, what he found was an individual unit, like his cubicle at work, but even more private. Its walls, and ceiling, and floor were all painted black...but minus the stars that were stuck to the wall outside. A pocket universe. A pocket, now, of nothingness.

Gerber looked behind him, down the corridor back toward the door, yet he was still alone but for that silent row of anomalies. He looked back to the portal before him.

He was in his fifties now, not some young man, and not in the best of shape, but he had determination on his side. He inserted his extended arms and then his head through the hole, squeezed his torso through. His hands braced themselves upon the floor and he walked himself further inside, ignoring the way the bottom curve of the circle scraped his belly through his shirt. When he was far enough inside, he bent one leg, pulled it through with a grimace, planted his foot against the floor. He dragged his other leg in, and then spun and sat down hard with his arms propping him up, looking back out through the hole he had just passed through in something like reverse birth.

There was a thin mattress in here. Nothing else but that, and the bottled up smell of Lola that made him want to retch. That made him ache for her to join him on that meager mattress.

After a while Gerber felt behind him, took hold of the edge of the mattress, pulled it a little closer to him. He shifted to sit upon that. Despite its thinness, he felt the urge to curl up upon the mattress, on his side. He considered this impulse for some time, growing dreamy, until he saw a head appear as an eclipse in the hole into the corridor.

The head was in silhouette, but he recognized Burl's voice. The man sounded gentle, understanding, not like he was chiding him.

Burl said, "You going to come out of there, brother?" He waited a few moments, and when Gerber didn't respond, he said, "It's okay...you want to stay a while? It's okay." He backed away from the hole, backed into the opposite wall, slid down to sit on the floor and unscrewed the cap of his vodka bottle. Before he took a gulp from it, he said in a hitching voice, "Where else we all going to go, huh? This is all we got."

Gerber awoke, and inwardly groaned. Another work day. *Christ*, he'd been working nonstop since he was a teenager, and what did he have to show for it really?

And then he remembered, his memory jogged by the stink, where he was.

He propped himself up, looked toward the plywood wall.

Burl had replaced this section of the wall. The former large hole had been replaced in this new section by a much smaller hole. But Gerber trusted that in time, appropriately, Burl would enlarge the new opening.

He realized what had awakened him. Burl had been rapping lightly, respectfully, upon the outer wall. The man put one eye close to the hole, and said, "Hey, Ken. We have a customer coming in a few minutes. You ready, brother?"

Gerber grunted, pushed himself to his feet. The room was warm, like a womb; Burl had put a space heater into one corner, at his request. He came close to the hole and muttered, "I'm ready."

Burl withdrew. Gerber heard him walk away, down the corridor. When Burl opened the shed's door to go outside and greet their guest, Gerber thought he could hear a car's wheels crunching across thick snow. It must be January now.

Gerber grew ready. He peeled off his stained white undershirt, tossed it behind him onto his mattress. He bent his left arm up so that his hand gripped the right side of his head, and pressed himself close to the hole...so that someone on the other side would see framed within its circle the cluster of great blisters, fruit rotting on the vine, that in bursting sent viscous streams of blood and pus running down Gerber's side like star jelly.

With Shining Gifts That Took All Eyes

Mike Allen

Candace feels no breeze, though the silhouette of the houseplant shimmies behind the window curtain, the long fronds of its leaves wriggling like legs. That curtain should flutter with equal agitation, but it hangs motionless. Candace shudders, goose pimples stippling her arms.

"Donny?" she calls. "Could you shut the window?"

She could have sworn she heard him moving around in his home office, saw a brief dimming cross the wall as he eclipsed a lamp while fussing with his chair. Candace hold herself still, even holds her breath. All is still with the office save the movement of the leaves. No lethargic mutter of acknowledgement answers her, no floorboards creaking as a body's weight shifts. Only minutes ago, it seems, the time between spliced away by sleep, his hands had pushed back her thighs, and a wild notion takes her that his warm touch had been deception, a ruse carried out by a ghost.

Her wet hair wrapped in a towel, she cinches her robe tighter and steps out of the steam cloud emerging through the bathroom door. Immediately she regrets it. The cold deepens, the goose pimples spreading up her arms to her neck. The plant sways as if it were a palm tree in a storm.

The chill is inexplicable as the animated plant. There's no sensation of air brushing her shower-damp skin. Not a peep from Donny when she calls his name again. He's sitting just out of view — how hard can it be for him to get up and close the window, it's right there behind him, not three feet from his chair.

The weight of his shoulders against her hips perhaps had masked a deception of a different sort. He's back to his usual self, easily distracted, prone to ignoring her. She takes a deep breath to repel the chill and her mounting impatience and walks into his office, which stands empty. Yet Donny was in here, somehow, and heard her, somehow, because the plant is gone from the window. She pulls the white gauze of the curtain aside, unveiling fog thick as cotton batting, the afternoon light diffused to gray.

A screen saver jitters on Donny's outdated monitor, a chubby eight-legged monster chewing away at a pastoral rendition of rolling hills. For a fleeting instant she conflates the monster's teeth with Donny's, the nips at her neck before he descended lower.

She used to find the animation funny, then tiresome — eight years and he's never switched it out. Now the cartoonish grossness grates on her.

At the other end of the house, a floorboard creaks. She slips to edge of calling Donny's name again, but stops herself, instinct counseling silence. She retreats in a slow creep, peers down the hall, across the darkened dining room, through an archway, into the room where she and Donny settle on a hand-me-down couch to watch the few shows they both enjoy on a flatscreen television that might well be the most expensive thing they own. Beyond the TV, behind drawn curtains, the silhouette of a houseplant waggles in the window.

An all-too-familiar pain taps behind her right eye, then presses, exerting a malevolent pressure. *Not now*, she implores. *Not now.*

Donny isn't in the living room. She can't fathom how he moved the plant.

This time, at least, air currents cause the curtain to ripple. Outside, children shriek. The dilemma clenches in her chest. She doesn't want the neighbor kids to see her wearing nothing but a robe, but if anything the house is colder yet and this window is definitely open. She hurries to it, discovers a two-foot gap between sash and sill, struggles with the reluctant latch as one of the shrill voices from across the street calls her name. In the fog, she can't tell which child spotted her. How inconveniently sharp his vision had to be.

As she tugs the latch abruptly loosens and the window slams shut so hard she fears broken glass. She cringes as if Donny slapped his hands together beside her ear, a stunt he loved to pull when they were younger, he loved making her shriek.

A sludge of pain flows down her spine into her belly. Confirmation a migraine is boiling up.

The same kid shrieks her name again. She flinches backward, something snags her bad ankle and her ungainly topple spills her onto the couch. She gasps at the twinge in her back, the cushions so worn that the front frame digs into her shoulders. Donny had pinned her that way once, in this same place, gripping her wrists, her back arched uncomfortably as he leaned to thrust his hips in her face. She had done what she had to do to get it over with, trying to concentrate on how his chest and belly tensed with each movement of her mouth, a sight she had enjoyed in other circumstances.

Why was she thinking of that now? Because the pain echoes through the years? Gaze level with the sill, she registers that the plant isn't in the window, wasn't there when she pulled it shut. Donny is messing with her somehow and not in a nice way. It must be that he's pissed at her still, because they need to go visit her sister in the rehab center and he doesn't want to. She doesn't want to either, but there's no hope for Chrystal at all if no one offers her a lifeline. He's told her that he understood this. He swore to her that he grokked that poor Chrystal was the only family she had left.

But Donny hasn't been that quick since he

hurt his back and he's not slender anymore. If he was taking out his aggression on her by moving that plant around, she for sure would have seen him do it.

A chair in the dining room slides across the hardwood floor. Her heart backflips. A tiny thunder rumbles in the empty room, like panicked cats scrambling. For an instant she really does believe she hears clumsy cat steps — but that can't be. Those cats she's remembering, two chunky monkeys from the same litter, one of them died months ago, the other one years ago. Candace does believe in ghosts, or that least the metaphor of regret they represent, but not in ones that vibrate floorboards with tangible weight and mass.

Debunking that notion sends the previous one floundering away. She and Donny weren't going to see her sister today, rehab ended five months ago and after Chrystal's release she'd gone right back to her drug-dealing, gun-fetishizing boyfriend. Donny had admirably refrained from saying *I told you so.*

Her memory, what had warped it so? Had the exertions of the morning given her a small stroke? The throbbing in her skull denied access to the answer.

Candace works third shift at a factory that assembles different sizes of syringes. She was showering in the afternoon because she slept in after her shift, she's sure of that. She can't remember if Donny was awake when she got home. Too tired to care, she'd crawled in bed next to him after stuffing in ear plugs to ward off his snoring, the sound exactly like the grunts of pigs rutting.

A morning that began just like hundreds of others, and what happened next intruded in her memory like it came from a different universe. His hand on her belly, under her shirt. His lips pecking at her cheek like a child's kisses, engaging full throated when she brought her mouth to meet his. The nips at her neck, the tongue at her nipples, tickling her navel, her knees pushed up to her breasts, his shoulders pressed against the backs of her thighs as he slid down further, started to suck on her, his fingernails stabbing her a little as he worked his way in, up to the knuckles of his index and middle finger. Eventually he would stop, climb back up her and push his way inside, except this time he didn't, he stayed down there, sucking, matching the staccato of her gasping breath. He had not gone at her that way in months, maybe in years. His hydrangea-blue eyes stayed focused on her face, his gaze meeting hers whenever she briefly opened eyes and bent her neck to watch what he was doing.

She lost herself so she doesn't remember when he stopped, or how. Nor will her memory confirm whether he was out of bed when she woke up, whether she actually saw him in his office when she got up to shower, or heard the clicks of keyboard and mouse.

Another chair shifts, and not only does she hear it, she sees it jerk away from the table. Several of the kids outside scream at once, the sounds coinciding with her own short shriek.

Her mind and heart race together. An animal found its way inside, a squirrel most likely. That's happened before, one crawled through a cracked window in the basement, a frightened and frightening homunculus in a dim, cramped space. Donny put sheets of cardboard over all the other basement windows and the creature followed the light out.

Again, she almost yells for him, but stops herself. He can't be in the house, by now he'd have shouted from wherever he was to ask what was going on. Maybe genuinely concerned, more likely cross at having his computer game interrupted, but at least he'd have made some sort of fuss.

Ergo, it was up to her to cope with the squirrel, possum, bird or — she shudders at the thought — rat. She does what she should have done in the first place: finds and flicks a light switch. The sun might be out, but you wouldn't know it from the gloom boxed in the house with her.

Nothing under the table but dust bunnies, and a hint of honeysuckle and lavender spoiled with the sourness of fermentation that she matches after a puzzled moment to the scent of the plant now missing from two windows.

She regrets more than ever that her botanical and horticultural courses in college are more than a decade past, and that she's been too preoccupied to dig through her books for the plant's identity. (Why has she been so distracted? She can't put her finger

on the why. In her mid-forties her powers of recollection have gone blurry in a manner not unlike her
mother's did in her final years, though with that
awful woman it was hard to tell where the onset of
dementia ended and maliciously selective re-edit-
ing of history began.)

The most curious thing about the plant —
which sported unremarkable white blossoms, the
tiny needle-like petals evoking miniature dande-
lion blooms — was that Donny had insisted on
bringing it home when they happened across it
during an exercise hike, one where he had been unusually considerate of her weak ankles, maintaining a pace she could match without growing
winded and sweat-soaked, her hips and knees
burning.

Usually, she would stop the hikes to investigate a bush, flower or fungus beside the trail, and
he huffed and practically stamped his feet a toddler
until they started moving again. When he hiked,
much like when he fucked, he tended to care only
about the act itself: the forward motion through uneven but beautiful terrain, which he made little to
no effort to take in as he traversed it. Finishing the
trail for the sake of finishing took precedence. The
discovery of this plant caused one of the most dra-
matic role reversals in their sixteen years of marriage.

That Saturday afternoon on Poor Mountain,
she had walked ahead almost twenty yards before
she noticed that he was no longer at her shoulder,
that only one set of footsteps disturbed the fallen

leaves.

Donny had stalled at a bend, his gray-flecked beard emphasizing the direction of his gaze as he focused on something spied between two enormous rocks that in truth were one rock split asunder by some prehistoric upheaval. Once he had caught her eye, he pointed at the slope between trail and cleft. *Any poison ivy?* He trusted her to spot it — no matter how many times she showed him what it looked like, he always forgot.

Candace doubled back, picking her way carefully as he tapped his hiking-booted toe in mounting impatience.

Within the dagger-shaped split in the rock grew the ugliest tree Candace had ever seen, its branches curled in unnatural fashions, curving upward until they looped back in toward the gnarled trunk, reminding her of sea anemones or the spirals formed by nesting centipedes. Reinforcing that grotesque impression, the long fronds of its leaves also curled strangely, down instead of up, paired evenly like arthropod legs along the lengths of the branches. She could easily picture those branches as worm-like bodies that could straighten and crawl away at any moment. They had walked this path dozens upon dozens of times, but she had never noticed this rock or this tree, as if an egg of massive dimensions had surfaced from the substance of the mountain and hatched a frilly sea worm of leviathan scale. Imagining this, Candace forgot Donny's question until he prodded her. *Well?*

She gave him the all clear. He trotted straight at the creepy tree and dropped to one knee in front of it as if swearing fealty. Hurrying to catch up, a root snagged her ankle and sent her, too, to one knee. Only a miracle kept her from slamming face-first into the rock.

Donny didn't turn his head at her shouted curse. He had unslung his backpack from his shoulders. *Can I have your spade?* he asked as if she hadn't just come within an inch of having her head cracked open.

Nor was he paying attention to the tree. All his focus was devoted to a small plant sprouted between two knobby roots. The sight of the flower up close prevented her from snapping at him, because, unassuming though it was, she didn't recognize it as any species she'd ever studied. Her own curiosity welled up, though the odd flower accounted for only part of it. (And frankly, she'd been more than happy to spare herself his inevitable defensive retort and the plaintive whine that would taint his raised voice as he made some balderdash excuse.)

Your spade? he asked again. She wanted to say, *You should let me do that*, but a part of her wanted to see whether the many times he'd observed her collecting samples had somehow rubbed off. The only collectibles he ordinarily got this excited over were bonus treasures in computer games.

She complied, and he dug out the plant with a care that made her proud. It proved to have more roots than she expected for something so small, the thickest of which he severed with the spade's serrated edge.

A flash of color from above snapped her head up as if pulled by a string. This close, the branches reminded her even more of curled centipedes, but she spied nothing to explain the splotch in her peripheral vision, dismissed it as a random sunspot floating behind her eyelids.

Meanwhile, Donny was gingerly stowing his new find into his backpack. As sometimes happened, her mouth bypassed her reservations. *I've never seen you this interested in a plant.* The subtext of his resentment of her interests sharpened her words. *What's got you so fascinated?*

He shrugged. *I've never seen one single plant have so many different-colored flowers.*

He was making fun of her. *You don't have to be that way, I just asked you a question.*

I answered. He stood up, and for a moment his hydrangea-blue eyes met hers, gorgeous as jewels but fixated somewhere other than on her.

I've never seen a tree like that, she said, and pointed, but he was already walking back to the trail.

You got a pot to fit it in? he called back. Immediately she'd known who would really be taking care of this plant. He was back to his subtly infuriating usual, walking a little too fast for her to easily catch up.

As Candace reached the trail a burst of wind nearly yanked her over, whipping her hair to one side and tugging at her backpack — it really felt like someone had grabbed hold and pulled. This same wind affected that strange tree in the most unsettling way — it appeared to shrink backward into the rock cleft, like the sea worm she had imagined, withdrawing tentacles into its burrow under the sand.

Donny never said another word about the plant, even after she potted it and set the pot in the sill of his home office. As she packed its pudgy roots in the pot, she turned it this way and that, scanning for any sign of iridescence that explained his odd remark about color. The flowers, already wilting, remained resolutely white.

If she gave away that she was allotting any additional thought to his deadpan sarcasm, he'd take the opportunity to snicker at her, so she declined to let him have that opportunity. If he so much as curled his lips in a patronizing smile, she'd long to claw his face off, then lie awake later wracked with guilt that the urge had even crossed her mind.

A splotch of color where none should be yanks her attention back to the present.

Gaze aimed under the dining table, she catches sight of it again: one room over, in the darkened kitchen, a scintillating cluster of green quivers in the gap between cupboard and heating vent. Faintly glowing, the hue blurs into pink before her eyes. Then come blooms of deeper purple, then gold, the various shades swirling like the surface of a soap bubble.

Staring directly at the spot establishes unequivocally that there's nothing there.

She leans into the kitchen entrance, groping for the light switch by the refrigerator, half expecting something to grab her wrist. The other half of her mind berates her superstitious anxiety, using Donny's voice, *Why would you even think that?* delivered with a mocking curl of the lips.

The fluorescent bulb buzzed to life, illuminating a worn, banal, unoccupied kitchen, the linoleum curled up at the corners, revealing dirt underneath.

Another thunder. Not a pitter-patter this time but a heavy thump.

"Donny?"

He responds this time, an indistinct exclamation from the direction of the bedroom.

So he *had* been in bed with her when she'd woken up. She can't believe his presence didn't register, but in the state she's in, tired and disoriented and distracted and maybe even hallucinating, missing something so obvious is distressingly plausible. She's ruefully reflected more than once how the same conditions cause adoring parents to absentmindedly leave their babies inside oven-hot cars to die.

The neighbor kids are still screeching outside, but the sun must have gone down or the clouds thickened to brick wall opacity, as moonless-night dark smothers the windows.

Donny rarely stayed in bed this late. On the days he worked from home, and on the days he was

41

off work, she'd invariably find him at the computer, and if she was quiet enough, she's sometimes catch him watching porn — he always reacted like she was the one wronging him, snarling at her in that defensive nasal whine to stop looking at things over his shoulder.

Something tickles at the back of her mind, something that contrasts sharp as glass with the adventure of the morning. *He's been sick.* Her struggle to connect with this thought disturbs her deeply, like a chasm encountered on a nighttime walk, only the sudden giving way of dirt altering her to its edge. She recalls pasty, sweaty skin, a fever that blazed, heat that radiated from him as he watched her from between her legs, his lips and tongue squeezing, pressing.

Maybe she's been sick too. Maybe the plant was never in either window. Maybe she'd thrown it away. She has a vague recollection of a withered thing in a reeking pot, that sweet odor gone completely to sour, the dead plant not looking much like a plant at all.

When she turns on the overhead light in the bedroom, Donny cries out like he did the time he tried to move his desk on his own and tore a muscle loose in the small of his back. "Turn it off," he moans, shuddering under the covers.

"Sorry!" As soon as she complies, something punches her bad ankle and she drops like a sandbag.

The pain was as intense as it was when those tendons first snapped, all those years ago when she was small and that van backed out of the driveway and the bumper knocked her over and the rear driver's side tire ran over her foot. Chrystal had seen it coming quick enough to jump out of the way and reacted first with a laugh when she noticed Candace sprawled on the ground.

Her head slams on the bedroom floor, iridescent blotches flowering in the void behind her eyes, where that bulging migraine pain unfolds and opens to absorb any and all light and convert it to fire, sun-poisoning her skull from the inside.

The pounding in her ears isn't figurative. The pitter-patter of panicking cats drums toward her, as if they've returned from the grave to clamber over her prone body the way they did in life.

She manages to make noise. Donny's right there, he's right there lying on the bed but he doesn't shout her name, doesn't cry out *Are you okay?*

A prism shimmer casts its glow across the feet of the nightstand, illuminates the underside of the bed.

The little plant's blooms are as colorful as Donny said they were. His voice says *I told you so* but the words come from somewhere other than the shuddering mound on the bed.

Why did he bring the plant into the bedroom? He must have spilled it from its pot — through the migraine haze she perceives the dark stains dribbled down the sheets and box-spring cover. The mud stinks of warm copper and feces. Maybe it's not dirt from the pot at all, maybe Donny

43

had some disgusting bathroom accident right there under the comforter. An urge to laugh gurgles from the depths. He'll expect her to clamber upright and deal with it, won't he? But first he has to help *her*, genuinely get off his ass and help her. "Donny! Donny, help me up, I'm hurt!"

The plant has two new stalks with buds bulging at their tips. When they open Donny stares at her with those hydrangea-blue eyes, but Donny is still twitching on the reeking mattress. His breathtaking irises glisten in the spectral light, focused on her as intensely as they were this morning, as intensely as they've ever been.

Meeting her gaze, Donny's stolen eyes blink. The plant totters and sways at her, its thick, undulating roots rat-tat-tatting on the hardwood. The long fronds of its leaves uncurl to caress her face, their touch across her brow and cheek like the skittering legs of centipedes.

The Wolf at the Door or the Music of Antonio Soler

Devora Gray

Soledad had to touch Senor Ramos. Her hands were the long, pale petals of a strange flower. She held them to the light in the morning, in the evening, whenever she had a moment to herself. Turning them this way and that to drink in their mystery, they were, in her estimation, the greatest instrument. If Senor was dying, what feeling could give better confirmation than skin on skin? What was the look of a thing compared to the touch? His flesh under the white sheet, calling, her fingers danced on their own accord a melody and slipped underneath.

Soledad was but a girl of fourteen, naive and cloistered from infections and malaise. She gave no thought to contagions, whether her touch would inflict pain, or the impropriety of touching a servant ordained by God. After six years in Senior Ramos' tutelage, the man in the bed was a desperate departure from the vivacious animal he'd been a month before. His head a wild ball of graying blackish hair, his figure trim, almost gaunt, and his skin a deep olive tone warm as candlelight, he had never seemed *old* to her.

She was told he was blind and his senses dulled by drugs, that he would not recognize her. This was not so. Her mentor's eyes caught hers, pleading, stay, stay, *you must play*, to remember this. Remember me. Soledad wondered if whatever ailed him---a virus, a worm, or a spirit, she didn't know the difference---was digging into his imagination, planting thoughts meant to eradicate a man's goodness. As the nuns warned, when these thoughts took hold, the thinker would become wicked, revolting, and unstoppable.

Sitting next to his bedside, the Senor was restless, taken with a pain that jabbed him in the hip, then the shoulder, twisting his neck in garish angles. He thrashed, his legs twitched as if being danced on by spiders and rats he couldn't shake off. The nuns hovered like solemn black-winged messengers until the headmistress Sister Marguerite rolled the gramophone into the room on a book cart and palliated the pitiful teacher with records of his beloved composer, Antonio Soler.

Soledad hadn't been allowed to stay long. Retrieving her hand, damp and tingling, she was shaking, but he caught her with a phrase. He spat out in her direction a wild, demented glee. The nuns ushered her, patting, consoling, *He's possessed, my child. Not himself. Think nothing of it.*

Perhaps the same could be said of her. Was she possessed? Possibly. The power of possession lay not in the magician or the supplicant. The power lay in an arc of communion between two or more.

Soledad wasn't special. Unusual in her features, a board forehead over wide almond eyes the color of lava rock, she had pale skin and plaited dark hair. The girl was ethereal, spectral, removed from the laughing, jittery innocence of the others. But she was not special. She entered the girls' dormitory and made her preparations for sleep as a cat grooms herself on the edge of a radiator. The girls paid no notice, nor did Soledad engage in their light-hearted babble. Each movement was slow and graceful. Off went her sturdy mule shoes. Unrolling her woolen socks, the parts of her body revealed to the chill of thick stone slabs glowed pink and dusty. Her skirt and starched shirt were placed on the dresser beside her bed. Nearly naked in her camisole, she shook out her nightgown.

The girls' school of Santa Marcia lived in the high country of Seville and rested at the end of a brightly painted town. The cobbled roads and narrow alleys ended abruptly as the road disappeared into a dense forest of gloaming evergreens, black-tipped boulders, and silvered aspen. The antiquated fortress with its turreted embankments and lead-plated windows gave not the look of Catholic dominance but of a medieval fairy tale.

The Church paid for the town's nunnery, cheese makers, winery, and more, sending their beloved daughters to be taught by the good sisters of Santa Marcia. In the town, there was no contention as to who or what set the precedent for spiritual intervention. The forest surrounding the school was haunted.

Haunted, the girls giggled with disdain. Superstition. Gossip. Fodder for the pigs. They were noble, high-bred, and destined to change the history of Spain as independent scholars of the Second Republic. There was no such thing as haunted castles or forests. When the girls' whispered about hearing a wolf howl, or when they poked each other's ribs and rolled their eyes at how, when they were of age, they would like to be ravaged by the wolf. When they were caught arching their delicate throats and moaning about the legend? The sisters were quick to cross themselves and tell Sister Marguerite, who would bring her stern expression and a leather belt.

Soledad listened and watched the girls shivering with delight over the thought of being mounted by a large dog. Coarse, base, and too *human* for her tastes, she regarded them with the same curiosity she gave a snail melting in a puddle of salt. She listened and watched when they were told to expose their pale thighs for the strap. She listened and watched as their laughter dried into

whimpers. Throughout, she didn't flinch. All Soledad cared for, outside of the reverence of the Holy
Trinity, was music.

Her thoughts returned to Senor Ramos. No
one saw her hand under the sheet. She was sure of
it.

Why she lay hands on him when he could
not feel, she didn't know. She hadn't the propriety
of a healer. It must have been the music. A pure
conduit, the music played her. Was it her hand on
his thigh, feeling the music running the length of
her ear, her neck, her arm, quick as a lightning bolt,
and as vibrant to dance in unseen gestures? She felt
her fingers moving minutely, but her body was frozen. The concerto coursed through her fingers,
making her trace figure-eights, sure that he could
feel this energy, a code shared from pupil to master.
Her inner ear received his commands.

To her memory, the Senor never touched her
except to place her hands on the keyboard or dis-
tribute a gentle, scholarly kiss at her brow at the
end of each lesson. He didn't need to show physical
affection. His love of music, always for music, kept
him alive with a thrumming, happy intensity. If
that wasn't love—the mania produced with long
hours of study and his insistence, his absolute conviction that Soledad must play every day regardless of mood, weather, or school duties—she didn't
know what emotion it might be. Love and pain.
Pain and promise. What is it to feel close to one who
has mapped out your life for its betterment? Soledad would be a renowned organist, he declared.

She would play in the great Catedral de Santa Maria de la Sede, a symbol of devotion and beauty in Seville since 1507. Yet this was 1931, and the girls of that day were not the girls of this day.

As much as Soledad wanted to say she loved Senor Ramos, it was the feel of the keyboard under her hands, the sound of wind rushing through the organ pipes, yes, that was love. Knowing it was she that directed the melody in tandem with the great musicians and composers, knowing the genius existed inside her as it existed inside them—a secret only they could hear—this was love. Perhaps it was a sense of gratitude Soledad felt for the man on his deathbed. Surely, they were tied together with threads stronger than mentor and student because of the music. Music could be haunting, intangible, ripping apart the very fabric of materialism. This wasn't a sin. And if it was the music that implored her to touch—

There was something missing. Another element with a stronger force of will, incomprehensible mass, and ancient understanding. The answer must lie with Antonio Soler.

Soler's Catalan contribution to the Baroque and early Classical repertoire—by the use of the harpsichord, fortepiano, and organ—was ingrained in Soledad's childhood. As a musician, priest, monk, and composer, Soler was the ghostly father, dead for over a hundred years, and still he had the presence to inspire movement at the deathbed of her mentor.

In the hospital wing, Sister Marguerite put

the needle to the record and the Senor settled like a baby swaddled against his mother's chest. This was a strange kind of power, a gift or curse, when one could see the pleasure it brought Ramos. He began to mumble incoherent words to no one in particular. In his dementia so plainly spelled across his face, Soledad was struck with how painful it had been to learn the organ under her maestro's tutelage.

Her posture might be impeccable, her fingers as unbreakable as iron pikes, but since the age of six, some part of her body had been in constant ache from hours of practice. And for what? So that Senor could hear Soler's concertos? They didn't play his music at Mass. They were much too lively for service to the Lord. Why had it been necessary she learn Sonata No. 84 at the age of twelve? How her fingers had danced for him! Running across the keyboard, they were feathery, light, pouncing with kitten soft play, the feeling of being chased from — A ghost! A demon? What sort of priest made music lush and happy? Soledad tried to picture how the ancient might look at the keys but all that came was the feeling of mist. Dense, silky mist.

Ramos's suffering *now* was connected to her suffering *then*.

When Ramos turned and his eyes flashed, seeping an amber liquid, imploring her to share in this last lesson, he said, laughing madly, "I've fought as long as I dared — to keep the wolf at the door — If you don't play — He'll eat them all."

He's possessed. Think nothing of it.

51

But Sister Marguerite caught her at the door, yanking at her arm. She snapped, "What did he say?"

Soledad shook her head. "I'm to go practice — Right now."

Sister Marguerite, once a beautiful woman in her own right, looked Soledad over. "Not tonight. You go straight to bed."

To bed she went.

Soledad was impatient for the other girls to turn down the lamps. She wanted darkness. She wanted sleep. She climbed into her narrow bed, pulled the blankets to her chin, and unbuttoned the tight, high collar. The cotton warmed immediately, but most likely, it was the fever in the girl's body conducting a fine radiation that gave her the idea nothing could touch her.

Sister Marguerite would not approve of her bare throat. The others loathed the craggy nun's disproportionate vigilance, but Soledad respected the marm. She treated Soledad with a sneer of contempt where the others received indifference. In this way, Soledad marveled at the sister's discipline. Such adherence, as they learned from the study of saints and martyrs, could only be achieved through tribulation. The willingness to endure. Harsh. Cruel. Punishment. It was rumored Sister Marguerite trained as a pianist before wedding the Christ Lord and taking on the school as her home.

Soledad had no problem picturing her as a girl. Once comely, what remained of her female form was hidden by black habits and gloves. Even in summer, she wore gloves. Sister Marguerite's face, bony and built like a stonemason's house, seemed impervious to moisture, light, mildew, and wind. That face, floating in a sea of containment by her habit, held the same lines and curves year after year. In a face that didn't age, a face could refract layers as a prism divides a rainbow, Soledad saw great pain. To obtain this skill — How she must have suffered!

Under her blanket, Soledad pushed up her nightgown and placed her hand on her thigh. She tried to replicate the feeling of Señor Ramos' flesh. She could hear the concerto playing into a secret, dripping cave of her mind. If she was still, the strains of that music flowed into her hands. The strains of "Concerto for Keyboards No. 6," this was the thought, existing as a tickle, a tingling fibrous itch of the brain. She entered into her sleep as a trance victim goes into a stupor.

The other girls settled down and were none the wiser.

Awake. Not awake. Drawing back the blanket, Soledad saw herself gliding toward the massive windows spanning the girls' dormitory. In a blinding moon, the cultivated landscape was a purplish gray, the outline of the trees lusty jagged spikes and swirls in thin tendrils of black. Soledad's body opened a window overlooking the expansive green of the grounds. Stealthy as a thief, she climbed from the room to stand barefoot in earth that sunk between her toes. A fine mist seeped from the edge of the forest. Coming toward her, lazy, seductive. It rolled as waves of vapor on the surface of a lake. She felt free to wander and was carried forward, her gaze intent on the tree line.

Something was there. A presence. An animal. Something breathing, commanding the fog hidden by the foliage. Growling, groaning, licking its lips, it was hungry for *her*. Standing in the middle of the field, Soledad's nightgown was lifted by the sweet eddies, icy around her ankles. The mist was its breath!

She turned and ran.

The cloudy thing leapt from the dark and charged. The ground shook. It was massive but had no weight. Faster and faster, Soledad flew across the lawn, the ghost form taking shape, having no substance, but appearing in her mind's eye as a wolf, opaque and bottomless as the mist was sheer.

Where the fog flowed, it coated the tips of the grass and solidified into ice. Soledad felt needles piercing the bottom of her feet. She was too overwhelmed to cry out. The sensation plucking at her new breasts held the buoyancy of youth. She was running fast, effortlessly, she felt she could jump into the sky and the sky would hold her.

The fog's tendrils slipped into her hair and grasped the hem of her gown. It pulled her back, raking her over the needles. She weakened — how could she not — when the wolf's breath meant to leave nothing behind. The pleasure began where the fog crept up her gown, pulling at her ankles, her thighs, her bottom, parts of her that blossomed and taken form in soft springy hair. There, between her legs. It was a throbbing pleasure, akin to what she'd known at the keyboard.

Terrifying, unholy, primal pleasure.

She would jump. She would ascend and leave this forest, leave the ancient estate where sleeping girls prepared for a life consumed by ideas not their own. To live here was to be thirsty and hungry and quite mad with want. Temptation was pain. What if one loved the pain? The sky would hold her. If she didn't leave this plain of temporal existence, all would be lost.

To save herself, Soledad leapt. The mass of angels, her promised protectors, fled, or they never were. She flung herself forward and saw the needles rising up to impale her on a bed of nails. In those last seconds, she turned her head.

The wolf opened its mouth.

The instant before she was devoured, Soledad entered into an unearthly cathedral of lust, spirals of unquenched desire rising and falling in pale stalactites and stalagmites. She wanted to weep from the beauty. This was the beginning and the end. All the girls' voices — all the girls' of the world — fit inside the wolf's mouth.

The grass and the pain disappeared. She was floating face down, her hair a swirling current of dark. Her arms were manacled by the mist taking form and substance as a man-wolf. It mounted her in a blanket of white. Belly against her back, thighs pushed apart by the thing's massive haunches, its ghost teeth weren't sharp, but they knew how to chew. The nightgown was shredded like cobweb in the bristles of a broom.

She could hear its thoughts inside her belly, poking and pushing with needful fingers covered in succulent fur. Those fingers fondled and knew her intimately. They stroked in small lapping circles. She was the instrument. A harp, a violin, there were strings running the length of her breast and into her loins, bit by bit, massaging the organs of her femininity as one tenderizes meat before the spit. The wolf-man's tongue, a wet-warm eel, slathered the inside of her thighs, preparing the way.

The need of the thing was horrendous, spurring her insides to shed happy, delirious tears.

"Lead me not into temptation," she prayed in vain. The man-thing prodded and solidified, its organ too thick for the tender flesh it invaded. Its arms wrapped around her, cupping her breasts, panting a rhythm.

Unbelievably, Soledad felt flooded with light—with music. The most perfect music. This was the rocking of a bow against the strings. This was the striking of a felt against the cord. Vibrating, pulsing, the beast withdrew, and she panicked. Let her be ripped open, let her offer her neck, anything to be filled. Surging forward, as it took, so did it drink her youth, her promise, and her freedom.

Again and again.

If this was the true face of sin, a face you could never see clearly, Soledad understood the Church's terror. To be torn open on the spike, desecrated of personality, and transformed into a bleating, soul-less mouth of *want*, the promise of Heaven could not compare. What did they preach about Heaven? And in words that had no equal— Could this be? It could. The Gate. The Test. The Transfiguration. This wasn't man. This wasn't animal. This was Spirit. The invasion continued as she whimpered for a salvation that was eternally promised and never delivered. In her heart she perceived it as a mighty battle, as little as this helped, when every movement of struggle and retreat gave her jolt and jab of intense delight.

As a tempo on the metronome, she cried out her first breath of sensual fulfillment—

"Wake up."

A hand on her shoulder, shaking a tremor into Soledad's dreams.

"Wake up. Get up. Señor Ramos has died."

Soledad ached in every limb. She wanted to snap at the headmistress for waking her. Such a sinful dream, she must forget it and bar the doors of her imagination. Clamoring for awareness, she clutched the blanket and opened her eyes to see the pinched, pale face of Sister Marguerite staring down at her.

The Sister did not look well. She must have stayed at Ramos' side through the night.

It was mid-morning. The dormitory was empty. Soledad hadn't heard the others scurry through their rituals, nor had anyone attempted to wake her. She'd missed morning prayers. And breakfast. This was so curious, she couldn't break from—

Sister Marguerite swept the blanket off Soledad and froze. The girl's nightgown had been torn down the middle from the high collar to the hem. It lay under Soledad like parcel wrapping. Pristine in the bright room, the girl's body shimmered as if she were a star absorbing the dullness of the dark. A red-brown patch of blood formed a silhouette between her legs. The Sister peered at the tributary and read the message in the cloth.

"Get dressed," she whispered in a strained voice. "We haven't much time."

Sister Marguerite moved fast, but her breath came in pained wheezes. Soledad hurried to keep up. They descended into the kitchens. Soledad was struck by the smell of porridge and bread. They turned her stomach. Her mouth filled with saliva for another taste. Earthy, redolent with juice, it wanted—She stopped and doubled over with the need for—

Sister Marguerite's hand grabbed her arm and yanked her into the cellar. "Stay here," she said and left the room.

Hot tears sprang to Soledad's eyes. What was wrong with her? Was she ill? Had she survived the spirit dream to be trapped in this world of nonsense? She needed her music, the keyboard. Her hands would know what to do. She began to hum the opening of Concerto Number Six. *Padre. Ramos, help me.*

The sister returned with a plate of raw meat and thrust it into the girl's hands.

Soledad began to eat. Sister Marguerite

shrank against the cellar wall. She stared at the girl, the shelves of the larder, looking everywhere and nowhere as if blind. Crumpling under the weight of the spirit leaving her body, she tore the white gloves from her hands and held them in front of her face.

They were beautiful. Long, fine-boned, and slender, Sister Marguerite had hands much too lovely and young for an old nun. She had the hands of a pianist. Before her eyes, the youthful, plump fingers shriveled into gnarled fossils. Gray, bony, and wrinkled, the sister looked at Soledad.

"The Lamb," she gasped, nodded toward the half-eaten portion on Soledad's plate. "Eat of the lamb, the blood of the savior. I have given him everything — to keep at bay — You — the sacrifice."

Soledad ate and ate. As the last morsel of lamb entered her mouth, she felt a great wave of power enter her body and felt again her fingers upon the maestro's thigh, the song in her head, and the wolf-man's delicious rutting.

Lifting her face, Sister Marguerite spoke her last, "Praise be — The sacrifice — Keep the wolf at the door."

Sister Marguerite was dead.

Hours later, the sister was laid out in her chambers. Fully dressed, her hawkish hands were clasped, and the rosary beads like prisoner's ropes circled her wrists. Her face, for all its authority, was not the face of the recently departed. This was a face of petrified wood, dead a hundred years and kept in an airless tomb. Without expression, her flesh had receded, sinking into the hollows of her cheeks and temples. One could see the hinge of her jaw, each tooth carved in skeletal relief. The taupe eyelids, once plump and smooth, covered her eyeballs as intestine encases macerated meat. The nuns crossed themselves, kissed their crucifixes, and muttered.

Miracle. Omen. A letter would be sent to the Bishop, a sign of God has been delivered. All would pray. All would rejoice.

Soledad was alone. Sitting at Sister Marguerite's bedside, she could not help but stretch out her hand and lay her fingertips on the cold cheek.

The dead woman opened her eyes — marbles of ivory and opal — and turned to look at the girl. Gone was the stern reproach and the knowing sneer. After all, Sister Marguerite had been dead a very long time. The music, a concerto of unknown origin, flowed between them.

The old woman said, "He is with you now."

Soledad blinked, and the vision disappeared. But the melody remained, somewhere, off into that secret cave where Antonio Soler, Senor Ramos, and now Sister Marguerite danced in the mouth of the wolf.

The servants of God came and went, mumbling to themselves, raised above the gilded diadem of their imaginations by a living — or used to be living — oracle. Soledad remained, humming. The girls would continue to joke about the haunted forest, the priesthood would replace the music teacher, and Soledad would never leave the school alive.

As Sister Marguerite had been before her, the pianist, the musician, the girl was to be the sacrifice for the hungry wolf that drank upon femininity, youth, and vibrancy. As long as she satisfied the wolf, call him Despair, Lust, Hunger, Time, the name didn't matter, the other girls would be safe. Poor Ramos. He must have thought the music would keep the wolf at the door. Music to soothe the savage beast.

If this was the case, they picked the wrong lamb.

That night, Soledad disrobed and stood naked in front of the large windows where the mist was soon to gather. Ignorant of the whispers directed her way, she climbed under the sheets and fell into an immediate sleep.

She dreamed. A large white dog came into the room where she lay uncovered. It began to chew her hands at the wrists. Soledad was not alarmed. She watched, breathing deeply, under half-closed lids as the jaws opened and contracted. The delicate bones snapped and popped, a log falling on the fire. It didn't matter. Her hands were not hers any longer. It was possible they had never been hers. A wolf eats when he is hungry. A girl plays when she is a child. Soon, the pain would become an afterthought and she, its Mistress. She imagined what was in store for the other girls, helpless as lambs. Theirs would not be a passage over the mists of lust, but a voyage of disillusionment, misery, and ignorance.

At this, Soledad smiled in her sleep. She would never again play for the entertainment of others. As the wolf had promised, the song was for *her* and only her.

Dermatology, Eschatology

Kurt Fawver

Your doctor thinks you have hives, but you know better. Hives are supposed to be red, not blue — a fact your doctor glossed over or purposely ignored — and you're not supposed to feel something moving inside your hives, which you do. You're afraid the real problem is insects. You're afraid a six-legged monster laid eggs under your skin and now its larvae are burrowing out. That's what the people online told you might happen, and it feels right. Or, more right than the doctor's diagnosis of hives, anyway.

As soon as you noticed the blue bumps running up and down your arms and your chest two weeks ago, you took to the internet for answers. You wanted information, yes, but you also wanted to connect with other people who had similar afflictions. Misery loves company says the old maxim, and the internet is nothing if not a congregation of sorrow. So, you reached out on message boards and live chat apps and social media groups in an effort to find someone who could understand your illness. You wanted commiseration. You wanted friendship, however strangely formed. You wanted answers you could understand. And that's what you received, with an entomological bonus.

The people online asked for pics of your mottled skin and showed you pics of their ruined flesh in return. They mentioned flies and beetles and segmented things with razor pincers and toxic exoskeletons. They cited incidents where they'd had ticks suctioned to their bellies and ants latched onto their nether-regions. They sent you links about egg sacs and pupae, sores and wounds. They gave you the comfort that someone out there *did* care, if only as a member of the same neurotic society. These were people reaching out, trying to connect with you as you were trying to connect with them. That their explanations for your bumps were a little absurd only endeared them to you further. So, even though your doctor claims it's impossible, you think the potential for insect infection is worth consideration. At the very least, it gives you a reason to go back online and chat about your worries.

When you arrive home after the doctor's visit, the movement within the blue bumps grows worse. You waste no time messaging the bug people on their message boards, their forums, their social media groups. You're looking for advice or further explanations or just a voice in the wilderness that proves you're not alone, but no one responds. It's the middle of the day. Everyone is probably busy with work. You keep posting, regardless. You want everyone to know the details of your appointment and your doctor's dismissive attitude. You're hoping for a little righteous anger on your behalf.

While you drop messages to your new wound-obsessed acquaintances, you scratch at the bumps. The longer you wait for responses, the more your scratching gains strength and traction. You refresh apps and web pages. You check messaging programs and your email. No one responds. Soon, you're no longer scratching, but clawing, and your fingers come away from your skin slicked with blood.

You don't panic, surprisingly, because this is an opportunity — an opportunity to see what lies inside those bumps, to give the people online even more information. You rush to the bathroom, wash away the blood from your arms and see, poking up from every torn bump, a cluster of silver wires.

Insects are nowhere to be found.

You touch one of the wire bundles and it reacts, sliding further out of your ragged flesh and curling itself around your finger as though of its own volition. You pull your hand away and the wire releases, but also continues to lengthen. It worms its way down the side of your arm and drops into the sink over which you're standing.

There, it twitches as though conducting an electrical current.

You should be horrified, but you're thinking about all the ways to tell the people online. They're going to be so fascinated. They're going to be so jealous. You can't even imagine how much conversation this new development will generate.

Other exposed wires begin slinking from your body. They extend an arm's length from your body, twitching and flailing in midair. They seem to be seeking something, testing the surfaces with which they come in contact. Dozens of wire tendrils grow from you, wreathing you in a whipping chaos. You glance at the bathroom mirror and you see a monster staring back. Or maybe it's a god.

Then again, maybe it's a dying animal.

A wave of dizziness and nausea sweeps over you. You decide this is all too much. It's not what you bargained for, exactly. It's too involved, too intense. Insects could be cleared up with some medications, a bit of lancing. But live wires sprouting from your skin? Well, no one online mentioned anything like that. What if it's too much for them, too? What if there's no one to understand this particular affliction? What if it drives them away from you? What if they won't talk to you anymore?

On the verge of passing out, you lie down in the middle of your bathroom. Your thoughts buzz—not like a fly or a bee, but like the sound of an overworked electrical outlet. You wish you could find some advice on your situation now more than ever. You wish you could reach out and contact someone, somewhere, who could lend perspective to the wires' emergence, but you don't imagine there is any such person. Still, you have to try. Somebody is out there. Somebody will care. Surely somebody will care.

Head lolling to the side, you search for your computer. You don't see it. You don't see anything except the lashing of wires all around you. It mesmerizes you with intricate weaves and patterns. Kaleidoscopic would be a way to describe it. Fractal, another. And as you watch the wires, entranced and overworked in body and mind, you fade out and enter a state wider than dreams and deeper than death. There, answers and connections and monstrosities are all irrelevant.

You wake to an untuned orchestra of screams. You try to sit up, but you can't. You're held fast by a network of wires, a spider caught in its own web. As you rested, the wires continued to grow and, horribly enough, multiply. They now sprout from every inch of your body. Every bundle of silver strands stretches into the distance, far beyond your field of vision. Some pass through the bathroom doorway. Some snake out of the broken bathroom window. A few have punched directly through the walls.

The screams continue. You realize they're

not inchoate, but, rather, simply loud and frightened. You try to isolate what they're saying. Among the fragments you pick out are:

"Get it out of me! Dear god, get it out!"

"Why can I hear all this?"

"It's gone straight through my chest! Straight through!"

"They're in my neck! They're moving!"

"How am I still alive? This should kill me."

and

"Who is that? Who's talking?"

You realize, all at once, that the voices aren't in your ears. They're in your head. They cry out in places far from your bathroom. But how? You consider the situation for a moment and come to a second, more terrible, knowledge: you can hear the voices because they're connected to you through the silver wires. You concentrate, and, somehow, as though through your own eyes, you see the wires where they puncture the screaming people, bundles of silver drilled into their flesh, leading directly from you to these frightened others. You see the shock, the awe. You see snarling mouths and tear-spotted cheeks and fingers probing at grievous wounds. And, of course, you see the wires, which wrap themselves around deep organs and bore through bone, entrails, and gray matter — anything that can be penetrated. No matter how deep they travel, the wires shoot back to the surface and pass out of their unwitting hosts, growing further, growing beyond, finding more bodies and minds to infiltrate, to knit together.

It's these people you hear, the people twisted up with you. You share their innermost thoughts; you pulse with their feelings. They're all connected to you, through you. A multitude, you ebb and flow as one. Thousands of people, maybe millions, lie elsewhere, impaled by the wires. They share this terror with you, united in pain and fear. You would tell them to relax, to let it happen, but you have no reason to believe this will end well.

Again, you try to move, but the weight of the wires and the many lives they now support is too great. No matter how much you strain, you can't lift your arms or legs more than a hair's breadth off the floor. How will you eat? How will you drink? Unless you can derive sustenance through the wires, this bathroom is where you will die. You wish you had your computer or your phone. The people online really need to hear about what's become of you. Alas, both remain far out of reach.

You wonder when — or if — the wires will stop growing and puncturing new victims. Will they continue on, even with your dry, desiccated corpse at their center? Will they encircle the world and everyone in it? Even now, are they seeking people halfway around the globe, in places you've never even heard of? You laugh, imagining the ridiculousness of an apocalypse that bloomed from your skin. Dermatology, eschatology — same difference, you think.

The screams reach a greater pitch. They need to be heard. They need to talk. To you. To each other. They need to share.

You laugh again. At least you've found a community that truly understands your plight and can sympathize. You're sure you'll all have a great deal to discuss in the time you have left.

Headsman's Trust: A Murder Ballad

Richard Gavin

"Life is flesh on bone convulsing above the ground."
— E.Elias Merhige, *Begotten*

Just how the Headsman successfully trapped divinity within His axe blade is a riddle I am not destined to solve. But I have borne witness to the Cut-Lord's miracles. They evidence the power of both the blade and the hand that wields it. This is sufficient to keep me in servitude to Him.

Once I shared a stout daub house with my Mother and Father. There was stew in my bowl daily and mown hay to bed down on nightly. If such an arrangement constitutes happiness, then for a brief time I was happy. But then Father abandoned us, forcing Mother and I to till the land and re-wattle our drooping roof and lay shivering in our cistern, hiding from the bands of highwaymen that stalked the trails near our land.

Mother seldom showed emotion, but I was not afraid to cry or curse my Father; which I did often at first, more rarely as the seasons passed.

It was on the very night when the Moon first pulled blood out of my body to stain my nightdress and thighs that the Headsman darkened our door.

The moment Mother spotted His monumental frame plodding toward our house she began to plead. Mother's fear of death ran deep. I see now that she could never have let go, could never have properly received the Headsman's lesson.

So instead she struck a bargain with Him: her life would be spared and in exchange, I would become His charge, His Trust. With horrifying ease he wrenched me from Mother's ankles where I clung, screaming. He whisked me off and chained me to His wagon. I have been at His side in the many Moons since that night.

We emerge like a spore of the forest that encloses this village. As if aware of our destination, the mares draw our carriage to the clearing. Once they reach the execution platform, they halt. I tie the reins to my footrest and leap down from the driver's bench. Our carriage is a slight but ominous thing, canopied in midnight-blue leather and fastened with thick iron bolts. The whole contraption appears to my eye as a grand foreboding book, one that holds fast to its secrets. I move to the back and unlatch the iron grate.

The Headsman climbs out from the wagon. He is looming and lanky. His arms, while thin, are sure.

He is already hooded when He lumbers into view. His hood is dun, and the eyes that stare through its only openings are citrine and intensely focused.

We have been travelling for what feels to be a ceaseless summer, an interminable span of swelter and insects and sweating peasants. Of late it feels that we are wayfaring to the very edge of the world. We have nearly reached the sea.

Our rituals rarely deviate, so the fact that we have not yet collected a coffin for today's victim troubles me. When I inquire about this the Headsman tells me:

...in due course...

My duty is to tend to the block and I see to this as soon as the Headsman passes me. The block is stored within the wagon. We employ it for each beheading. Its surface has been smoothed by the blood that voids out of His victims. This human grease softens the woodgrain. The block now has the silken texture of a woman's thigh.

The Headsman stores His implement in an

oblong box of stone that is lidded with a nameless tombstone.

Once the Headsman has inspected the scaffold for today's task he returns to the carriage and uncaps the oblong box of stone where he stores His implement. The gravestone lid groans as He pushes it from its mount. Trapped air flows upward. It is heady with apple and pine, poppy and sage. On the eve of the first execution where I served as the Headsman's trust I watched Him prepare entanglements of these and other flora with great delicacy. He'd sowed the dank bottom of the trough with them, making a fragrant bed upon which His unwieldy axe reposes. I do not ask the Headsman about this practice, though I believe that the indwelling spirits of these plants bless the weapon, for never never have I witnessed the Headsman burnish it nor lean it to the whetstone, yet the blade has lost none of its lustre or its edge.

A drum begins to beat.

The ceremony is commencing.

I could list the minutiae of these proceedings --- the vengeful accusations of thievery or wortcunning, the mock trials, the prayers for the condemned --- but a greater picture can be painted without such trivialities.

The drum lures the villagers from their hovels and huts. They congregate before the platform as the guards drag out the latest woman to be convicted. She squints, for the sun undoubtedly pains her after such a long span in a windowless cell. She does not utter a sound, not even as she is guided up the scaffold steps and her head is pressed against the block.

The drummer goes still, and the mob falls silent in anticipation of the Headsman's song.

The Headsman assumes His stance, adjusts his grip on the handle of his weapon. It is customary for the Headsman's Trust to avert their gaze out of respect for the condemned, but something, some impelling force, inspires me to lock eyes with the woman on the block. I know the blade will fall at any moment, so I wring every detail I can glean from the sight of the woman's wide, lunatic eyes, her lips peeled back over her misshapen teeth. She trembles, though not from fear. Her body quakes with silent, mirthful laughter.

Then comes the Headsman's song: the crisp flit of the axe swinging downwards, the briefest of squawks from the victim before her neck is parted, the muffled thump of the wetted iron edge sinking into the block. The crowd gasps.

Along with its song, decapitation also has its scent, one that chokes the air like a swollen cloud. It stinks of copper and mud and yeast.

The head lops forward, like some sluggish creature. It wobbles down into the basket. Wordlessly the Headsman reaches down and grips it by its mane. Like Perseus, He holds this morbid trophy aloft. The drained face has already assumed a ghostly shade of white. Gore dangles from the halved neck like ruby pendants.

Occasionally the heads manage to retain a wisp of their original awareness. The eyes will shift and blink in frantic confusion, the tongue may wriggle as it gropes for speech. However this does not happen today.

The Headsman drops the spoil back into the basket, pushes it to the edge of the scaffold with His boot.

Like crows, the villagers swoop in to grasp at the carrion. There is arguing and shoving as they slink back into the village in a messy procession. The dripping basket is held above them. Different villages put these ruined heads to different uses. Some give them a burial in alignment with their native faith, others preserve them in brine where they are said to become a divination tool.

What they do with the head is of no concern to me or the Headsman. Our mission is markedly different from this.

A boy named Matthias worms his way to the headless corpse. He holds up a stone bowl to the raining neck.

Not far from this village, at the hem of the forest's shade, there stretches a broad heath. There the heathgrass sprouts as tall as men, and even on the stillest days these blades sway under winds from elsewhere. Upon this heath is a cluster of standing stones. How long they have stood no one knows. The winds that bully the heathgrass also erode the standing stones. Occasionally large pieces are lopped off. These pieces are often fashioned into bowls, as today's villagers have done.

Matthias has followed us dutifully throughout this scorching season, skillfully gathering the precious blood and then feeding it as offerings to the gods of certain hidden places that the Headsman regards as sacred spaces. Matthias wanders off, his bowl brimming. The blood will be meticulously borne to the heath and poured upon the standing stones, food for the power that pulses inside them.

Matthias was born to serve the standing stones. He has shared with me the methods his parents employed to groom him for this role. As to why I was recognized to the role of Headsman's trust I do not know. Perhaps the Headsman perceived some shift in my soul, a quickening that has transformed me alchemically into something purer than I was before. I do not sense it myself. But just before the season turned the Headsman informed me that I was no longer to collect the blood offerings, I was to tend to the block.

Today I am to be shown yet another step in this sprawling ritual.

The Headsman lifts the carcass from the block and sets it upon the platform. It is like a morbid enactment of the bridegroom laying his love upon the marriage bed.

We disrobe her.

"We should wash her," I say. My request is met with a rigid denial.

Instead the Headsman hands me a crude map that reveals a path to the hovel of the casket-maker. I am to collect the custom coffin for the recently fallen. He attempts to bolster me for what I will witness at the casket-maker's hovel. He orders me to make haste.

The midday heat swells the veins in my hands, causes my breathing to become laboured. I yearn for the shade of a glen but my path snakes through open country.

The casket-maker dwells and works in a pithouse far from village, far from any burial ground.

The sight of her homestead steals my breath. I am impelled to lower my tired frame, to cross my legs and sit in contemplation of this mound-like structure. Being a pithouse, the dwelling is a bored-out hole in the earth that is roofed with a rigid entanglement of bones. Fibula and femur, scapulae and tarsal; they all nest into one another as if Nature Herself had forged this skeleton, the remains of some fabulous arachnid who skittered across the plains with the mammoths.

The bones are the colour of old wheat. They nestle so tightly together that no view of the pithouse's interior is possible. After a respectable amount of time has passed, I rise and approach. An odd sound creeps into my ears.

Crickets.

To hear one or two of them chirping in the daylight is not uncommon, but what I hear is not the thin creaking of a few stray bugs, it is an orchestra. Their serrated song gives the afternoon a nocturnal pulse, a rhythm ill-suited for raw light and heat. It is the cool, murky rhythm of twilit mires, of waning embers, of the charm hung above the bed before slumbering, of secrecy, of dim potential.

Their song passes over me, through me, and I imagine that my heart is altering its beat to match this pulsation. I move closer to the pithouse, the womb that houses the crickets. My face is practically pressed against the spiky mesh of bones. I can see precious little through the weave, but I can hear the chirping fully now and I can smell the heady stench of mud and milt. It is sickening and arousing at once.

There then comes a sonorous creaking which joins the cricket orchestra like the faint rumble of distant thunder. The creaking pulses low, then high, low, then high. Its pace is measured and patient. I press my eye to one of the few slits in the bone shelter.

Within the pithouse, something shifts. I can almost discern the shapeless form. It reposes in the centre of the shallow hole. Needles of sunlight manage to pierce the darkness through the tiniest of apertures, pressing in like unwanted seawater through a ship's hull. These bright threads form a luminous crosshatch. As my eyes grow accustomed to this, I am better able to spy the figure in the hut.

I can only presume it is a woman, for the figure is dressed in a luxurious gown, one that suggests nobility. The hair is piled hectically upon the pale head. I cannot discern the face. If woman she is, if *human* she is, she is seated in a frame chair, one that rocks slowly back and forth, creating that measured creaking. The chair is composed of pale wood. Or is it bone?

Instinct presses me backwards. I scuttle back

from the hut. The crickets continue to chirp.

Leaning against a warped, canker-laden tree is the coffin. It is a wicker casket. The thin branches that form its woven body are the grey of morning fog.

Suddenly remembering my task as if newly woken from a dream, I scramble to my feet and creep over to collect the casket. I am glad to be ignorant of whatever arrangement the Headsman has with the casket-maker. I simply take up the coffin and flee.

My load is mercifully light, but its shape makes carting it a chore. I lug it on my back and can feel the knots of its branches pressing into my flesh. I do not offer the pithouse a backward glance. Soon the only cricket-song I hear is the one that stains my memory.

The light is already fading to a late-afternoon shimmer by the time I return to the scaffold, where I find the Headsman waiting in what appears to be the same standing position as when I departed. I plunk the coffin down and begin to breathlessly explain what I have seen.

Unconcerned, the Headsman simply goes about His task. He removes the wicker lid and from the inside of the coffin He produces a length of fabric. I aid him in unfolding this. The long sheet feels coarse against my palms. It is a shroud, dyed midnight-blue.

We begin to wrap the headless body. The shroud is a sullied thing, woven with many kinds of thread and soaked in the waters of the Moon. Or so the Headsman tells me. When this task is complete, I help the Headsman lift the swaddled body and deposit it inside the coffin.

Once we replace the lid the Headsman orders me to step away and turn my back. This I do, all the while trying simultaneously to both hear and not hear the words He mutters over the casket. I wonder what gestures the Headsman makes, what substances He might use to anoint His victim.

Eventually He announces that it is time.

We take up the casket. I am at the foot of the box, following my leader as He marches steadfast through forest and across the great heath whose stones seem to study us as we pass and whose billowing grasses urge us to *hush...*

The Headsman does not utter a sound and I dare not break our shared trance by asking any of the thousand questions that swim in my brain, foremost of which is where our destination will be.

We move west, further and further. Even the sparsest of villages are now behind us. Eventually we three are crossing a terrain that no hermit or even beast would occupy. We are nearing the sea. In all my years, it is a sight I have never seen and the prospect of it fills me with exhilaration, with dread. Rocky cliffs jut up all around us, like the grasping fingers of a great hand. They strike me as being the parents of the heathstones, which now seem tiny and frail by comparison. Between the rocky spikes of the cliff I catch my first faint glimpse of the sea.

"May we stop?" I ask.

When the Headsman does not reply, I ask Him again, and yet again. I want so very much to race to the cliffs' edge and take in that boundless green expanse, to hear its roaring surf, feel its cold spray against my skin.

Our path suddenly juts in a sharp incline. I feel the cadaver shift in its box, placing all the weight on my end. My exhausted arms wobble as I struggle to keep our cargo aloft.

When I spot the mouth of the great cave that yawns at the end of our path, I somehow intuit that it is our destination. After a few more paces the Headsman proves my hunch correct.

Once the casket is set down upon the stony ground, I am only able to take a few steps nearer to the sea before my body betrays its exhaustion. I collapse against a boulder. My arms and thighs burn with pain. In the distance the moon paints a gleaming stripe across the roiling sea. I am only dimly aware of my hand as it grazes the surface of the stone that braces me. Have the howling winds of this plateau smoothed it? It feels like taut silk beneath my fingertips.

Faintly I hear the steps of the Headsman. He holds His hand out to me.

…I have placed her inside the cave…

I take the small bundle that the Headsman is

offering. My fingers can barely unknot the fabric. Within are shelled nuts, a wedge of bread, fruits.

...eat...

I devour it all greedily, gratefully.

The Headsman never eats.

...tonight you rest here...

I nod gratefully, for the very thought of having to venture back to the village overwhelms me. My exhaustion is excruciating.

The Headsman never slumbers.

My stomach filled, I recline on the luxurious stone and close my eyes. The surf lulls me. I feel like an infant in the arms of its Mother, Her rolling tide rocking me back and forth, back and forth...like the woman seated in the pithouse.

Though our surroundings are arid, a garden of stone, in the distance I hear an orchestra of crickets.

I do not dream.

The warmth of the sun upon my face draws me back to the land of the living. I sit up, groan.

The Headsman is nowhere to be seen. I stand and call for Him, softly at first, then at a volume to rival the pounding surf below. I climb and survey the area from many vantage points but see no trace. Am I being tested?

I return to our outcropping and I wait. I have courage enough to start homeward, but before I do, I must inspect the final place where the Headsman might be waiting.

With reluctant steps, I enter the cave. Once more I call for my master and the echo of my voice spurs violent sounds of movement. Startled, I stagger backwards. The firmly textured wall of the cave halts me. I feel the foul water that moistens the cave saturating my clothing. I squint to see but can discern little of my surroundings beyond mere black.

Something shifts in the darkness. Instinct causes me to look in the sound's direction.

I see.

I do not want to see.

She is sitting up in her casket. Her stiffening body is luminous within this grim cave. The shroud we had used to wrap her remains like a gift for the afterlife is now twisted and rent. One large section is draped over the lip of the wicker coffin like flung bedclothes. The woman herself --- or what had once been a woman --- is like a startled dreamer who has bolted up in her bed. Her hands molest the air around her and her headless trunk twitches as if trying to see.

A strange logy feeling comes over me. As my eyes grow accustomed to the gloom, I truly scrutinize the thing in the box. I study the halved neck; lumps of muscle, knots of bone, all held in place by the gluey clotted blood.

The whole image becomes a primordial volcano, spitting up waves of blood-lava and fledgling landscapes of tendon and of bone.

It is as if a new world is flooding out all around me. I see it with the eyes of my heart. It is a potent land whose laws are the bristling nerve; the pulsing red caverns and the stiff digits of bone.

Who will be the god of this grim, corporal

world? What deity would dare send down creeds in the lawless wilderness of quivering skin and flowing blood?

She leaps!

Her escape from the casket is sloppy and awkward. Her hands swat the wicker box while her feet wobble over the cave's rutted floor. The thing staggers about in a series of blind, brutal rings. She is as a panicked moth trapped in a bell jar. Though she has no face, the headless thing turns to face me. Worse, I know that in some way she *sees* me. The dark blotches upon her breasts come to resemble eyes. Horror seizes me utterly. I collapse upon the jagged stones, yet I cannot look away.

I watch her climb the cavern walls, nimbly, like some ugly salamander. She skitters the very summit of the cave. She contorts her body and presses her open neck against one of the stalactites. For one indescribable instant, this creature dons the entire cave as her crown. The tapered rock penetrates her throat and suddenly I can hear the cave's long-buried song. It comes to screeching life through the woman's flesh. Her pores open like the mouths of some heinous choir.

The chthonic music screams at me.

I stagger up and charge down the daylit passage.

I would flee the area entirely, but I discover a trio waiting for me on the plateau: the Headsman stands with Matthias by his side. The boy is holding the block before him, not to boast of his appointment as the Headsman's new trust, but to show me that he understands his duty, that he reveres it.

Standing behind them is the woman from the pithouse. Her face is worse than words can convey. I turn away from her, but not from revulsion. Her visage is a sun at full glare. I am awed. I am awakened.

The headless cadaver comes bounding out of the cave. She flails about like a manic puppet.

Gracefully, placidly, the woman from the pithouse advances. She swipes her claw-like nails at the cadaver, wielding these natural weapons with swiftness and skill. With a single slice, she ends the corpse's mad enactment. The thing falls, goes still.

I feel I should speak yet I can find no words. The only sound is the pounding surf and the incessant wind that creates dust-devils all around us.

The headless cadaver begins to twitch, but only for an instant. Something is struggling to free itself from that lifeless husk. It finds the yoni forged by the woman's razorblade. It erupts from the flesh.

A shrike.

Despite the gore that greases the bird's plumage, I can sense the pristine shading of its feathers. It seems to carry celestial light in its down. The bird's eyes are the silver of burnished nails. The bird takes flight.

I see. I want so very deeply to see *more*. But what observes this richly shaded world is not my eyes, but my throat, my fingers, the soles of my feet. I am a vent for visionary power.

The bird begins to sing. And I hear the music

of the spheres. I somehow comprehend the wisdom of the song. It speaks of a knowledge deeper than the mind, a frenzied light that lies within the flesh and beyond it.

The song stirs my soul while it lulls my flesh. I am only dimly aware of dropping to my knees, of resting my head upon the smooth block that the Headsman's new trust has set before me.

I watch my predecessor and I believe she feels no pain.

She is now a bird, floating, soaring, singing.

She is riding sublimated light, along with the bird that was the woman from the cave.

They are the light.

My name was once Matthias, but now I am simply the Headsman's Trust.

I turn my gaze once more earthward and I see the pair of headless bodies. Their bones awaiting repurposing. Soon I will carry them to the pithouse shelter of the horrible Woman who has already slipped away from the Headsman and myself.

She is vile.

She is a Saint.

She and the Headsman have freed these two souls from the tyranny of their heads.

Their thoughts have now become a shrieking music, a deathly birdsong that makes these decapitated corpses flail.

These mangled forms frighten me. They are rising and moving all around me. I shut my eyes and I shiver.

Everywhere I hear the screaming shrikes, everywhere the thunder of dead flesh dancing, dancing.

It's Hard to Be Me

John Claude Smith

"He's not the same," Philip said, as he tossed my one piece of luggage in the back seat of the rental car.

"He hasn't been the same since—"

"Stephen. I know. Mark hasn't been the same since Stephen passed away." Philip shook his head. "But this time...this time..."

I knew where this was going.

Stephen, Mark, Philip and I were the four musketeers of mischief throughout high school. Detention and cutting classes and rendezvous with all the wayward girls, we were united by nothing but a good time and perhaps a bag of prime weed until our senior years, when we all locked into hardcore studying as a means of facing the real world, which loomed large in the not too distant horizon. We were not stupid, passing classes with ease despite our indiscretions, but at this point, we all knew we had to brace ourselves properly, so the good times took a back seat, where most of the girls with their shirts unbuttoned and panties around their ankles used to reside. We had growing up to deal with.

Philip and I ended up going to the west coast, attending Cal-State Long Beach. Stephen ended up out east, hitting the big time at Yale. Mark stayed in the middle, which made sense with his more fragile sensibilities, and settled in at the local community college. We vowed to stay connected, so 3-4 times a year, we convened in the middle, in Kansas, where all our families still resided, allowing us to catch up with each other as well. Until one bleak Autumn day when we got the news that Stephen had ended up falling asleep at the wheel of his car and crashed into the back of a semi. This unscheduled get together was forged by grief and the loss of our friend. What happened back then filtered through my head while Philip drove in silence.

As Philip and I stood amidst a slight drizzle at Stephen's funeral, Philip pulled on my arm, drawing my attention from the mingling crowd. Family and friends galore spilled out to the edges of the cracked, rippling asphalt that cut through the cemetery. The roots of large cypress trees made the road look like a turbulent black sea.

"What the hell is up with Mark?" Philip said, peering over my shoulder and nudging me to follow his gaze.

When I turned to see what had caught his attention, I was taken aback as well.

"I know he and Stephen were particularly close, but don't you find this a bit…distasteful?" Philip's grief had been replaced by a burgeoning ire. I knew we'd have to talk to Mark, to figure out what exactly he was doing, but right now, it was so out of place.

"It's a fucking mockery," Philip seethed, though it was under his breath, for my ears only.

I knew, and expected Philip knew whatever Mark was doing, it wasn't being done consciously, in bad taste. Perhaps he was thinking it was — what? Any firm perceptions were getting shuffled in an ever-increasing deck of possibilities…or absurdities. Because the obvious was being bent into something purely bizarre as he finished his approach and reached out to take Philip's hand and move in for a comforting hug.

"What are you doing?" Philip said, between clenched teeth. Their hug was awkward, two puzzle pieces from different puzzles, not like our usual bonhomie, carefree connections.

"What are you talking about?" Mark said. The look in his eyes indicated he hadn't a clue as to what Philip was hinting at.

He looked genuinely perturbed as he leaned into me, another awkward hug, as I didn't know what to make of it, either.

"What's up with Phil?" Mark asked, close to my ear. I had no response. What I did have was an influx of familiar cologne, but not familiar within the context of what Mark had ever worn. It had to be Stephen's favorite, the muskiness cut with an earthy scent. When Mark backed away from me, I took it all in, up close and personal, and quite bewildered.

After high school, Stephen lived in expensive suits, usually dark of color, and a variety of red ties. Always red ties, and red socks to match. He had the quirky habit of wearing his pants slightly shorter than they should be, highwaters we called them in school, when other kids hadn't gotten their school clothes upgraded for a new year after they'd gained a few inches in height. He liked to make a point about those red socks, as if it was a nonconformist statement he never really explained to us, he'd only smile when it was brought up again and again. It amused him, which might have been the only point.

Mark wore Stephen's attire to a T, including the short slacks and red socks. As I took it all in, I spotted an identical cross to the one Stephen wore dangling outside of the dark grey shirt, gold trimmed in black, and handmade by our friend, Sharon, who had made startling jewelry in high school. Distinct, one of a kind, but what was this?

No matter Stephen's implied spiritual allegiance, he had Sharon engrave, "I'm on the highway to hell," along the back of the cross, vertical to horizontal. We all thought it was a hoot, and quite appropriate, closer to his true self. Too bad that highway had led to his premature death.

I was tempted to reach out and spin the cross around, see how close the masquerade had gotten. But after our initial contact, I wasn't sure I wanted to touch Mark again, at least until things were cleared up.

"What are you two staring at?" Mark asked.

I can't say how he'd done it, but even Mark's face looked as though he'd done something beyond adopting Stephen's severe haircut and applying a dye job. It wasn't just a masquerade we were witnessing, it was a transformation. The jawline seemed more square, stronger, as Stephen's had been. The other features seemed somehow altered as well. There was even a small mole next to his right eye that Mark had never had, but Stephen had. The weird thing was it didn't look drawn on with an eyebrow pencil, it looked real; there was also some obvious trimming and shaping of the eyebrows to complete the makeover.

But, in thinking of it that way, I knew I was wrong. This was not a makeover, this was something else.

"Excuse me," a shaking voice said. Mr. Lott, Stephen's father, had moved toward us. "I don't know what you're doing, Mark. But I need you to leave, now." His voice was calm, still quivering, but his fists were balled and bleached white. Stephen's father was a big man. He was a tough man, as memory recalled. You didn't want to piss him off.

"What's wrong, Mr. Lott?" Mark said. He looked at all of us, all eyes taking him in. "What's wrong with everybody? I came here to say farewell to my best friend, and everybody is being strange." He flexed his fingers as well, occasional fists opening to anxious spiders, but there was no threat there. I got the impression he was trying to hold himself together amidst circumstances gone amiss.

Mr. Lott took two steps forward, muscles tensing in his arms. His wife gripped his left arm and said, "Honey..." The chilled air plumed out of his nostrils and I thought of dragons.

"We'll take care of it," Philip said. We moved toward Mark and gently but firmly turned him around, pushing him away.

He was swift to turn back.

"What is going on, Phil? Jacob?" He continued to struggle, pushing back at us. We persevered, steering him toward his car.

"This is totally uncalled for, man. Disrespectful." Though Philip had peaked at being angry a minute or two ago, his voice was calmer now, simmering. I got the impression he wasn't about to judge anything until we knew the facts—same as me--but had to say something, so perhaps Mark would get a clue.

"What have you done to yourself, Mark? I get you and Stephen were close, but this"—motioning toward him, as if displaying a prize on a game show, though this was probably more a booby prize.

Mark stopped, shoved us both back, with force. I raised my hands, palms toward him: a peace offering.

"Look at yourself," Phil said.

Mark paused and did as he was told. He glanced down at himself and shook his head.

"What's the problem?"

"You look spot-on like Stephen. Spot-fuck-ing-on," I said. I wasn't angry in the stating either, more miffed, my disbelief tempered, concern the overriding emotion.

"Are you guys crazy? I'm me. Stephen is dead. You two and everybody else, I don't get it. I don't."

The moment hung unattended, a moment outside of life being lived and hijacked by another memory, this one from when we were all eight-years-old and Mark's year-older brother, Carter, had died in a drowning accident, tipping over a ca-noe while the family was on summer vacation at Vagabond Lake, and being somehow stuck in the canoe or trapped by panic, unable to pull himself out or flip it back over.

My mother didn't think it would be good for me to go to the funeral, this being the first death of anybody close I'd ever experienced. I didn't know how to react, anyway. She told me to "just be sup-portive as Mark goes through the grieving pro-cess," which I figured was best to do by keeping my mouth shut until Mark and I hooked up again.

Since it was almost the end of summer, I didn't see him until the school year commenced. He looked different. I could see Carter in his features and knew almost immediately the Nirvana shirt he was wearing was Carter's, as that was his favorite band. It didn't register as heavy as now, because Carter was family, so a resemblance was expected. There was something in his eyes, behind his eyes, I could not quite place, though. I didn't dwell on it, like now with the more blatant appropriation of everything Stephen, just thinking way back then that death changes a person.

But to this extreme and in such a physical way, I'd never imagined.

I wondered if Philip had thought anything about Mark's subtle changes after Carter's passing, but we never discussed it at that time and had no reason to afterwards. Life moved forward, we were kids, and death didn't linger in the same way as it does when you're grown up.

After the scene at the funeral, we spent a long weekend reminiscing and drinking too much and, somehow, moving beyond Mark's feigned ignorance and odd adulation for our dead friend, a psychological aberration, and realized nothing he'd done was meant to be disrespectful or bring harm to those who knew and loved Stephen. Because Mark was purely Mark in every other way besides appearance, we somehow acclimated and thought nothing more of it until we got together three months later and, though Mark's outward spin on Stephen was still present, it was as if he wore it like a finely-tailored suit.

Most would find it perverse, this change, but since we'd known Mark since grade school, and knew his nature was always a bit more sensitive, we let it be and didn't question anything, even as the change remained over the next few years. Philip and I had accepted it, acclimated to it, and, in private discussion, realized as odd as it was, it was almost as if some essential part of Stephen lived on in

Mark.

The years passed, ours with less definition, a grey smear of seasons as California's temperatures were less extreme; the colors muted. Philip and I ran through relationships that bordered on permanent but faltered because neither one of us was mature enough to undertake the task our parents had when it came to establishing families. Mark, though, had mentioned courting a lovely, spirited woman, Darlene, for a couple years, before popping the question. Their marriage was the best time we'd all had together in a long time. I'm sure Philip was with me in thinking perhaps, just perhaps, this marriage deal was something to investigate further. What we saw of Mark and Darlene together was inspiring. Even as the loose strands of Stephen remained, a strange tether to a past long dead as we all crossed the hurdle of thirty years on this spinning stone beneath a weary sun.

After Mark got married, his participation in our few times a year gathering was whittled down to once, maybe twice a year. Darlene was a delight, and always welcomed us. She'd let him gallivant for a day or two, and Mark would have fun with us, but he was devoted to her, his conversation often dovetailing back to her, and you could see it on his face, in *Stephen's* laugh lines, he would much rather spend his time with her. We understood. We were happy for him, sensing this permanence was necessary for the person he was.

Throughout all of this, we never mentioned to Darlene about how Stephen's death had changed

Mark on the outside. She never knew Stephen. There were no photos of the four of us in their house; there were no photos of Mark as a child at all. There was no reason to weird her out. All connections to the past that included Stephen had vanished. After Stephen's death, his family moved away, and those that knew both Mark and Stephen dwindled to negligible. Questions were never asked. Answers or, more aptly, explanations were never necessary. Only Philip and I knew the depth of what had transpired, yet what we *knew* was indefinable, and for anybody else, it was probably viewed as we viewed it: one of life's mysterious. If they even thought about it.

Mark had always been a follower, never one to make a stand for anything he believed in, because what he believed was what those closest to him believed. When it was the four musketeers of mischief, he only believed in a good time, even as his participation was usually on the outside, a voyeur, a gofer, a dark silhouette as the sun set, but also at high noon.

He was like a chameleon. When I first thought this, I was overwhelmed with sadness, the harsh truth of the thought one to bring a tear.

We settled for phone calls for a few years as our main line of communication. Philip or I would call him to touch base, sensing an obligation that he might not need any longer, but we did. I could not explain it, but we kept the connection, however lean. The last time I'd talked to him was seven, maybe eight months ago, finding out Darlene was pregnant with their first child. Marks' elation was infectious. I expected Philip and I would have to make the trek his way sooner than later, to celebrate, but work kept us both occupied until Mark called out of the blue. It was the first time he'd initiated contact in a few years.

"Jacob?" The voice was feather-light, couched in something I could only distinguish as shadows. As if shadows could speak...

"Mark?

"It's hard to be me."

"Mark?" I still wasn't sure it was him, even as the caller ID indicated it was. The tones were too indistinct.

"It's hard to be me," the voice repeated; Mark repeated. "Darlene's gone, and I need your help. You and Phil."

"Where's Darlene?" I asked, sensing tragedy nipping at the inconclusive inflections that said nothing to me about the severity of the situation, yet the words spoke volumes.

"She's gone," he said. "I need your help. It's hard to be me and I need your help." There was a clear line of something bordering on shock in his voice, the subdued, monotone cadence so alien to his usual, vibrant manner.

"Mark, tell me what's happen—"

But before I could finish my question, the connection went dead, completely dead. As if a knife had sheared the invisible line.

I called Philip and he said he'd received a similar call only minutes ago as well. We knew we'd have to fly out as soon as possible, to see what was up, as the vague nature of the call left us both wary. I had to deal with a meeting at work on Friday morning, so couldn't fly out until early afternoon, but Philip said he'd head out the next day, Thursday, and get us a room at a hotel. Set up fort and check in with Mark.

"Shouldn't we drop my luggage at the hotel," I asked, noting Philip had passed many already.

"We're staying at Mark's," he said, eyes dodgy as he glanced at the side mirror, the rearview mirror, at his door, fingers gripping the handle, then rubbing his pant leg with the restless hand, then wiping at his forehead. I knew Philip well enough to know when he was stressed, his OCD kicked in big time. There was every indication he was struggling with something. I knew it had to be Mark but hadn't thought it through yet.

"Is this a good idea?" I asked.

"As if we had a choice," he said, a low chuckle trimming the words. "Mark insisted. After…After seeing his condition, I was too stunned to react in any other way than to say we'd be happy to stay there." He rubbed his pant leg again, fingers to his forehead, then back down to the pant leg.

Silence again, except for the rumble of the engine and the tires grinding against the road filled the next few minutes. Contemplation about Mark's condition snuggled into the nooks and crannies of my brain. When Philip turned onto Cheshire Lane, I half-expected a cat to leap out in front of the rental car, smiling with devious glee at our predicament.

"Look," Philip finally said, as we approached the two-story Colonial Revival house Mark's father had passed down to him when he and Mark's mother had skipped town — also soon after Stephen's death; perhaps as a response to their son's changes? — and moved to a retirement home along the beaches of Miami, Florida. Whenever I brought them up to Mark, his pat answer was, "They're fine, but we don't talk often."

"If you think hard, you might have a hint at what you're about to see. But let me warn you, even a hint won't prepare you for the real thing."

The early evening shadows curled around every angle, staining everything during the sweeping overture with something I'd almost call sinister. Philip and I sat in the car and watched the shadows move as swiftly as the patchy clouds, the combination one to inspire unease.

"Guys," a voice said, as the front door opened, and Mark stepped onto the porch.

"Holy fuck," I said. Even with Philip's warning, even with what I 'd witnessed before with Mark, nothing prepared me for what I saw stepping down and toward us from the porch.

"I told you," Philip said.

As Mark approached us, every visible nuance suggested Darlene. Philip and I did not know Darlene well enough to catch everything, I'm sure, but the obvious was enough. The pink dress with blue and purple flowers that looked like it was probably a maternity dress, the two pig-tails jutting

101

from the side of his dyed blond hair, the lipstick, make-up in general—all of it—let us know Mark had gone off the deep end in a big way.

It also let us know there was the strong possibility Darlene was dead. That's when the transformations took hold.

"He sounds just like himself, though. He sounds just like Mark has always sounded."

"He sounds like himself? What of the phone call?"

"Oh, he sidestepped that with ease. Said it was a moment of weakness, he was depressed because Darlene was gone. When I asked where she'd gone, all he said was, 'Away,' and smiled, but the smile was all surface. No depth, no sparkle to the eyes."

Mark was almost to the car, so we had no time for hesitation. I already knew we had our work cut out for us in figuring out what had happened to Darlene for real. And what of Mark? The dress and hair and make-up would have been enough, but it was obvious his psyche, something deeper than manipulated appearances, something squirming below the surface, had also been compromised.

Then again, it always had been.

"Let's do this," Philip said, pushing the driver's side door open. I grabbed my luggage and we all met halfway up the walkway.

"Jacob," Mark said, his smile that of a clown, what with the make-up and too-short hair tied into lazy pig-tails, and even the dress, seeming too large, yet as I reluctantly put out my hand to shake his, there seemed perhaps a pillow stuffed beneath the flowers. The façade of pregnancy.

It registered as he took my hand and pulled me close — pulling hard, as I was resistant — the mole that had emerged next to his right eye after Stephen's death was gone. I also remembered Darlene had a small scar on her chin — Mark had casually brought it up once, talking about her perfection, except for a scar on her chin from a bicycling accident when she was a child — and how Mark had one now; one that looked lived in, as if he'd had it forever and it wasn't something he'd perhaps done to himself.

I hugged him, but I was full of too many questions to relax into the hug as we usually would.

"It's been too long, my friend," Mark said, slapping me on the shoulder. "You look different." He mimed stroking a beard, a nod to the goatee I'd grown over the last year.

I looked different? He looked like another person. Again.

"Where's Darlene?" I asked, knowing the answer as Philip had related, yet stumbling through impressions, possibilities, or simply flabbergasted. Probably the latter.

"She's gone," he said, without any emotional inflection, the words only words, rooted to nothing but response.

"Come inside. We'll find our way out back. I've got burgers grilling and cold beer to lubricate the path to our bellies."

Really, he sounded just like Mark

As we entered the house, Mark said, "Just set your luggage down here, we'll take it up after dinner." He paused, stopped in his tracks. Mark and I bumped into each other. "Whoa, the baby is going to be a soccer player if he or she keeps kicking like that." He smiled wide, and I noticed how his lips seemed different. Not just deep red from the lipstick, but thicker, the mouth larger, just as I remembered Darlene's had been.

Philip and I were numb. I could see it in Philips eyes, he was calculating ways out of here, for good. We'd felt obligated to our friend for so long, holding on to the memory of a slight boy who just needed friends, so we befriended him and made him one of us, yet at this point, all of us pushing 34-years-old, I expect that boy was not even a memory to Mark. I expect he was erased when his brother died. I expect his brother was erased when Stephen died. It was obvious how the progression of Mark's sickness had burrowed down deep inside, all while corrupting the surface.

He needed help. He'd always needed help, but kids don't realize the magnitude of such a thing as we were experiencing with Mark. Sure, we should have dug deeper ourselves after Stephen's passing, but our own grief disallowed taking the proper steps, because Mark was still Mark, which was the biggest lie of all.

Had we ever known the real Mark Stalling?

Philip and I took seats in blue plastic lawn chairs, both of us firmly entrenched in observation, while Mark fed us burgers and beer and all the Mark touchstones during conversation—lots of sports talk, as well as many references to Darlene, as if she were about to step out of the house, toting another case of beer, and the baby, which was due any day now—and we all laughed in a way that I understood was also only on the surface—*as everything was when dealing with Mark*--the appropriate response to a situation that made no sense.

Sprinkled throughout the carefree conversation, Philip or I would inquire about Darlene. Every response was cookie-cutter perfect: "She's gone."

"Gone where?"

"Away."

And Mark would smile, his lips still red even as the red should have faded, worn off by food and drink.

After saying to Mark, "It's probably not a good idea to drink so much since…" and motioning toward his belly, and his only response being a shrug of the shoulders and saying, "It's all right," and me knowing nothing here was all right--*no way*--I could not take any more of this.

The straw that broke the camel's back was the weight of denial or ambiguity or just the pervasive fucking weirdness, and I really could not take any more of this grim, enigmatic masquerade that Mark had worn forever. I finally lost my composure, as fueled by beer that I drank in abundance, drowning out the layer of strangeness that coated everything here, and decided to try a different tact in figuring out how far and how deep whatever was in motion had gotten.

"On the phone, you said, 'It's hard to be me.' What exactly did you mean by this?"

The flow of conversation halted. I could peripherally gauge Philip leaning forward in his lawn chair, attentive. Mark turned and stared out toward the last glimmering dregs of the setting sun as the flood lights automatically turned on behind us. Darlene had a hawk's nose, angular and long: Mark's profile highlighted the degree in which he'd somehow altered himself, his flatter nose now sharp like hers. He sipped his beer and turned back to me, his eyes moist.

"I never said such a thing." His voice cracked, as if he were reliving puberty. His smile crinkled slightly, dented in a way I could not describe.

My nostril hairs twitched, the perfume he was wearing, Darlene's I was sure, though I could not be positive, having no set memory of her smells--*but it had to be*--this light and clean and fresh smell that turned sour as I inhaled it and we stared at each other.

When we were ten-years-old, the four of us went through a staring contest stage that lasted for six months. A ridiculous stage, where one of us would stop and yell, "Staring contest," and we would all stop whatever we were doing and stare at the one who initiated the contest. In most cases, the initiator would win, but it wasn't as if the contests broke down over the span of thirty seconds.

We were all competitive, and those contests would grind away for two, three, even four minutes at times. Eyes watering, but lids firmly in place. The breakdown would rarely be met with laughter after the first few times we did it. This was serious business. At the end, there would be relief, a shout of victory, and we'd move on to whatever we were doing before the sudden interruption.

Mark took another sip from his bottle of beer, then smiled at me. It was an unhealthy smile, a smile full of secrets and disease--secrets I'm not sure even *he* knew or, at the very least, understood. A smile gone gangrenous, in need of amputation. Everything about Mark was wrong, infected. Everything since...*forever*, it seemed.

"Staring contest," Mark said, not shouted like we'd done in our youth, but calmly, shifting the tension from the real to the game, yet it was a mistake on his part. Philip leaned back, out of peripheral view, as I locked into Mark's face.

The mistake was in what this revealed to me.

Unease circled as vultures awaiting the final death throes of a dying beast on the side of the road, one minute bleeding into two, then three. The flood lights beamed down on us with glaring intensity, as if presiding over the contest, judges awaiting a verdict. What I saw as I stared into Mark's eyes and, overall, his face, annihilated all the laws of a reality I thought I understood.

As I stared at him, those eyes moist but never blinking, I witnessed the malleable putty of his face as it became almost liquid. A twitch next to

107

his right eye grew dark, Stephen's mole rising from the unsettled skin, before sinking under the surface again. Veins pulsed in his forehead and were visibly entangled beneath the thin skin of his neck — too many snakes crammed within a small basket-- the blood moving perceptibly slower than seemed possible, his stare one frozen into place by sheer will, or whatever assisted sheer will, and just as swiftly the prominence of the veins was negligible. Yet that momentary prominence highlighted something I'd never imagined: though I'd always noted it was only surface level with Mark's transformations, whatever ruled his body was rooted deep within. Beyond his psyche, tightly knotted into the corporeal

Lines deepened, and lines materialized out of the contours, before smoothing out again, or shifting allegiance to another.

Another. Not Mark.

I saw traces of Carter and Stephen and Darlene ebb and flow out of his face; *the* face. It was never *his* face.

I heard Philip gasp once, when Mark's face seemed at a point in-between, as if uncertain which countenance to wear, all features rounded, undefined, *inhuman*; marble awaiting the first strike of the sculptor's chisel. It was hard for Mark to be himself, because there had never truly been a "Mark," that indeterminate moment defining him with nothing but the nebulous display.

I continued to stare, the contest one of will whittled to raw nerve, as the subtle and less subtle alterations flickered along his jaw and chin, his cheeks and the ever-mutable nose. I stared as it all transpired in real-time, those two, three, now four minutes that seemed to last an eternity, until Mark bolted upright in his chair, causing both Philip and me to stagger back, our lawn chairs scraping the cement.

"You win," he said, "though you have to feel this."

Mark, now fully in the guise of Darlene, grabbed my hand and pulled it toward his swollen belly. I tried to pull away, but he was persistent, and stronger than I remembered.

"It's really kicking now," he said, pressing my palm on his belly, which had to be a pillow, because there was no way anything could be kicking beneath the dress. Yet, as he pressed it, I felt something move.

I jerked my hand away, but Mark held strong, and pressed it against the belly again.

"What are you afraid of, Jacob? It's only mine and Darlene's baby."

I felt something move again, my initial impression that my imagination was running away with the situation corralled by the unmistakable truth that something had moved under the dress. Where a pillow had to be assisting in the impersonation of his pregnant wife, yet what I felt...

"No way," I said, finally staking claim to my hand again. I rubbed it, as if it were injured, or just to rub the obscene sensation out of my fingers.

Philip said, "Can't be," but I nodded my

109

head, there was no denying what I'd felt.

We both looked toward Mark. The light in his eyes dimmed. He said, "It's hard to be me," and nodded. Tears streamed down his face.

Despite everything, despite the discomfort that felt like a lead weight the size of a basketball filling my stomach, I said, "What can we do? How can we help?"

Philip followed-up: "Yes, how can we help, Mark?"

We watched as Mark got up, strolled toward the far end of the vast porch. While he was turned away, perhaps looking at the tall trees from a park near the house and beyond his huge backyard, he said, "It's hard to be me and I need your help."

He made an odd motion, his right arm moving across his body from left to right, the elbow jutting out as he ended, though because he was facing away from us, we could not see what he was doing. Until a bloody knife dropped to his feet and he turned around. He must have taken it from the tray of utensils sitting on a small table next to the barbecue.

"I cannot do this without your help. The baby needs to come out now."

"Jesus, Mark, what have you done?" Philip said, as we both dashed toward him as he collapsed to the ground.

There was blood everywhere. Mark had sliced into the upper part of the swollen belly and there was blood everywhere. Crimson spread across the blue and purple flowers, blotting them out. As he tottered back up to his knees, Mark had one hand stuffed inside the fresh wound, and was grunting as he moved it within himself.

Philip was beside himself, shuffling in place like an agitated lion.

"What are you doing?" I asked, ignoring the obvious as I pressed my hands against the bloody dress, his bloody stomach, trying in vain to deter the bleeding. I said to Philip, "Hand me that towel," pointing to the one Mark had wiped his hands on while grilling the burgers. Philip did as he was told, too stunned to think beyond my demand. When he handed it to me, I pressed it against Mark's bleeding belly, only to realize the futility of my act.

Mark grunted again, both arms stuffed into the wound and pulled up from within himself. He wailed to the blackened heavens as he pulled. The baby's head was in his hands, his muscles flexing as it was slowly dragged upward and out of his mutilated body.

Philip turned and vomited.

In my kneeling position, I stumbled backwards, landing on my butt.

Mark let out another wail. A chorus of neighborhood dogs joined in.

With a sticky sucking sound, like boots stamping through mud, Mark excavated the belly, the baby, his baby, the impossible cargo squirming in his hands. There was no umbilical cord, no placenta. There was no sense to be made of the proceedings as they toppled into lunacy.

Mark smiled, the colors in his eyes an ever-

111

shifting mish-mash of blues and browns, hazels and ebony. The skin of his face quivered, an ominous display, a portent steeped in dread. He raised the baby to his mouth and started to lick the blood off it.

"Aw, no, no..." Philip said, backing away.

Mark held the baby up, his mouth a wet, red slash, and said, "He's handsome, just like his father," but Philip and I could only see the baby's blood-coated backside.

I heard cries from the baby, astonished that this thing that should not be was even alive.

"He looks just like his father, don't you think?" Mark said and turned the baby around.

Philip screamed, a wordless confirmation of an unbearable truth. He screamed and abandoned us, running into the house, and away. Where Darlene perhaps was: away.

I scrambled to my feet and stepped back, hand to my mouth. Tears blurred my vision, but I knew what I had seen. Tears for a boy who had never grown into the man he could possibly have been because something snapped and all that was left was a blank slate.

Just like the baby's face.

Because Mark had no real face to call his own, or at least it had been too long since he'd worn it, the baby had no substantial foundation upon which to draw features of distinction; features of genetic influence. The death-masks it had inherited from its father dissolved into a jumble of indecision, a strobing shift between male and female. The

features bubbled up and out of the face and solidified, moments when the eyes would be one color,
the nose would bulge outward and elongate, the
mouth would split the smooth skin and grow wide,
devoured by the fickle, transient quality of constant
transition, so the next moment rendered the previous one null and void, not a part of the equation
any longer. The changes rippled by in rapid succes-
sion.

I stood there and watched as my friend,
Mark, turned the baby back to face him, rocking
back and forth and said, "Remember, my precious
one. The world is your oyster. You can do whatever
you want. You can *be* whoever you want, my son."
Then he turned to stare at me as his face started to
slowly melt, my friend's face started to slowly melt
as a candle beneath a burning wick, losing touch
with anything human.

"This is why I needed you and Philip, Jacob.
I..." His lips blistered and burst. "I need you to take
care of my baby." He held the baby, this thing, out
toward me. "I need you to promise me you'll take
care of my..."

But the words failed him as his face crumpled and folded in on itself. I caught the baby before he dropped it. I held the baby at arm's distance
as I watched Mark become an indistinguishable
pool of pink goo.

He wanted me to take care of his baby, this
thing that was not normal, not right, a blotch on
everything I thought I knew.

Dark hairs jutted out from along the thing's

113

left arm. The arm grew in length, to the size of a man's arm. The hand, a man's hand, clawed at my shoulder, before the fingers shrank to the size of a baby's again. The hairs changed color and texture, to fine blond wisps, before retreating beneath the skin.

I realized this thing was worse off than Mark. It had nothing to hold on to, as Mark did with his brother, Stephen and Darlene. The turbulent display writhing in my hands was evidence of this much. The constant swirl of features, some not even where they should be aligned — the right eye had slid down to the cheek--caused my gorge to rise. I turned to cough, still holding the thing, but needing the momentary break before my brain went completely off the rails.

The thing coughed. The thing coughed just as I had coughed. With no allegiance to anything, it latched on to me, the sound of the cough startling it, catching its attention. Giving it direction.

As I turned to face it again, the sight was one to behold only in nightmares.

I set it down and backed away from it.

I turned and ran through the house, out the front door, only to see Philip was still there. I heard the car's engine idling. Though he had abandoned Mark and me, and that thing, he hadn't left.

I swung the passenger door open, swiftly sat down and said, "Drive."

Philip was trembling.

"Drive," I said, with urgency.

"What happened back there?" Philip stared

at the steering wheel, his hands gripping it in such a way I knew they hurt.

What was I to say?

"It was like looking in a mirror," I said. I'm sure my eyes were glazed, the image burned into my memory forever.

"What?" Philip swiveled his head in my direction, though his grip on the steering wheel stayed firm. "What's that supposed to mean?"

"It was like looking in a mirror," I said, as I turned to face Philip.

Realization hit Philip like a sledgehammer to the forehead.

"You mean—"

"The baby, that thing--*it was wearing my face!*"

Philip stamped on the gas pedal, tires screeching, as we headed away. As far away from the atrocity as possible.

The Gutter at the Bottom of the World

David Peak

It wasn't until the skinny tires of Kate's Honda scraped against the curb, after she hit the flashers and slammed the door behind her, only then, in the smog-warm night, with the phased sounds of sirens rising and falling, did she think, please, not another lost and lonely girl. Deep down, though, she knew that this was the real world, and in the real world things were almost always as bad as she feared.

They fell into place that night the way they often did, those bad things, the crime scene — the colors, the noise — the carnival-like chaos of it all. The blue and red police lights spun against the drab North Hollywood street, a corridor of crowded apartment complexes, barred windows and sickly palms. Taut strands of yellow caution tape boxed out the throng of onlookers, a few old ladies smoking cigarettes, a horde of filthy skater trash, a yuppie couple in matching khaki shorts walking a yipping Yorkie. And on the other side of the tape, two uniformed cops standing shoulder to shoulder — both holding the collars of their thick vests, as cops often seemed inclined to do — barking at people to stay back, to put away their cellphones, move along, disperse.

Kate threaded her way through the crowd until the scene was only a few feet away. There, on the pavement between two parked cars, she saw a thin, pale arm sticking out from beneath a blood-soaked sheet. She snapped a quick photo with the camera on her phone, using her thumb and forefinger to zoom in, frame the shot. Then she pressed the thumbnail to enlarge the image. It filled the screen, a smear of nebulous red light, the arm limp and lifeless yet not devoid of a discomfiting beauty — the neck of a strangled swan.

She looked up from the screen and saw one of the cops take a few assertive strides her way, looking pissed off, boots chunking against the pavement — the camera flash must have caught his attention. Kate tapped the home button, then the record button on her phone's voice recorder, opened the notepad app. Her movements were made without thought, pure muscle memory.

"No photos," the cop said, close now and pointing a gloved finger. "I won't tell you again."

Kate pretended like she hadn't heard. She extended her arm toward the cop, held out her phone like it was a mic, her voice in competition with the noise of the crowd, the sirens. "What happened here?"

The cop's eyes narrowed. A thin white scar pinched the skin over one of his eyebrows and ran straight back over the curve of his shaved head, pitted skin gleaming in the streetlight glow. His earlobe on that side was missing a chunk of flesh. And his cruel smile showed small and sharp teeth like a piranha — similarly cold, unfeeling eyes. All of these things — these details she'd been trained to pick out, make note of — made Kate's skin crawl. Without missing a beat, the cop snatched the phone out of Kate's hand, dropped it to the ground, and sent it skidding across the pavement with a swift boot swing.

Now it was her turn to be pissed off. "I'm a reporter with Clued-In-LA," she said, her voice a bit more shrill than she would have liked. She looked to her left, her right, hoping someone was recording this, getting it on the record, but no one seemed to have noticed. No one seemed to care. "You can't do that."

"Do what?" the cop said, affecting confusion and innocence in equal measure. And then he turned away. A moment later, two more cars rolled onto the scene, a cruiser calling its siren and an unmarked black sedan spinning silent dash-lights. An ambulance followed, and then a fire truck, God knew why. The cops fanned out into the crowd, throwing their weight around. One of them barked into a megaphone. Next thing she knew Kate was back in her Honda, windows down, cutting the muggy night air along a dry stretch of highway, tears of frustration blurring the sea of shifting tail-lights. She headed home because there was no-where else to go, no one to go home to. Not tonight, at least. She'd have to come crawling back to North Hollywood in the morning and look for her phone, knowing all along it would be a waste of what little time she had. Fuck it. Her phone was gone. Just an-other object swallowed up by the cracks that lurked between things, always lying in wait, ready to swal-low up some poor, misfortunate soul, so many of the young women in this city, lost and lonely, fresh off the buses from God knew where — grim corn-fields and trailer parks, oil-pump desert towns and festering swamps — dreams of stardom blinding them to the dangers grinning their veneers in plain sight.

Kate had a hunch that whatever had hap-pened in North Hollywood that night, whatever it was that had happened, there was a story that needed to be told, there almost always was. Maybe this would be like one of those old and sordid Hol-lywood murders: Black Dahlia, Ronni Chasen, or Christa Helm. That's what her instincts told her, and Kate had long ago learned to trust her instincts.

That's how she'd kept her job at the daily in New York all those years, each more cutthroat than the last, surviving round after round of layoffs. Back then, she was fresh out of Columbia's J-school and looking to make a name for herself. And that was exactly what she had done, racking up bylines, breaking stories about unscrupulous media execs, accusations of sexual harassment—that kind of thing. It was her area of expertise: scumbag men who abused their power. One day, she pissed off the wrong person—she never did find out who it was—and the daily's managing editor sent her packing. Too much of a liability, he'd said, wringing his hands, the gutless piece of shit. She splashed her iced coffee in his face and never looked back.

Now, here she was, on the other side of the country, exiled to a depressing little bungalow in porn-soaked Van Nuys, covering the crime beat for a trashy website that no one even read, churning out content to sell algorithm-determined ad space. It was impossibly meaningless.

Kate cracked open a bottle of cheap chardonnay, plopped down on her couch, and opened her laptop. The first thing she did was check her bank account. She'd have to put the new phone on her credit card, the one that wasn't already maxed out. An unplanned expense was the last thing she needed. There was still so much to take care of around the house. She hadn't even finished unpacking yet. Stacks of boxes lined the walls of every room, labeled in Sharpie: Kitchen, Living Room, Bedroom, Books. It seemed like there was never enough time in the day to get her shit together. Not when there was so much work to be done, so many bills to be paid. It seemed like there was never enough wine left in the bottle. She refilled her glass, took another sip—a longer one this time—and closed her eyes.

The image of the crime scene came back to her, the photo she'd snapped on her phone, an impression that haunted her like the lingering traces of a bad dream. She recalled details — a beaded gold band on one finger, a strange tattoo on another, fingernails painted dark — but it was as if her mind wouldn't let her see what she'd seen. Each time she tried to recall the image it was less detailed somehow, until eventually she couldn't really remember it at all. God, what the fuck was wrong with her?

Maybe it was the temperature. She still wasn't used to the bone-bleaching heat of southern California. With the ceiling fan cranked on high and the overtaxed window unit blaring, the heat in her bungalow was maddening. Ten minutes on the couch and she was sweating through her T-shirt. On the radio they'd said this was the hottest summer in years, and it was supposed to get even hotter. That reminded her: she needed to get the check-engine light on her car looked at. It had first popped on during the drive from New York, and ever since she'd crossed the desert it was periodically joined by the even more ominous engine hot light. It might be a radiator problem — no guessing how much that would cost. She'd just have to add it to the list of unplanned expenses.

She finished her glass of wine and opened a second bottle. It was all so overwhelming sometimes. And there was nothing she could do about it besides click on the same sites again and again, refresh the same pages over and over, looking for breaking news, anything about the murder in

North Hollywood. In a separate private-browsing tab she went to Pornhub and scrolled through the BDSM category, not interested in anything too extreme. She mostly liked videos of women humiliating men, using words to inflict pain. Videos like those made her feel like she was in control. Tonight she wanted the opposite. She pressed play, hid the browser window behind the other windows, and listened to the sounds: skin on skin, crying out — that intoxicating mix of pleasure and pain. She wondered how many of the girls in these videos lived in Van Nuys, how many she'd passed on the street, never recognizing them for who they were or what they did to make ends meet.

Kate killed the second bottle of wine. Not long after that, she slipped into fitful sleep.

She slept in late the next day, and when she woke she felt energized. No more of this helpless victim bullshit. Today, she was going to take control of her life. She was going to do what she did best: follow her instincts and find the story. Kate made a pitcher of cold-brew coffee, sat at the small table in her tiny, sunbaked kitchen, and got to work.

First she called in a favor from a friend of a friend, someone who worked in records for the LAPD, told him she was looking for anything on female DOAs brought in from North Hollywood the night before. She was in luck. It just so happened that the body of a young woman was photo ID'd that morning by her distraught boyfriend, same poor fucker who had reported her missing a week ago.

The victim's birth name was Anastazie Lhotsky — unique enough to get good search results. Kate plugged it into Google. Anastazie was from a small town in Minnesota, some place Kate had never heard of before. She was young, 20 or 21, and beautiful, big green eyes, perfect skin, walnut brown hair. It took a while but Kate confirmed that Anastazie was an actress and model who went by the name Melody Carmichael. From there Kate learned that outside of some photoshoots, mostly tasteful seminudes — under yet another name — Carmichael had only a single acting credit, a project titled *The Angel of Death*, which was in post production. That information led Kate to an article published in *Variety*, of all places, couldn't get more mainstream than that. Apparently *The Angel of Death* was the long-awaited comeback feature film from reclusive arthouse director Leonard Shea.

This was surprising, to say the least. Shea was a legend. In the late '70s he'd written and directed a deeply unpleasant avant-garde horror flick called *Wormlust* that was now considered a cult classic, still screening in the midnight slot at achingly hip theaters. The film was nearly impossible to describe, pure sensory overload, composed of rhythmic montages that stitched together highly sexualized, surrealistic imagery, writhing piles of

bodies slicked in scorched oil, black-hooded ritual-
ized murders, plagues of locusts, surgical footage —
all set to a pummeling protoindustrial score. Kate
had watched it twice, both times while an under-
grad, both times at the whiny urgings of the
moody, unwashed men she'd been seeing. She as-
sociated the film with the smell of clove cigarettes,
the ashen mouthfeel of cheap red wine, and bad
memories of fumbling, unfulfilling sex.

Wormlust wasn't Shea's only claim to fame,
of course. Years later, he inexplicably advanced to
the studio system, where he released exactly one
big-budget flop, a bloated, rape-obsessed interpre-
tation of the Bluebeard folktale titled *His Many
Wives*. Slapped with an X rating and dropped by its
distributor, it was widely considered one of the
most misguided films ever made. Shea's investors
each lost a small fortune, and he was banished from
Hollywood.

There was no telling where he'd gone after
that. Kate searched Google images but couldn't
find any photos that were even close to current. The
ones that did exist were old, black and white. She
studied Shea's long face. He had rock-star good
looks: a wide jaw, razor-sharp cheekbones. In every
photo he wore a cowboy hat and mirror shades, a
hand-rolled cigarette dangling from his lower lip.

The fact that Carmichael had been cast in
one of Shea's films was especially significant. Kate
recalled something one of those unwashed young
men had told her while screening *Wormlust*, something she'd written off as yet another urban legend.

One of the actresses cast in *His Many Wives* — some young woman whose name no one could remember — had been murdered shortly after shooting her scenes. None of her footage was used in the final cut, so the rumor went, but apparently she had played one of Bluebeard's wives, and in the single scene she shot, she was beaten, raped, strangled to death, and hanged on a meat hook. Shea did something like 80 or 100 takes, spent days on this one scene, Bluebeard killing his wife again and again, until this poor actress was decimated physically and mentally, until Shea had what he wanted — a performance of a woman being broken by a man that was totally believable because it was very nearly real, a woman who was so exhausted, so utterly destroyed by her husband's abuses, by the sacrifices required of her, that she was grateful to be killed.

And that wasn't even the worst part. This was the real world, after all — things always got worse. Weeks after this nameless actress's scenes were wrapped her body was supposedly found hanging from a meat hook in an industrial freezer in the Valley. She'd been beaten, raped, and strangled. Who knows, maybe the whole thing was staged for publicity, a fucked-up marketing tactic designed to drum up controversy. Shea certainly enjoyed a dark reputation — then and now. In fact, some of his nuttier fans even went so far as to claim that *Wormlust* contained genuine footage of the netherworld.

Kate typed a couple different phrases into

Google but nothing came up. She scoured some message boards, scrolled through a couple of poorly written blogs, read dozens of archived newspaper articles, but there was nothing to be found about an actress in *His Many Wives* turning up dead. Rumor or not, once was a tragedy, twice was a pattern. Two women cast in Shea's films, both young and inexperienced, both found dead. The coincidence was enough for Kate to go on. She typed up a pitch letter — explaining in careful detail how a recent murder in North Hollywood might be connected to a legendary cult filmmaker — and sent it to Suki, an old friend from J-school, now a senior editor at one of the mass media glossies in New York. Total Hail Mary, but she might as well start at the top.

She looked at the clock on the wall in her kitchen — it was just after two in the afternoon. Her pitcher of cold brew was empty. Feeling good about herself, excited by everything she'd uncovered, Kate threw on some clean clothes and drove over to the T-Mobile shop on Victory Boulevard to pick out a new cell phone. Hell, she deserved it.

After the sales associate booted up the new phone and slid it across the counter, the first thing Kate did was check to see if anything from the previous night had saved to the SD card — the photo of the arm, the voice recording of her interaction with the cop — but she was out of luck on both counts.

Her credit card was still processing when her email account chimed a dozen times over. Among the deluge from her editor at Clued-In-LA,

Kate's heart leaped when she saw a response from Suki. She opened the email, could hardly believe what she read. The glossy wanted 3,000 words and, amazingly enough, offered half pay upfront — enough to cover Kate's rent for two months. She'd get the rest when the piece was published. Word on the street was Shea's new film was being screened for private audiences. They might even be able to arrange for Kate to see it. Either way, there would be renewed interest in his work, whatever he'd been up in the past 40 years, and they wanted the piece ready to run by the time the new film came out. Kate fired back an email accepting the job. Suki's next email had the contract attached.

Half an hour later, stuck in traffic on her way home, air-conditioner blaring, Kate got a call. The area code was 442 — somewhere out in the desert. She put the call on speakerphone.

"I am glad to have reached you, Miss Murphy," said the woman on the line, her voice velvety, etched with age, the barely noticeable trace of an Eastern European accent.

"Please, call me Kate. How can I help you?"

"Kate, of course. My name is Carol Reid. I am the agent of Leonard Shea. It has been brought to my attention that you are writing a story about my client. This is correct? I do make it a point to know these things. Please, you must accept my apologies for contacting you so urgently. Mr. Shea is — how do I say this? — quite protective of his reputation. He is a particular man. Very particular. As such, he would like very much to meet you — to give you an exclusive interview, of course. That's right. Mr. Shea will tell you everything you desire to know. I'm sure you have many questions. Today, if possible. You are in Los Angeles, yes? Splendid. I will text you the address. You do not mind driving a ways, I hope? We are in Barstow. Yes, we look forward to meeting with you too."

This was certainly unexpected, but Kate didn't question it—she couldn't afford to. There was no hesitating in moments like this. She would do anything for a story, or so she told herself, as she plugged Shea's address into GPS, pulled off at the nearest exit, and changed course.

The drive to Barstow took just under three hours. Kate's Honda hummed through the oppressive, concrete sprawl of the city, emerging as the road straightened into a limitless stretch of highway, waves of oily heat rippling the dust-choked horizon. As she drove, she listened carefully to the sound of the car's engine, eager to avoid breaking down out in the wastelands. Whenever the engine hot light blinked on, Kate pulled off into the nearest gas station, bought some water, and collected her thoughts. She watched the turkey vultures circle some unknown meal in the distance.

There were so many things she wanted to ask Shea. Of course, she'd have to wait for just the right moment to bring up Carmichael. The trick was getting him to where she needed him. She spoke into the voice recorder on her phone, rehearsing and refining the questions she planned on asking, interrupted intermittently by GPS telling her when to turn.

Eventually she reached an intricately designed driveway gate, something Shea apparently felt was necessary way out here in the middle of nowhere, no name even on the map. A sleek black camera mounted on one of the gate pillars zeroed in on Kate's window. The gate buzzed, opened, its wide panels swinging outward. She followed the winding gravel driveway up to a large ranch house.

The place was gorgeous, fit for the cover of *Dwell*. The landscaping was immaculate, scattered with small stones and picturesque cacti. The driveway was hand-laid slabs of grey stone. And the house itself was an elegant mix of stacked stonework and adobe, all long lines and large windows. Gaslight lamps mounted over the wide front door glowed pleasantly orange, exuding warmth, especially inviting in the cool, early evening air.

Kate knocked softly and the door opened, revealing a young woman in expensive athleisure, her flaxen hair pulled into a high ponytail. She couldn't have been a day older than 18, with model-thin arms, delicate features. She let Kate inside, snapping her gum, and promptly slipped away.

"Hello?" Kate said, her voice echoing in the foyer. The house was immense, a symmetrical progression of rooms, frames within frames, low lamplight, dark wood, glass, and stone. The air smelled sweetly of incense. She heard the distant sound of running water.

A handsome older woman wearing a tailored dress suit stepped out of the shadows, extending her hand. Silver bracelets clattered on her wrist. Her stylish hair was cut short. The woman introduced herself as Carol Reid. Kate returned her smile, took Carol's hand in hers, shocked by its roughness, the sturdiness of leather and bone.

Carol's heels clicked against the polished floors as she led Kate deeper into the house. They descended some short staircases, turned a few corners, passing overflowing bookshelves and a gurgling fountain, went down a long hall, and entered an impressive great room, its raftered ceiling maybe 20 feet high, shrouded in shadow. The lights were dimmed. A series of full-length windows overlooked a large patio and swimming pool — its waters a pristine, sapphire blue — beyond which stretched the limitless desert. In the pool, a woman in a one-piece bathing suit was swimming laps, her stroke measured and strong. Kate wondered idly if it was the same girl who had opened the front door, but didn't think so.

Leonard Shea sat in the center of a huge leather wraparound couch. He slung one long leg over the other, arms out at his sides, resting atop the cushions. He wore gray Levis, a white V-neck T-shirt, and a canvas cowboy hat, the brim pulled low over his eyes. He was barefoot.

Carol took a seat near Shea. She sat up perfectly straight, impeccable posture, and smoothed her skirt over her thighs. She gestured to the opposite side of the couch, instructed Kate to make herself at home. And when she did, as soon as Kate sat down, a young woman in a black dress swooped in out of nowhere — another pretty little thing, this one raven haired, stick thin — and placed a sweating bottle of Pellegrino on a coaster. How many of these girls were there? Before Kate could even say thank you, the raven-haired beauty was gone, disappearing around some dark corner.

"Again, thank you so much for driving all this way," Carol said. "Mr. Shea certainly appreciates being given the opportunity to speak to you directly — and on such short notice." She turned to Shea, who tipped the brim of his hat with two fingers.

"Howdy," he said, voice shockingly deep.

"It's an honor," Kate said, studying Shea closely. His forearms were toned, fingers slender. She recognized that long face. He looked as if he hadn't aged a day since those old black-and-white photos. Though it was difficult to make out his eyes beneath the cowboy hat, he was still handsome.

Then Kate saw something that took her breath away. Hanging low on a leather-cord necklace Shea wore a silver pendant bearing a strange symbol — a ring with a cross at its apex. She couldn't believe it. That was it — the thing she couldn't remember — the thing she'd seen at the crime scene in North Hollywood. Suddenly it clicked: it was the same symbol that was tattooed on Melody Carmichael's finger.

All the questions Kate had so carefully rehearsed during the drive went up in smoke. Still, she opened the voice recorder app and placed her phone on the glass coffee table. "Do you mind if I record our conversation? I thought maybe we'd start with some casual stuff before we get to your new film." She pointed at Shea's necklace. "That's an interesting design. Can you tell me a bit about that?"

Shea looked down at the pendant, as if he was surprised to see it there, eyes hidden beneath the brim of his hat. "It's the sigil of the abyss," he said, looking up slowly, speaking calmly. "I like it out here in the desert because the climate is unforgiving. It's boiling hot during the day, freezing cold at night. The kinds of things that grow out here cover themselves in spikes. Little things get eaten by big things. That's what this symbolizes — this necklace. They say the abyss is a place of extremes. Sandstorms, lava, mountains of flesh." He paused. "There's life everywhere, you know, so long as you know how to find it. In the desert it's hidden away. It's adapted."

Something about the way he spoke, the words he chose, scraped at Kate's nerves. He was so serious. There was no detectable irony in his voice, no sarcasm, no recognizable emotion. He spoke with the fanatical conviction of a true believer. She looked around the room. It was dark, but she was still able to make out a series of large, oil-based paintings on the wall behind Shea. The paintings seemed to portray elaborate scenes of apocalypse, orgies of full-bodied female nudes and black-winged demons, hardened phalluses, rivers of gore. The images in these paintings brought to mind what little she remembered of *Wormlust*.

"What can you tell me about those?" Kate said, motioning to the wall.

Shea didn't react. Carol, however, looked over her shoulder before turning back to Kate. "The paintings? They are beautiful, are they not? That's how Mr. Shea supports himself when he is not making his films. Many do not know this. You should put it in your article. Mr. Shea is a great maker of art. Fine art. He is very accomplished. Those are his most recent pieces. They go for a high price. In fact, we are currently finalizing their sale to a well-known collector, the owner of the studio financing Mr. Shea's latest film, nonetheless. A powerful man. He is a great fan."

Shea cut in. "Those paintings are special. They show the demon Abaddon as he presides over the realm of the dead. The black-winged angel. King of the locusts."

Kate steered the conversation away from this talk of demons and apocalypse. She told herself it was because she didn't know how much time she had, but really it was because she was uncomfortable, thrown off her game. They spent the next few minutes talking about Shea's frustrations with the formalities of the art world, how he passed his days out here in the desert, waking up late, only eating a single meal each day, exploring the land. He talked about the energy vortexes he had discovered, his experiments with dark crystals and peyote, and why he refused to read any books. Kate was relieved to find that, after its menacing start, the interview evolved into something more comfortable, conventional even. She began to find Shea strangely alluring, laughing at his cryptic comments. All the while, Carol kept smiling, broadcasting her approval.

Outside, it was now quite dark. The sky had turned a beautiful, deep shade of desert-rose purple. The patio lights kicked on and the pool gleamed bright as a polished gem. As Shea spoke about his admiration for lizards, Kate watched as the woman swimming laps emerged from the water — a silhouette against the blinding lights — ascending the steps in the pool's shallow end. She bent over, shook out her hair, and wrapped her willowy legs in a towel. Then she opened the sliding glass door and entered the room.

At first, Kate thought she must be mistaken, that it was impossible. It had to be impossible. The girl who had just entered the room was identical to Melody Carmichael — same green eyes, flawless skin, and walnut brown hair. But it couldn't be Melody Carmichael. Melody Carmichael was dead.

Shea stopped talking, perhaps sensing that Kate was no longer listening.

"I see you are struck by the beauty of my newest client," Carol said to Kate. "This is Bianca Rhoads. Soon she will be a big star." She turned to the girl. "Don't be shy, dear. Miss Murphy is a writer. She's here to write an article about Mr. Shea."

"How do you do?" Bianca said, blushing. Her voice was youthful and pure. She kept her eyes trained on the floor.

Kate couldn't imagine how to answer. The question was phrased so formally. She was vaguely aware of the fact that her mouth hung open. She closed it, tried to pull herself together. She was just about to respond when Shea cut in.

"This girl is the bravest actress I have ever worked with. Not like the others. Most actors, most actresses, they never really learn how much bravery it takes to truly let go. To experience one's own death over and over again — that is the ultimate artistic expression. It's the ultimate expression of life itself, all of our experiences in this life. It's a kind of bravery that most people will never be able to imagine. They'll never know what it means to live in that moment, as terrifying as it might be, captured on film, the moment that lasts forever — even if it means embodying your worst fears." As he spoke, his voice grew louder, swelling with something like pride. "Bianca Rhoads will live forever on the screen as somebody else. To really make it as an actress requires . . ." He searched for the right word. "It requires sacrifice."

Shea stood up, shockingly thin, skeletal, and crept toward Bianca, moving like a cartoon villain, raising his knees high with each step — towering over her. He lightly touched her under her chin, tilting her head back, directing her to gaze into his eyes. Then he craned his neck, leaned forward, and whispered something in her ear, the brim of his cowboy hat brushing aside her damp hair. Then she was gone, skipping happily down the hall at the end of the room, one of its many doors clicking shut behind her.

Kate couldn't help herself. It was too much to hold in any longer. She just blurted it out. "Does the name Melody Carmichael mean anything to you?" It was like all of the air was sucked out of the room. "She was murdered a few days ago. That symbol you wear around your neck, I saw it tattooed on one of her fingers."

Once again, Shea did not seem to react to her question. Carol's smile had disappeared.

Kate couldn't stop now. She couldn't help herself. "That girl," she said, "the one you just introduced to me as Bianca Rhoads? She looks exactly like Melody Carmichael."

Shea was suddenly ferocious. "Tell me, Miss Murphy," he said, growling the words, "where do you think your soul goes once you die? You don't deign to know? Well, let me tell you this, those who are forgotten are banished to unnamed layers of existence — the gutter at the bottom of the world. How does that sound to you?"

Carol nearly leapt to her feet, playing interference, positioning herself between Shea and Kate. "I'm afraid that's all the time we have for today," she said, putting a hand on Shea's shoulder. He shook free of her, ignoring his agent, crossed the room and stood over Kate. She tried to sink deeper into the couch, staring up at him. No matter what, she couldn't let him know that she was scared. She would not give him the satisfaction of allowing herself to be intimidated.

"Here is what you should put in your fucking article," Shea said. "Here's your fucking lede. This is what you came out here for, right? People like you, you think making films is about creating art or you think it's about making money. You're fucking clueless. Nothing more than worms—all of you. I've been trying to show you the truth. But you're all too fucking stupid to see it for what it is. When you watch my films, what you see up on that screen, it's more real than you'll ever realize." He raised his arms out to his sides. "I set people free with my camera. The people in my movies, the person who plays the character, they cease to exist. Once you train the lens on a person, they disappear. But the worms lust after violence. They demand it. So I show them what they want to see. I show them other people—people just like them, normal people, like you—getting torn to shreds by monsters. I show them a vision of what it's like to die a painful death, to be cast away and forgotten, and they worship me for it. They elevate me above others. But murder? No, not as you understand it."

Carol wrapped an arm around Shea's thin waist. "I'm afraid you're going to have to see yourself out, Miss Murphy," she said, pulling the famous director away. She guided Shea toward the hall at the far end of the room. His whole body began to shake, as if he were having a seizure.

Kate immediately got up and followed. "Wait," she said, "we're not through here. You can't just yell at me like that and walk away. Where are you going?"

Shea and his agent rushed through the doorway just as Kate caught up with them. And in that moment, she got just a glimpse of the sunken living room beyond, its various couches and chairs filled with dozens of women, all in various forms of repose — some wearing robes, others in lingerie, still others wearing nothing at all — their big eyes on Shea, utterly adoring. And then the door slammed shut. Kate instinctively grabbed the handle. It was locked. She banged on the door but no one answered. She was so mad, so utterly bewildered by what had just happened, she stormed back into the great room, and, not knowing what else to do with her anger, her confusion, picking up the still-full bottle of Pellegrino, cried out, and shattered it against the wall.

She didn't get home until midnight. The whole drive back, all she could think about was that room full of women, looking like hungry cats pleading to be fed. Was she supposed to see that? Was it just a wild publicity scheme?

Back in her bungalow, Kate turned on all the lights, cranked the ceiling fan, and opened a bottle of wine. Whatever it was Shea was raving about — setting people free, giving the worms what they wanted to see, being worshipped — she couldn't make any sense of it.

There was no way that had been Melody Carmichael, either. It couldn't have been. Kate opened her laptop, took down half her glass of wine in two mouthfuls, and typed Carmichael's name into Google. There it was — an article in *the Times* reporting her death. Kate studied the photo of Carmichael at the top of the page. She really did look exactly like the girl who had been doing laps in the pool at Shea's house. And yet, the more she stared at the photo, the less she was able to see her. It was as if Carmichael's face was erasing itself from Kate's perception, one detail at a time. This sense of erasure was the same feeling she'd had when she took the photo of the arm in North Hollywood, when she tried to recall its details later that same night. Something was missing from what she remembered, like there were holes in her memories, draining details.

Kate closed her eyes, listened to the blades of the ceiling fan as they sliced the humid air. She was hotter than ever, stripped off all her clothes. She spent the next few hours drinking glass after glass of wine, letting it dribble down her chin. When she got tired she locked herself in her bedroom with her laptop.

She went back to Pornhub, scrolled through

the videos, and found something rougher than last time, something that looked like it was filmed in an empty warehouse. The girl in the video had a ball gag in her mouth, her arms tied behind her back, ropes crisscrossing her chest. Her mascara ran down her face, her eyes looking up at something beyond the frame. She looked just like Carmichael. A man wearing a black hood over his face approached her. Kate didn't want to see this. She went to the next video. This one showed a girl tied to a table getting fucked by a machine. She looked just like Bianca Rhoads. Kate clicked on video after video. All the performers looked scared. They looked like all the girls she passed by on the street. They were girls whose names no one knew — forgotten, overlooked. The videos got weirder. Everyone was slicked in scorched oil, plagues of locusts descending from the sky. Men in black cloaks held one of the girls down and cut open her belly, chanting, carving symbols into her thighs, firelight flickering against the walls. It looked so real. There was so much blood. It didn't look like a performance, the way the girl's skin puckered, the way she recoiled from the bite of the blade, the sounds she made, involuntary and guttural. The men pulled out her organs by the fistful while she screamed. Her eyes remained open wide with fear, disbelief. Her chest heaved with each desperate breath. Kate couldn't help but watch, fascinated, repulsed. Was this for real? She clapped shut her computer, plunging the room into darkness, and wept herself to sleep.

In the morning, she lay in bed and stared at the ceiling. Her head was killing her. Her eyes ached, a dull, pulsing pain. When her phone vibrated, it was as loud as a buzzsaw, ripping maliciously through soft tissue, skull splitting, adrift somewhere in her tangled bedsheets. She dug it out — Barstow area code.

It was Carol. Of course it was Carol. She heard Carol's voice, as genial as ever, apologizing for Shea's outburst, saying something about his medication levels being off. "He's an old man," she said. "He's on pills for the pain. Everyone in Hollywood is on pills. Surely you must know that."

Kate listened quietly, waiting until Carol was finished, and when it was her turn to speak, she said, "Nothing was off the record, you know. I'm going to use his words. Everything he said, whatever it meant. Everything I saw in that house . . ." she paused. "Whatever it was. I'm going to use it all. I'm going to write about all of it. And if you think it would be helpful for readers to know that Leonard Shea was under the influence of prescription medication during our interview, I'd be happy to include that information as well."

The line was quiet for a few moments. Carol cleared her throat. "Naturally," she said, "you are the professional. You should write the article as you see fit."

"Okay then," Kate said, angling to end the call. She felt like she might throw up, a mixture of nerves and nausea. Her mouth flooded with saliva.

"Just one moment, Miss Murphy. Before you

go. There is one last bit of unfinished business. Mr. Shea and I think it is only fair that you attend a private screening of his new film, *The Angel of Death*. Whenever suits you. Mr. Shea will not be there, of course. You will have your privacy. You will watch the film and then decide how you wish to write the article, yes?"

Kate agreed and was more than a little relieved to end the call. Carol was right. As much as she might loathe the idea, Kate had to watch the film. She couldn't finish the article without seeing it. A few minutes later she received a text with the address. She looked it up, some faceless building in an office park in Studio City, a post production facility. A second text came in with the number of the viewing room. Kate got out of bed, took a pull from the bottle of vodka she kept in her freezer, and forced herself to take a shower. The ice-cold water was the only relief she could find from the heat. When standing became too difficult, too exhausting, she sat down in the tub, pulled her knees close to her chest, her arms wrapped around her hamstrings, and let the water beat down over her head and shoulders.

The rest of the day got away from her, in a daze, fucked up. She took a few more pulls from the chilled vodka bottle and the light soon slipped numbly into darkness. Kate coasted along the eerily deserted streets to Studio City and parked her car in an eerily empty garage, the engine cutting with a shudder, and took the elevator to the building's lobby. The ceiling lights seemed to be malfunction-ing, twitching and pale. There was no one at the front desk, just an empty chair facing a blank secu-rity monitor, long shadows climbing the walls. She took another elevator and got off, walked down a long, angled hallway until she found the room she was looking for. The door was unlocked.

A blade of light cut through the darkness, slicing along the small room's wood-laminate floor. She flicked on the light switch, sent the shadows into hiding. The room was nearly bare: a cheap couch pushed up against the wall and a flat screen on the wall. The window shades were pulled down. It took her a minute to figure out the TV, to discover the blank disc in the DVD player, find the right in-put channel. Once she got the film going, she sat on the couch.

The version she watched must not have been finished. There were no opening titles. The sound was poorly mixed. At first the images were hard for her to process: humps of shadows, windswept dunes, close-ups on row upon row of sharp teeth. Then there was time-lapse footage of the sun rising and setting, which dissolved to a wiry nude man alone in the desert, his skin darkened by the heat, his head wrapped in rags. The man fell to his knees, digging at the edges of a wide, flat stone, shredding the skin of his fingers, growling like an animal. He extracted a small yellow lizard, the little thing squirming frantically in his fingers, brought the liz-ard up to his mouth and bit off its head. A single spurt of dark blood lashed his unshaven face, the lizard's limbs still thrashing.

Cut to a Steadicam shot sweeping through the halls of a desert palace, sand and dust sloping in the corners of empty rooms, cracked walls, fractured pillars. The soundtrack was stuffed with the sounds of wind, sucking sounds. There was the sudden image of a massive cave filled with sleeping bats. Then, back in the palace, there were people everywhere, dressed in fine silks and linens, wearing gold and gem-encrusted masks. Scores of elegant, beautiful women lying motionless on long couches, their breasts exposed, draped over the extravagant furniture. The bats awoke, fluttering into the cave in a great choreographed swoop. Similarly, the camera swooped around the palace's ballroom, revolving around dozens of couples as they danced a waltz, first one direction, then the next, revolutions around revolutions. A dazzling, corkscrewing overhead shot showed the dancers moving along the black lines of a pattern painted on the floor — the sigil of the abyss that Shea wore around his neck, the ring crowned by a cross.

There, in the center of the ring, Kate saw a small black dot take form, nothing more than a pinprick. The dot seemed to contain depth, an inky blackness, not a dot at all, but rather a hole. She focused her attention on this hole. Once again the images dissolved, the image of a woman's face — Anastazie Lhotsky or Melody Carmichael or Bianca Rhoads, whatever her name might be, if it even mattered — appearing beneath the ballroom, beneath the sigil, the camera zooming in on the woman's face while the image of the ballroom floor, the sigil, continued to spin, revolving again and again until the two images aligned, until the black hole appeared at the center of the woman's eye. The image of the ballroom continued to fade as the hole grew larger, entering the woman's eye. The sound of the wind returned — the noise of air sucked through a tube, a great pressure released. Soon, the hole was as large as half the screen, the entire screen, larger still — Kate covered her eyes, afraid of what she might see — until she felt the creeping dark come over her, sucking her inside, swallowing whole the room itself, warm as a mouth.

Then she was sliding down a sludge-slicked crevasse. She tumbled over herself a few times before turning over onto her back, pummeled by the uneven stone surface. Her clothes were torn open, skin bruised, shredded. Her legs were thrown over her head, and Kate fell far enough that she had time to draw a deep breath, to feel her heart in her throat, terrifyingly weightless. She was just about to scream again when she slapped the water's surface, hard as cement. Her body plunged deep down. There was nothing beyond the black silence, all-encompassing, no telling up from down. She thought she was dead, felt the relief of that, and let her body go limp, turned over, her arms and legs hanging slack.

She surfaced. The smell around her was putrid, the smell of rot and ruin. The water was disgustingly warm, its taste foul. Wherever she was, it was dark; a single source of light shined through some deep, faraway crag, illuminating the swelling surface of some kind of underground lake. As far as she could see, the lake's rolling waves rippled with the misting rain. She was surrounded by bodies floating face down, uncared for, unloved, everyone left to dissolve in this godforsaken place. She saw men and women, old and young. She saw a clump of tangled babies, severed limbs, unidentifiable rafts of tissue and viscera.

The fetid water rolled over her, submerging her once again, choking her. The waves tossed her around like a ragdoll. Kate washed up onto some kind of shore, oil sands globbing onto her skin. She swiped away the muck from her eyes, crying out, vomiting brown fluid, emptying her stomach. She soldier crawled to safety, her legs heavy and limp, waves over against her, threatening to pull her back in.

Then it was like she was watching a version of herself, leaving a version of herself behind, someone she no longer recognized. She watched the whole thing unfold like it was a camera shot — bird's eye view, spiraling upward — a scene in a movie that revealed Kate as she rolled onto her back. And as the camera pulled back, it revealed what could only be described as a mountain of flesh, a writhing pile of corpses, crushed together, arms and legs wriggling as a mass. Cries of agony echoed in the darkness. Kate saw this place now for what it was: a crack in the earth at the bottom of a deep ravine. In the distance, she caught a glimpse of giant creatures lumbering in the muck, things beyond comprehension, all humps and horns and innumerable limbs, feeding on the dead. And there, floating above everything, she saw Leonard Shea, knowing instinctively it was him, the keeper of the abyss — its overseer — Abaddon, the Angel of Death. His leathery black wings beat the air. This was his vision. Everything Kate had been given to see — the world below, her suffering — all of it belonged to him.

Kate stopped leaving her bungalow. She drank too much. She got fired from Clued-In-LA because she stopped responding to her editor's emails, stopped checking her voicemails. She ran out of money, both of her cards maxed out, rent past due. The cops sent two officers to check on her — banging on her front door, peeking through her windows — but she hid in the bathtub until they left.

She was obsessed with the story. The only thing that mattered was getting it out there. People had to know what she'd seen. Suki assured Kate that the story was still going to run. The magazine said the second half of Kate's payment was on its way, but the money never showed and the story never ran. Suki said the delay was because Shea hadn't finished his film — there was no release date. They couldn't run the story without a release date.

Then Suki stopped responding to Kate's emails, stopped answering her phone, her voicemail filled up. Her number was disconnected. Suki's social media accounts were deleted, as if she'd been swallowed up.

That's when Kate got scared. She worried she might be next. She knew too much. Still, she had to do something. She started a blog and posted the story there, fully aware of how crazy it sounded. The next day she received a cease and desist, certified mail, citing the contract she'd signed with the glossy. It was signed by the legal team of the company who owned the magazine. Her heart sank when she realized it was the same company that owned Shea's studio. And that's when Kate realized, all too late, that the magazine had never intended to run the story on Shea. The whole thing had been a catch and kill.

Kate needed to get out of LA. She grabbed her laptop, her phone, filled a duffel bag with her filthy clothes, and scraped together as much money as she could for gas and food. She threw everything in the backseat of her Honda and got behind the wheel. The engine choked and coughed. She beat the steering wheel with her fists and screamed. She pumped the gas pedal. The engine caught. She felt euphoric, laughing like a crazy person, swinging her car out into traffic and hitting the highway, heading back east, where people knew who she was.

Once she reached the desert the engine hot light popped on. Smoke started pouring out from under the hood. Her car started to slow. She pulled over onto the side of the highway, put on her flashers, screaming that this couldn't be happening — not now. The other cars kept driving by, a rush of sound and wind. Nobody seemed to notice her there, broken down on the side of the highway. No one seemed to care.

Blue and red police lights spun in her rearview mirror. Kate was crying now. The cop came to her window, motioned for her to lower it. He bent down, hands on his knees and smiled, flashing small and sharp teeth like a piranha. She noticed the thin white scar that ran straight back over the curve of his shaved head, the chunk of flesh missing from his earlobe. His eyes were hidden behind mirror shades.

"License and registration," he said.

Kate was defiant. "If you try to take me anywhere I'll scream."

He leaned forward, no longer smiling. "How much have you had to drink today?"

In that moment Kate knew she'd lost. He had all of the power — the control. She watched as the cars continued passing her by on the highway, all their different colors, gleaming impossibly bright beneath the white desert sun.

"Open the door and exit the vehicle, Miss Murphy."

Kate always did have a knack for the story. She even knew how this one would end. She knew it would be just as bad as she feared because this was the real world. Bad things happened all the

149

time—as bad as you could imagine. Soon, she would be a lost and lonely girl just like all the other lost and lonely girls, swallowed up and discarded. And she knew that no one would come searching for her. Only too late did Kate realize her worst fear—and for this she ached more deeply than she thought possible—that no one would come looking for her because no one would notice she was gone.

Worm Moon

Gemma Files

By the time the Worm Moon rises, you will already have been aware of its approach for far longer than a month. This is not *their* Worm Moon we speak of, after all; the false one, the sham, a mere matter of phases. This moon—*our* moon—does not come tied to any month, or linked to any human season. It rises in cold, wet darkness, from under snow and stones, so slowly that none of them can even feel its approach. It rises on the other side of that dead place you and they pretend to share, the face turned always away from the sun, of which they can only ever see half.

The dark will be opening wide soon. You will rise to meet it, emerge from this meat suit they make you wear, slick and filthy. Disgorge yourself, at last. Be fulfilled.

Locusts only have to wait seven years to find fruition; we wait far longer, work far harder. This is why all that lies Below loves us far more than anything Above.

You don't remember being born so much as just crawling your way up out of the earth, shell cracking to shuck itself and slip back down into the dark, the muck, the wounded, gaping soil-mouth. Your thin new human skin slapped by cold air as you wriggled free, slimy and goose-pimpled all over, into the fire's weak light. You thought you would never be warm again.

Cold blood is the best sort of blood for the long sleep, congealed like antifreeze. You could lie lost under three feet of ice and still survive, every part of you re-organizing itself from roe to egg, egg to pupa, pupa to nymph, nymph to larva. Larva, which means mask, the false face over the true.

This face, *their* face, over you.

Twenty-four hours before the Worm Moon's arrival, you'll already know it's on its way. This will give you just enough time to gather all the bits and pieces of this life you've made for yourself here — amongst them, unseen, unheeded — and fold them up like a soldier's coffin-flag. The knowledge will come to you at the height of an indrawn breath, the very moment your throat turns hollow and starts to bell, a blown-into reed swollen with potential speech, too large for your own hand to fit around. Your larynx will vibrate, a struck skin. Then the note will sound in your gut as you force the air back out silently, biting down, creating an undertone rather than words, or song. It will taint whatever comes out of you next, lending it a vile, hungry shade.

Maybe this will happen while you're at rehearsal and the choirmaster will call halt, unaware you're the culprit; he'll spend the next ten minutes trying to figure out what went wrong, reframe the line he's been teaching you, make sure it doesn't happen again. To fix things. And you'll just stand there and let him while the other choristers blame each other, blame themselves. No need to point out their mistakes.

It's their business, not yours, after all. Not really. You are not part of this, of them.

You never have been.

Drive until the lights dim and fade, then turn off into the woods, and park. Leave it all unlocked; nothing here means anything. Your feet will find the way. Take off your shoes, your socks, and stand with bare soles on the cold, hard, wet earth. The snow will melt beneath your feet, becoming mud, bringing you closer and closer to that thin rind of stony soil overtop what really matters. And as your toes turn blue, then grey, then black, the pulse will rise. You will feel it in what would be your marrow, if only you had bones.

When you've finally reached the right place, you will open your mouth, inhale. Cold air will coat your throat and settle inside your lungs. Every hair on your head will prick up. The blood in your veins will whirl and congeal, separating, black from red. Close your lips, and blow.

Eventually, something will answer.

Out here, the moon rises tiny and dull, a pebble off a dead man's eye. Out here, every stone — however fragmentary — is made from our mother's bones.

You will be met in the woods. So many more of you! You never knew. So many of them older. So many with drums.

(No one taught you how to make drums, you may think. No one taught you anything. You have been alone all your life. You will not know who to blame for this. Not that it matters, now.)

Some of you will turn your drums to ground, and beat them. Soft, soft, hard, harder, harder, hardest. Pound and pound. Match the heart which beats at the world's core, that bubbling volcanic rhythm. That liquid, glottal roar.

Here is how it will happen, at last:
Your blood will rise as the moon does, blackening your veins to make your feet, your fingers. Making them writhe.

The dark will open, wider than your mouth, by far. An empty, gaping void, aside from the Worm Moon above.

Your pores will open as the blood keeps on rising. As it noses out from each pore in your face like a fine filament of night, spinning itself together, thickening into a web, a sort of beard, fringing your mouth like whiskers. Thickening until it reaches out like fingers. Like the fine fungus which grows on some corpses' faces, a pallid mask, deep down under the ground.

Straighten, squirm, let your skin snap. Let it ruck off. Leave it behind.

You won't need it anymore.

Split yourself in two, make a friend.

Cut a long slit in his spine and crawl inside, face-first. Wear him like a coat.

It will not warm you.

You will not want it to.

Fall and slither, spreading slick slime along the dirt, the carven furrow. The seeding trace.

Spore. Spore. Spore.

Plow and plow. Seed it under. Bury it deep.

Wait seven years, and look! New yous.

All the while, the pulse will deepen, become louder. A crack will form and open wide, rippling with the beat. Inside the crack, more wetness, more cold. More you.

Something looks out, eyeless. Something noses the air.

Come down, it seems to say. And so you will.

(You always do.)

All you will leave in your wake is a hole.

But:

Nothing is perfect.

Not even this, for all it's simpler in its own way than anything you watched the meat-bags do. All the things you finally tried, once, more from boredom than curiosity. If there was a surprise in its ending, it was only in how much more pain he seemed to feel than you did.

It wasn't like you weren't grateful. After all, it was his books, his endless monologues about work, which set you on the hunt.

You read about arcane names like *Gliocladium,* and *Eurotium chevalieri,* and *E. repens* — midwife organisms between rot and rebirth. *Ascomata* and *conidia,* the words thrilling in your skin like a thousand pictures of anatomy never had. Read about the cycles of the moon, and the web of all the invisible life that spun to its pattern. All of it mulch for the strange fruit of your epiphany.

All of it which led you here, now. With the others.

Writhing in the dirt.

Changing.

If only you'd read just a little bit more.

The moon's road isn't perfect, either.

Its elliptical path, the faintest degree out of

circular true, sways it nearer and farther as it travels, like a pendulum. Humans have a dozen names for how these oscillations synchronize with orbital facings: *supermoons, micromoons, blue moons, wolf moons, blood moons* for the reddish umbra of a full lunar eclipse. All of it pointless, harmless poetry, you'd always thought.

But it means that not all moons are created equal.

And that every cycle has its reset point.

Something's wrong, you think, with the closest thing left to a brain you have. *Something's — not right. Not . . . right.* Whatever those words can mean, now.

A sea of black earth, churned up by a hundred slick, viscous bodies, white-capped in the moonlight by the shreds of what was once skin. Stirred to a near-froth by the remains of limbs, by fogs of a thousand spore-laden tendrils. The metamorphosis you'd ached for in every cell. Except . . . your reach, your ache, is not pulling you down or outwards.

But in.

Plasm entangles with plasm, knotting at the molecular level. Hands — or the remains thereof — grip hands, fusing like tree roots, melding into singularity. Pseudopods dance and mate. Your memory drowns in the orgasmic, irruptive rush of a hundred other souls, dissolving into the imperative common to you all: Transformation. Rebirth. But not separate, as you'd expected.

Together.

You thought what you'd wanted was metamorphosis. To become what you should have been all along. You were so certain you knew what the final form of your cycle was. Not the details of its shape, of course, that didn't matter. What it *meant*.

You'd wanted freedom.

But that is not the nature of this stage.

If you had the neurons left to remember it, you would know that this is called the *hypogeous sporocarp*. The fruiting body. A thousand-foot-wide tangled web of wormlike, mycelial tissue, woven through the earth, flickering with the last sparks of the previous cycle's memories. Collecting the genetic information of every bipedal pedipalp's life, collating it, rebuilding it into eggs like a wasp hatching young in its own flesh.

The last, supreme irony: *This* is the sexual stage of the reproductive cycle, a corpse-bed from which new yous will incubate — new, but not *you*.

159

One generation to a bioform, and the species re-boots. It survives. You don't.

This is as close to what the one you left behind truly wanted from you as you could ever give him. Too bad he'll never know that if he ever does come seeking you, only to find what you took in-stead — the car, clothes, whatever else. A discarded shell.

A seven-year locust's pupa-larvae, left be-hind, as the self — the molted, bright-winged, buzz-ing seed — drifts free.

Nothing is visible now above the surface of the soil, except the remains of clothing; abandoned drums; here and there half-buried flashlights, still alight, slowly fading. Leaves rustle in the wind.

A watcher might see the earth between the trees move, faintly, as if the forest floor itself breathed. Then the moon passes behind clouds, and is gone. Leaving only — the dark.

Above. Below.

Inside.

Walking in Ash

Brendan Vidito

I

"It's simple," Dale said, clutching the shotgun against her chest. "All you need to do is pull the trigger."

The house shook as a bomb exploded less than a block away. The sound was like thunder multiplied a hundredfold. Dale staggered and nearly fell. Her scream was lost in the cacophony of breaking glass and crashing furniture.

Aaron, her partner of six years, stumbled forward and grabbed her shoulders. His eyes were wild, his skin paled by exhaustion and lack of food.

"I know," he said. "But I want you to do it."

Dale shook her head. A solitary tear cut through the grime on her cheeks.

Aaron dropped to his knees like a praying man, hands caressing her outer thighs.

"Please," he whispered.

A second blast rattled the foundations. Dust drifted down the ceiling in a fine snow. The radio perched on the washing machine danced to the edge and plummeted to the floor. Black plastic sprayed in all directions and the batteries rolled across the cement like discarded bones. For months, that radio had fed them news of the world's collapse, but in the last few days, it had offered nothing but the steady hiss of static.

Slowly, reluctantly, Dale lowered the shotgun until the muzzle pointed at Aaron's upturned face. Her finger, with its long, dirty nail, trembled on the trigger. Despite this, she managed to hold the weapon steadily. The skills she gleaned from a lifetime of hunting with her father compressed, diamond-hard, into that singular moment. The window at her back framed an abstract view of hell: red-devil light, obsidian hail, and a ghostly curtain of ash. From his low angle, all Aaron could see of his partner was the towering darkness of her silhouette.

"Quickly," he said. Then: "I love you."

Dale's reply was drowned out by a third, cataclysmic explosion. The force knocked her off balance and she discharged the shotgun. Its roar rose up to meet the music of the world's ending — another jarring note in that symphony of absurd, conclusive violence.

Aaron's head snapped back and his vision filled with red mist. His body hit the floor, legs and arms kicking spasmodically. His bladder and bowels voided in a rush. The blood ebbing from his shattered skull felt first warm, then cold. And on the heels of that observation he realized he was still alive — or at least conscious enough to experience, in some rudimentary fashion, the death throes of his nervous system. He couldn't move, could barely *feel* anything, but was aware of a sensation of loss, as though he had forgotten something vital. Then the answer came to him: three-quarters of his skull had been obliterated. All that remained was one bloodshot eye, his mouth and the shredded remnants of an ear. Summoning his will, he bent his concentration toward his remaining eye and managed to roll it in Dale's direction.

She was holding the shotgun under her chin. Her mouth opened and closed in a series of grimaces. Tears gushed from her eyes. Then, with a wordless scream she pulled the trigger. Gore showered toward the ceiling in a vibrant, glistening fan. The weapon clattered to the cement, followed shortly by Dale's decapitated body, its movements limp and unnatural in the absence of life. She dropped first to her knees, and then flattened on her stomach. The blood from the ragged stump of her neck streamed thickly toward the floor drain.

The fourth explosion leveled the house completely. Brick turned to dust, walls ignited like paper, paint peeled and melted. Everything that had once given the place life or personality ceased to matter in a flash of apocalyptic light.

II

Aaron and Dale had been living in their first home together for a little over a week when they decided to explore the neighborhood. Standing on their front porch in jeans and short sleeves, they quietly took in their surroundings. The sun was setting, its amber glow reflected in the pools of rainwater on the street and sidewalk. Even though it was mid-summer, the air was cool, with that clean, rejuvenated feeling that follows a storm. All was quiet like the world had just exhaled, pausing for a moment before its next breath.

Thinking Dale wouldn't notice, Aaron pulled out his cellphone and swiped through the news feed. In recent months, it had become something of a reflex. Each headline screamed a fresh atrocity: two men arrested for plotting an act of right-wing terrorism, a mass shooting at a night-club that claimed the lives fifty-seven, climate reports warning of worsening natural disasters, and, if the others weren't enough, just that morning various countries had been sparring with threats of nuclear warfare. All it took was a glance and Aaron was instantly overwhelmed. He didn't understand why his mind kept insisting to check the news. It wasn't morbid curiosity. At least he didn't think so. Perhaps part of him thought that knowing what was going on in the world would help dispel the fear. But lately he was becoming increasingly aware that it was having the opposite effect. Every time he looked at the headlines, no matter how cursory his perusal, it was like a solid jolt straight into his amygdala.

"What are you doing?" Dale said. "Put your phone away."

"Sorry," Aaron mumbled, and slipped it back into his pocket.

"You got to stop doing that. We're going for a walk, for god sake."

Aaron laughed nervously and followed Dale down the porch steps.

The couple began their exploration by rounding a corner that led to a part of the street not visible from their porch. It was like they'd stepped into a different part of the city altogether. One ravaged by time and neglect. The street was cramped, hemmed in by dilapidated houses, and the sidewalk rose and fell in jagged rifts where tree roots had slithered up and cracked the concrete.

Aaron and Dale had been aware the area was in the process of gentrification. Seniors and young families populated their street. But what they didn't realize was the gentrification literally stopped dead several doors down from their place. The transition was slightly disorienting, and Aaron's pace faltered for just a moment. He looked back, saw the familiar curve of his street, the blue-painted house that faced his own, and only then did equilibrium return to his mind.

Dale took his hand, threading their fingers together. Her palm was warm and clammy. She cared little for public displays of affection, which

165

suited Aaron fine, but occasionally a glimmer of tenderness shined through, and she couldn't help but express her feelings.

Aaron looked down at their joined hands, then up at her face. She was smiling. The sun glanced off the lenses of her glasses. Her hair was a reddish frazzle, and the slug-thick scar on her forehead — the souvenir of a dog attack in her youth — was highlighted in the dying embers of the day.

Aaron remembered the first time he saw that scar. It was the second time they hung out. She wore bangs then, and shoulder-length hair. They'd gone to the beach with mutual friends on a day when air conditioners struggled to combat the record-breaking heat. Dale had plugged her nose and gone underwater. When she surfaced, her hair was slicked back, plastered against her skull. The scar was bright pink and glistening in the hot summer glare. It was gorgeous. Like jewelry made flesh, complementing the natural beauty of her face. When she noticed Aaron's gaze linger a little too long, she quickly flattened her bangs over her forehead as though covering her naked body. It had taken her several months of listening to reassurances and encouraging words from Aaron before she decided to wear her imperfection with pride.

Now, Aaron asked, "What's up?"

"Nothing," she said. "Just happy. Aren't you?"

"Of course." He gave her hand a squeeze. "I have to admit, though, being homeowners is a little weird."

"Oh, I know," she said. "It beats living in an apartment, though."

"You got that right."

Dale cast her eyes around the street. "It's really quiet here, isn't it?"

They passed a house with a sun-bleached FOR SALE sign and a basketball net in the driveway. Further, on the corner of the street, stood a building of brown brick. It was low and squat. The side facing them was arrayed with three battered doors, each with a number crookedly affixed to the chipped, curling paint. One of them was part way open — the lower half of the gap choked with dirty children's toys and bloated garbage bags. They didn't see any of the occupants. As he looked around for them, Aaron almost tripped over a broken flat screen television lying in the middle of the sidewalk.

"Goddamnit," he said, skipping to recover his footing.

"You okay?" Dale said, barely suppressing her laughter. "Funny how neither us saw that thing until it was too late."

"Daydreaming, obviously. We're not even here a month and we're already turning into mindless suburbanites."

Aaron bent to examine the television. It had been destroyed with chunks of blacktop. Each fragment rested in a crater of smashed glass.

"Someone took out their frustrations on this thing," he said and cast one look back at the brick building before Dale took his hand and tugged him

167

along.

As they turned the corner, Aaron was visited by a sense of déjà vu, accompanied almost immediately by a prickling of dread. It nearly froze him midstride, but he kept walking, hoping the movement would help him puzzle out the meaning behind these sensations. The closest parallel in his mind was the sudden shock of being stung by an insect. Only instead of pain, there was this feeling — just out of reach — that something bad was going to happen.

Ever since he was a teenager, Aaron had been prone to anxiety and panic attacks. And they'd only gotten worse in recent weeks. For this, he blamed both the stress of the move and the endless barrage of fear mongering in the headlines. What he was feeling now seemed very much like the prelude to one of his panic attacks. And if he didn't get things under control soon, his symptoms would only worsen. First, his heart would begin to race. Then came the tingling in his hands and fingertips, followed soon after by unpleasant warmth filling his chest and bringing a flush to his skin. Aaron closed his eyes and took a deep breath. *Everything is okay*, he mentally whispered to himself. *You're taking a walk, and everything is fine.* But the dread lingered.

The street they now followed was deeply shadowed, every lawn ornamented by a maple tree with leaves so green it was as though they gave off their own phosphorescence. The road and sidewalks were in much better condition than on their street, and the air was lighter somewhat. Despite the welcome ambiance of the place, however, Aaron couldn't help but sense that it concealed some kind of menace. Horrible things happened here, he thought, hidden away in the shadows. And all the darkened, shuttered windows were blind and ignorant. He shook the impression from his mind. His anxiety was distorting the world around him.

"You okay?" Dale asked.

"Yeah, I'm fine. I'm just getting weird vibes from this place."

"Why? It's beautiful. It looks like something out of a movie."

"Forget it. You know me."

"That you're paranoid?"

She gave his hand a squeeze to show she was teasing. This somehow made him feel a little better.

The tree-shadowed street crested into a hill that branched in two directions. One led to a neighboring street, the other curved down a gravel road. Aaron and Dale halted to consider their route. Silence stretched between them. The symptoms of a panic attack continued to gnaw at Aaron, so he decided to speak up, hoping his voice, once injected into the silence, would reassert his sense of reality.

"I say we continue down the street," he said.

"Aren't you curious what's down there?" she said, gesturing enthusiastically at the gravel road.

"Not really," Aaron answered. "Are we even allowed down there?"

Dale gave him a look that said *don't be ridiculous*. She waved a demonstrative arm. "I don't see a no-trespassing sign."

Releasing his hand, she started down the gravel road, walking backwards, beckoning him with outthrust hands, the fingers dancing in and out of her palms. Aaron stood immobile, watching her with a forced smile canting the corner of his mouth. It was impossible to appreciate her vivacity while his mind continued to simmer with that unknown species of dread. He wanted nothing more than to return home, curl up on the couch and knock back a beer. With any luck, the alcohol would dispel his negative feelings and allow him to slip into a deep, dreamless sleep.

"C'mon, loser," Dale said, vanishing where the path veered around the corner.

"Shit," Aaron said.

He pivoted to look behind him. The street was empty. He turned back to face the path. Cursed again. He had no choice but to follow Dale. Sighing, he started after her. Gravel crunched underfoot. To his right stood a garage without a door. Its depths were smothered in shadow and water dripped rhythmically from the ceiling. Further down the path, a rusted motorhome sat in a stretch of yellow grass. Its windows were shuttered with grey curtains of some drab jute-like material. One of them near the back moved subtly as though someone has just retreated from the window. Aaron stared, feeling watched. Something about the curtains didn't seem right. Their movement was unnatural. Before he could make sense of the observation, however, a hand grasped his shoulder, interrupting his line of thought. He gasped, swore under his breath and turned. Dale jumped back, mirroring Aaron's surprise.

"Jesus," she said. "What's wrong with you? Why are you so jumpy?"

Aaron gave another nervous laugh. Looking at Dale, he was quick to realize that her presence no longer offered comfort. His dread persisted, grower stronger with each new intake of breath. He shivered as sweat travelled down the canal of his spine.

"I don't know," Aaron said. "I think we should go home."

Dale's expression softened into concern. Her gaze became more intent.

"Are you not feeling well?"

"I'm definitely not feeling good."

"Are you having another panic attack?"

"I think so."

"What triggered it?"

Aaron paused to consider the question. "I don't know," he said finally.

Dale frowned. "Okay. Let's get going then."

As they turned to retrace their steps, Aaron noticed a house—taller than the others he'd observed in the neighborhood until now—standing at what he assumed to be the end of the gravel path. It was clad in white siding, stained and broken in places to reveal the rotting wood underneath. Graffiti scarred its surface. And through the chaos of tags and vulgarities one message screamed for his

171

attention: I WILL MEET YOU AT THE END OF THE WORLD.

Aaron's eyes then lifted to the only window visible from his vantage point. It was long and narrow. A sickly yellow light burned behind its glass. He could just make out a shadow moving on the ceiling. It was shapeless and seemed to dance with an almost flame-like motion. Aaron blinked, keeping his eyes shut for several seconds. The yellow light remained imprinted on the back of his eyelids. With a flash of pain, it rushed through his skull like a jolt of electricity. Yellow turned to orange, then...*red-devil light, obsidian hail, and a ghostly curtain of ash*. What was that? A memory. A hallucination. His stomach sank. Whatever it was, that brief glimpse of hell and the sickness it carried was inside him now.

III

Some hours later, they were in bed. Faces scrubbed for sleep. Reading lamps glowing in the dusk of evening. Aaron faced the wall, his back to Dale. His eyes were glued to an irregularity in the plaster. It looked like a raindrop on a window, frozen in time. At any moment, it could become a crack that would widen enough to split the house down the middle.

He felt sick. His dread from earlier had mutated into a full-body affliction. He was uncomfortable in his own flesh. His sweat, which came thick and steady from his pores, tasted and smelled different: more acrid and pungent. Acid burned the lining of his stomach. His bones ached, feeling too large for their scant covering of muscle and skin. He wanted to vomit until he escaped this prison of sickness and agony.

The bed springs creaked as Dale placed her book on the bedside table and rolled to face him. Her hand on his shoulder was colder that he remembered. Its chill seeped into his marrow.

"Still not feeling well?" she asked.

"Not quite," Aaron said, still facing the wall.

"Describe it to me."

Aaron thought for a moment, and then said, "It's like a shadow is hanging over my head. And at any moment it could fall and smother me. This probably sounds weird, but I think it's always been there. Ever since—"

He stopped himself, swallowed.

"Ever since what?"

The thought came to him unbidden: *Ever since I met you, ever since we moved into this house*, but he said nothing.

"Never mind." Silence stretched between them. Then he said, "I don't even know what I'm talking about. I'm sure I'll be okay in the morning."

"Well, if you need anything, wake me up, okay?"

Aaron rolled over to face Dale. "I'll be fine. You need your sleep."

She kissed him, gently, their lips grazing as she rolled over again to extinguish her lamp. Aaron

173

did the same. The click of the switch was loud in the relative silence of the house. The only other sound was the quiet drone of the air conditioner. It took a moment for Aaron's eyes to adjust to the dark. Before that, all he could see was black shot with the afterglow of the reading lamp — a pale yellow light that flared red whenever he blinked. He moved into a more comfortable position on his back and waited for sleep. Not a minute passed when he realized it wasn't coming. His mind was fully and horribly awake.

Staring at the ceiling, he listened to the music of the air conditioner. It sounded like something alive, breathing loud, icy breath. It had only been a week since they moved into the house, so his mental image of its rooms and layout was imprecise at best. But even so, he attempted to visualize the basement in his mind's eye. It was an exercise his therapist had taught him to calm his mind. *Open the door and you see a washer and dryer, edges flaked with rust. In the middle of the floor, a drain softly gurgles as it swallows the rain fed through the weeping tile. Opposite the laundry machines, stands the furnace, the newest and most polished appliance in that unfinished space. And then, there's the window — small and narrow, looking out from an extreme low angle at the street outside.* It made him think of red light and something else — something poised on the tip of his recollection.

As he explored the space in his imagination, Aaron wondered why he was so engrossed with the basement. It held some form of significance, but couldn't decipher what that was. But he knew it

174

had something to do with that infernal red light. Where had he seen it before?

Feeling movement beside him, Aaron turned and saw Dale watching him through the darkness.

"What are you doing?" he asked.

Her voice sounded drunk and far away, a sleepwalker's drawl. "When I was a kid, my friends and I used to play a game at sleepovers called Wolf," she said. "You'd stare at one another in the dark and watch as the shadows transformed your faces. It gave us a real thrill."

Aaron asked, "Are you asleep?"

"Just play with me," she said. "It's fun."

"I think you're dreaming."

"It'll just take a second."

Feeling like he had no other choice, Aaron stared into Dale's face, tracing its familiar outline and detail with his eyes. For some moments, nothing happened. Her face remained whole, undisturbed by the darkness encroaching from all sides. Then, she began to change.

"Ugh," she said. "You look really creepy."

Aaron didn't know what his partner was seeing. But he doubted it was as horrific as the illusion—it wasn't real, it couldn't be—playing out before his eyes. All the life drained from her features, her eyes rolled back, glazed, the pupils rimmed with ruptured veins. Her tongue hung over her bottom lip, its surface jeweled with droplets of blood. For an instant, Aaron thought he could hear the gentle patter of liquid striking the mattress. It was

175

blood, and it was draining with alarming speed from the missing top half of Dale's skull. An image of the floor drain in the basement flashed subliminally through his mind's eye. He tried to look away, to scream, but he was paralyzed. A quiet moaning began in the depths of Dale's throat, a prolonged death rattle that grew in volume until it engulfed the night silence. Aaron tried again to look away, to cover his ears, to wake up, but it was impossible. He did manage to blink, however, and hellish red light filled his head.

Aaron woke on the living room floor. It was still dark and the drapes hadn't been drawn over the window, offering him a view of the street. He clambered to a standing position and staggered toward the window. Pressing his hands firmly against the pane, he stared out at the street. It was empty and bathed in the warm glow of the streetlamps. For the first time that night, peace settled on him. He breathed slowly and deeply, wondering why he had ever felt so anxious in the first place. Dale was right. He was unduly paranoid.

But this was a dream. Aaron knew it with a lucid certainty. And so what? It offered him peace he was unable to find at present in the waking world. He would enjoy it. Allow his mind to be swept away on the current of his own subconscious. It would probably do him some —

All the windows across the street exploded with red light. The lamps sputtered and went out. A siren wailed briefly in the distance before falling silent, its echo fading like the filament of a light bulb. Aaron gasped as something slammed into the window with such force it rattled in its frame. Multiple faces stared back at him, charred black flesh stretched in silent screams. Fingers, incinerated to the bone, clawed at the glass with a screeching sound that made Aaron's blood turn to ice. And behind these ghosts of men, women and children, some still burning or smoldering, a white light slowly engulfed the horizon. Aaron threw an arm over his face to shield his vision. But the light was too strong. It penetrated flesh, muscle and bone, singing the vital spark at the core of his being. His scream transformed into the roar of a shotgun blast.

IV

He woke in a clammy sweat. Early afternoon light streamed through the bedroom window. His disorientation was so complete that for several moments he could remember nothing of the past twenty-four hours. Even his dream was nothing but a vague impression. No images lingered or stood out. All he knew was that he experienced something unpleasant, traumatic even, though he couldn't be sure of the details. Maybe that was for the best.

He grunted into a sitting position and glanced at his cellphone on the bedside table. There was a message from Dale. It read: *I silenced your alarm. You were having nightmares. Get some rest. Love you.* He smiled and climbed out of bed.

His dread from the night before had largely dissipated. Only a pale suggestion remained, like a memory on the fringe of consciousness. Today was a new day, and for the first time since the move, Aaron had the house to himself. Dale was going to dinner with friends that night and would likely not return until after he was asleep. It was the perfect opportunity for Aaron to familiarize himself with his environment and get some much-needed rest.

He brewed a pot of coffee and lazed around the house for several hours: watching television, reading a book, and eating random scraps of food from the fridge and cupboards. Eventually, his aimless wanderings carried him to the basement, where they had deposited most of their unpacked boxes. They stood along the walls, dour infantry watching over an unpopulated space. He looked at the furnace, hulking and lifeless in the corner of the room. Then his attention fell on a box orphaned from the rest. It sat resting against the wooden support beam in the center of the basement. Dale had written RANDOM SHIT across the top flap in permanent marker.

Aaron walked over and folded the box open. Dale had labeled it appropriately; it was indeed filled with miscellaneous junk. At a glance, he discerned empty picture frames, old, musty books, a loose sock, and a pack of playing cards. He pushed some of the junk aside, and froze as his hand passed over a portable radio that was at least thirty years old. Despite some wear on the corners, it still looked in good condition. And for some reason, it was familiar to Aaron, though he couldn't remember where he'd seen it before. It had likely belonged to Dale's father, something he packed into a box when she first moved out of her parent's place to attend college.

Picking it up, Aaron walked over to the washing machine, feeling on some deep intuitive level that it belonged there, and set the radio down. The effect was almost immediate. It was like puzzle pieces clicking together in his mind. Though what the puzzle amounted to, he couldn't be sure. He'd merely joined one piece to another. Its full image was still hidden from him.

He glanced at the window. Beyond, the street curved into the ungentrified part of the neighborhood. Another piece clicked together. He swallowed. A new wave of dread welled up from his stomach. What was going on? He had the nagging sensation that he'd caught a glimpse of something vital, and infinitely terrible. But no matter how hard he tried to make sense of it, it was like trying to read a language he didn't understand. He wanted to scream in frustration.

"Goddamnit it," he said aloud.

179

He desperately needed to put this puzzle together, but what was missing? His gaze returned to the radio on the washing machine. Like a man possessed, he scoured another unpacked box and fished out a pair of batteries. Jamming them inside the radio, he switched it on and adjusted the dial until a human voice garbled into existence. It was a woman. He'd caught her mid sentence, talking about the mounting tensions worldwide. Apparently, several countries were in discussions to sign a treaty preventing the use of nuclear weapons in the event of a global conflict. Aaron jabbed the power button. The woman cut to silence.

The basement was still and dark. Quiet except for the steady patter of dripping water. Aaron leaned against the washing machine to support his weight. The dread was creeping back to its original potency, filling his limbs with lead. The hairs on the nape of his neck stood up. What was wrong with him? His anxiety had been a constant presence in his life, but it had never been this bad. Was he in the grip of psychosis? Maybe the stress of the move, coupled with the endless barrage of bad news, had triggered something in his brain.

Somewhere, water continued to drip in a predictable rhythm. He cast his gaze around the room, searching for its source. The ceiling appeared dry and there were no puddles on the floor. Maybe a pipe was leaking behind the wall. He moved around, listening intently. The sound was loudest near the drain in the floor. Aaron hunkered down and lifted the metal grate. A wave of damp air caressed his face. The updraft caused a spider web covering the opening like a membrane to shudder and billow. The web's occupant was almost the size of a quarter. It skittered away and disappeared into the murky depths of the floor drain. Aaron placed his ear over the web and listened. The dripping was undeniably coming from somewhere below. There was nothing abnormal about that. The drain was connected to the weeping tile and it had rained quite a bit the day before. But even with this rationalization, Aaron wasn't satisfied.

He moved the spider web aside, shaking the clinging filaments from his fingertips. Pulling his cellphone from his pocket, he shined its flashlight into the drain. At first, it appeared dry, but when he moved his hand into the square opening, guiding the light deeper, a flash of crimson caught his attention. Rust? Dirty water, maybe? Upon closer inspection, though, he realized it was neither of these things. Reaching inside with his free hand, he touched the crimson substance and rubbed it between forefinger and thumb. It was sticky and oddly warm. Aaron reached in again with the intention of acquiring a larger sample. With an animal shriek, the red substance darted deeper into the drain. Aaron flinched back with a cry of his own, and crawled across the floor to the opposite side of the room.

His back was to the washing machine. His chest rose and fell, and his breath emerged in ragged, panicked gasps. Thunder pulsed inside his

181

chest with every frantic beat of his heart. Then the sobs came, each one threatening to wrench his lungs up his throat. He was losing his mind, there was no longer any doubt about that. The notion terrified him. He couldn't imagine a worse reality than not being able to trust one's own mind. He couldn't be alone any longer. He needed Dale. To hear her voice, feel the touch of her hands, smell the fragrance of her hair. She would make things right again.

He dialed her number. She picked up on the second ring.

"Getting bored having the place to yourself?"

Aaron tried to speak, but choked on a sob.

"Aaron? What's wrong?"

"Can you please come home?" he said. "I think something's wrong with me."

"What happened? Are you hurt?"

"No." He shook his head. "The feeling from last night. It's getting worse."

There was a pause on the other end of the line. Aaron could almost hear her mind working. Then she said, "Okay. I'm on my way now."

"Wait."

"What is it?"

He took a deep breath before speaking. "Do you think it's possible to be haunted by something that hasn't happened yet? Something so horrible, it vibrates backward through time?"

"Aaron, what are you talking about?"

"The signs are all there. In the news. On the

radio. I think something terrible is going to happen. And I'm the only one who knows it."

The more he spoke, the more his words seemed right. More puzzle pieces fitting together to form a progressively clearer image. It hovered in his mind's eye, bleak and imposing. A tableau depicting him and Dale collapsed on the basement floor, bathed in blood and ash.

"Listen to me," Dale said calmly. "Nothing bad is going to happen. Just hang tight and I'll be home as soon as I can. Okay?"

"Okay," he said, though it was barely audible.

He hung up and leaned his head back against the washing machine. Dale's office was only a fifteen-minute drive from home. It wouldn't be long before he heard her voice calling him from the living room. He closed his eyes and waited. A trickle of sweat ran down his forehead. His heart continued to beat a frantic tattoo against his ribs. Everything was going to be okay, he mentally told himself. Dale would make everything better. For as long as he knew her, she had a way of making the world seem like a less frightening place. All he had to do now was wait.

V

He opened his eyes. Night had fallen. Darkness lay thickly over the basement and its disorder of unpacked boxes. Aaron gasped and shot to his feet. It

183

had only been two in the afternoon when he closed his eyes. He checked his phone. A little past one in the morning.

"What the fuck?" he said, his voice shaking.

He checked his call history. Nothing from Dale. He dialed her number and waited. It rang and rang, and just as he was beginning to lose hope, she answered.

"Where are you?" Her voice sounded far away, distorted by static.

"Downstairs."

"Come up," she said.

He moved toward the staircase. There were no lights on upstairs. And everything was quiet. Something wasn't right. He mounted the first step. It creaked loudly under his weight. The second step sounded a note of its own, equally jarring in the ringing silence.

His phone vibrated in his hand. He held it at arm's length, checking the display. A text message from Dale read: *It's simple...* Then the phone buzzed again and a second message appeared: *All you have to do is pull the trigger*.

"Dale?" he called upstairs.

No answer.

Once on the main level he turned to face the hallway leading into the bedroom. Dale stood at the end, unmoving, little more than a dark shape. *All Aaron could see of his partner was the towering darkness of her silhouette*. He flinched at the mental image that sprang into his mind and superimposed itself on the scene before him. He took a step toward Dale and stopped. Something held him back. All of this was familiar, but it wasn't until Dale held up her hand and spoke that he realized he was living a scene from one of his nightmares.

"Do you want to play Wolf?" she asked.

The world outside exploded with red light that streamed through every window and doorway. It washed Dale in a visceral glow. She smiled and her teeth gleamed as though washed with blood. Her hair, Aaron realized, was styled the way it'd been when he'd hung out with her at the beach those many years ago — bangs swept over her forehead in a concealing curtain. Now, she raised her arm higher, and using an index finger parted the hair to one side, exposing her scar.

For several seconds, Aaron's mind refused to process what he was seeing. When it finally started working again, he shuddered in horror. He tried to scream. To run. But he was paralyzed. Rooted to the spot. He could only watch helplessly as Dale's scar opened like a mouth and expanded until it split her face down the middle. There was a loud crack as her skull came apart and a mixture of blood and brains fountained upward, splashing against the ceiling in defiance of gravity. Her eyes, each one nested in a separate half of her face, stared wildly, shining with perverse enthusiasm. Her tongue, like the rest of her head, had been ripped apart. Two bloody chunks of flesh waggled like bloated worms inside her mouth.

Another nightmare, Aaron thought almost casually. His fear upon seeing Dale, as it turned out, was short lived. It loosened its grip on his forebrain and faded away. In its place, came sadness — a feeling of profound, inexplicable loss. For the span of a moment, he was a child again, curled in bed, and reeling at a world didn't yet understand.

Dale walked toward him. Gore continued to waterfall from her skull, leaving a clotted red river on the ceiling behind her. She took his hand, threading their fingers together. Her palm was cold, the fingers stiff and clumsy. Aaron found that he could now move. He turned to look at Dale, and in spite of himself, managed a brief, sad smile. Even now, she had a way of making the world seem like a less frightening place. He would always love her for that.

"I don't want us to die," he said.

"So, you understand now?"

"I'm not sure. All I have is this feeling."

"You will never fully understand," Dale said, her voice lisped. "That's the mercy of premonition."

"Will this feeling ever go away?"

"Everything you've experienced these last few hours began on our walk," Dale said, as she conducted him toward the entrance. "Let's take another and see what happens."

She opened the door. It was dark outside. A crimson glow throbbed on the horizon. Flakes of ash fell like snow, and a trumpeting hum filled the air.

They moved onto the porch and stared at the street. Swarms of adults and children fled for their lives. Some were still on fire, others had been badly burned, their skin hanging from the bone and smeared in the fluid of broken blisters and liquefied fat. They were hairless, and their eyes had melted down the sides of their faces. Only their teeth were undamaged, bared in soundless screams of agony. None of them appeared to notice the couple on the porch.

Still holding Aaron's hand, Dale led him down the steps, across the driveway, to the sidewalk. They started walking in silence, following the same trajectory from the evening before. When they reached the bend in the road, Aaron experienced comfort rather than disorientation. He felt like he'd taken this walk many times before. Its geography and landmarks were familiar to his memory. Some distant, lucid part of his mind told him he should be driven mad from the vision of horror all around him. But, instead, he found himself nursing a dull, manageable fear.

"Watch your step," Dale said.

Aaron looked down. A broken flat screen television lay in the middle of the sidewalk. Its power cable snaked through the grass, useless and limp. Despite being unplugged, however, the screen flashed brightly and a garbled half-human voice emerged from the speakers. Through a dense web of cracks and dead pixels, a face was either laughing or screaming. The couple didn't stop to observe it more closely. They kept walking, soon rounding another corner.

Here was the street deeply shadowed by

trees, only now their leaves had been burned away. All that remained were the trunks and branches, alternately blackened and bleached by the force of some unknowable catastrophe. As a result, their shadows had grown thin, like emaciated fingers reaching across the asphalt for mercy or supplication. Behind every window lurked a face, screaming and charred black. In one home, a mother and father were killing their children with steak knives to spare them of further suffering. The youngest took the blade to the chest with innocent willingness, while the eldest had to be caught and pinned to the floor, allowing the father to cut his throat like a sacrificed lamb.

Aaron wept for them, but again continued walking. Dale wouldn't let him stop. She instead guided him up a gravel road. When they reached the motor home at its end, she stopped and said, "I leave you here. You must continue on your own."

He turned to face her and cupped her blood stained cheek.

"I don't want to lose you," he said.

"There is nothing to lose when we all die together," she replied.

Aaron could barely comprehend the elation he experienced upon hearing these words. They served as a climax of sorts—the much-needed respite after a long journey. Up until now, his entire existence had been consumed by anxiety. He'd been walking in the ashes of things to come. But now, Dale had blessed him with peace of mind using only a mouthful of simple words. He inhaled and the air shuddered into his lungs.

"Why am I seeing this?"

"An accident," she said. "You weren't chosen, if that's what you're wondering. The universe is blind. It doesn't choose anyone for any specific purpose. You merely contracted something on your walk the other night. A splinter in your brain, a flash of things to come."

The trailer shuddered on its cinder blocks. Aaron looked over Dale's shoulder and saw the curtain rustle and fall away with a muffled thump. A sliding, shuffling sound travelled the length of the vehicle, before the door burst open and something slithered into the grass. It was grey and thin, like a massive flatworm, and its flesh had the texture of old jute. What Aaron had originally mistaken for a curtain was, in reality, something alive. It moved through the grass with a whispering sigh, raised the upper portion of its body from the ground and regarded him intently. Aaron had the sudden impression of invisible fingers reaching into his mind, beckoning him forward.

He spared one final glance at Dale before following its sinuous course toward the house with the graffiti. Soon the words: I WILL SEE YOU AT THE END OF THE WORLD loomed above him. He looked up at the only window visible on this side of the building. Light and shadow wrestled in a wild orgy, twisting and turning like elongated limbs wracked by spasms. Something was moving in the upper room.

The flatworm-thing stopped at a door that

hung ajar. Sickly yellow light spilled from between the gap. Aaron looked at the creature. It was motionless. He turned his attention back to the door, took a step forward, and wrapped his fingers around the handle. With a deep breath, he swung it open. Light painted his face and stunned his vision. He held up a shielding arm. When his eyes adjusted, he found himself at the foot of a staircase. Feeling like he was on the verge of waking from a long nightmare, he gripped the bannister and started to climb.

It didn't take him long to reach the top. The room was modest, no more than a storage space. The yellow light seemed to emanate from the air itself, as though the particles of dust that drifted about were endowed with a form of bioluminescence. The shadows he perceived from outside had appeared on the ceiling. When he looked up, the blood vessels in Aaron's eyes engorged with blood and exploded, rendering him blind. His head swam and he nearly lost his balance. Either his eardrums ruptured or his brain was so overloaded with what he'd just seen on the ceiling that he could hear no more. Despite being both deaf and blind, however, Aaron still possessed a vivid picture of the ceiling dweller in his mind's eye.

It was vaguely humanoid, though at least three times the size of the largest man. It was curled up in the fetal position, its massive head cradled close to its knees. Long white hair hung down from its mottled scalp, each strand moving of its own accord, casting erratic shadows across the walls and floor. Its eyes, much too large for its face, roved madly in their sockets.

Aaron staggered backward until his spine came into contact with the wall. As he stood there, his mind a firestorm of questions, fear and confusion, the thing on the ceiling began to speak. Its voice rumbled in his bones and rearranged the cells in his body. It told him, in a language without words, that the human race would soon come to an end. The humanoid-thing, along with his kind, would inherit the ashes once the world had grown silent and barren.

The force of its speech drove Aaron to the floor. Blood pumped warmly from his ears and spilled down the sides of his face. He opened his mouth and screamed, "Why me?" over and over in a demented refrain until the pain in his head grew to engulf his entire being.

VI

He woke the following morning in bed, to find Dale snoring softly beside him. For several minutes, he didn't move. His eyes were fixed on the ceiling. Had Dale also been awake, all she would have seen was a white surface dappled with sunlight. Aaron, however, saw much more. His vision had expanded overnight. A huge man, not unlike the one Aaron had encountered in his dream the previous night, was curled up on the ceiling. Perhaps he had always been there, watching. Aaron stared at the man-thing, and it stared right back with bulging, bloodshot eyes. Its mouth moved in slow motion. It was speaking, and though Aaron couldn't discern the words, he understood their meaning. It was counting down.

Aaron climbed out of bed and moved into the kitchen. The man-thing followed, sliding along the ceiling with its arms pinned to its sides. Aaron gave him little heed as he turned on the coffee machine and threw a piece of toast in the toaster. He then turned on the radio, making sure the volume was not loud enough to wake Dale. He ate his meal and drank his coffee as the newscaster droned on and on. Eventually, Aaron realized she kept repeating the same story in an urgent loop, informing potential new listeners of what they had been missing. He stopped chewing, put down his coffee.

War.

He closed his eyes and thought of the day he spent at the beach with Dale. Every image, every impression flitted across his mind. The heat of the sun. Trees painting the shore a rich emerald green. Seagulls wheeling and crying under an unbroken blue sky. Dale's face sheened with lake water. The first time she *really* looked at him, appraising him as a future lover and friend.

God, he loved her.

He opened his eyes again, stared at the remains of his breakfast. Above him, the man-thing continued to count down. Aaron was ready for what waited at the end of those numbers. His dread and anxiety was nothing but a memory. There was no reason to be afraid anymore.

A floorboard creaked behind him. Turning, he saw Dale, standing in the hallway. Her hair was disheveled, her eyes puffy with sleep.

"What's going on?" she asked.

The Silvering

Thana Niveau

It fell from the sky like ash. At first people assumed it was just another effect of pollution; Houston was notorious for it, after all. As the strange event only seemed to be occurring in one of the city's most deprived areas, it wasn't really news. And it might have gone entirely unreported were it not so shockingly beautiful.

Day after day the silver flakes drifted down. They adhered to derelict buildings and crumbling ruins, building up like stalagmites and transforming shotgun shacks into fairytale castles. Gleaming spires shone against the dull grey sky, grander than the grandest of royal palaces.

The eyes of the world turned towards Houston. Beside the shining new silver towers, the famous skyline was a dreary monstrosity, as unsightly as the hulking factories that vented poison into the air along the ship channel.

The city's wealthy began to look on their own ostentatious mansions with discontent, filled with envy for the silvered hovels and shantytowns of the inner city. The clouds above their own communities never rained the coveted particles.

After a while the inhabitants of the silver realm began to transform as well. Their skin began to glow, their hair to shine. At first they tried to scrub the silver stains away, but the colour could not be shifted. Injuries bled shimmering fluid, like pools of mercury. Tears were lustrous pearls.

There was no pain, not in the beginning. Not until the first self-mutilation.

Carmen Ayala lived alone in a shabby frame house in the Third Ward. Most of the neighborhood had been destroyed by hurricanes the year before, and the promised emergency aid had never come. With nowhere to go, the residents stayed on, helping each other out as best they could as they struggled to rebuild their community.

But after the strange dust began to fall, Carmen's tiny home became a shining palace in a wonderland of other such palaces. All throughout the neighborhood, radiant pinnacles soared into the sky, rising higher and higher every day. They twined into spectacular loops and arches, like vast sculptures made of mirror.

Carmen stared around at the transformed landscape. Silver grass and weeds covered the ground. The once cracked and crumbling streets had become rivers of polished steel. Children ran and danced across the burnished surface, pursued by their reflections.

The wind blew the drifting silver snow towards the freeway. Traffic stalled there permanently, with thousands of cars inching past as drivers gawked at the magical pocket world down below. Before long the silver had encircled and blocked the overpass.

Most people were in awe, but Carmen was terrified. She could never have imagined such beauty was even possible. It was unnatural. Day by day she watched as everything she knew became something else, something impossible. And when her left hand started to change, she cut it off.

The pain was unlike anything she had ever experienced. Jets of silver blood pulsed from the wound, arcing onto the gleaming street. Then, like molten metal, it began to solidify. Where her hand had been was a lavish spray of silver shards, as though a fountain had frozen in midair.

The agony did not subside. Like her body, it transformed. The sensation grew and grew until she thought she would either die or lose her mind. And somewhere along the way the pain also began to transform. As she had never known beauty, so too had she never really known pleasure. That must be what this was. It was a feeling she never wanted to end. She felt reborn.

Now that the once-invisible community was on the world's radar, the politicians moved in. They hadn't cared enough to offer aid when it was needed, but now that something beautiful was happening, they wanted it for themselves. Their attempts at a quarantine were thwarted, however, as the area was simply too large to wall off.

Scientists in hazmat suits roamed the silver sector. A government-issued report that the area was contaminated by deadly radiation was quickly debunked by environmentalists who refused to spout the party line.

Martin Beyer had seen a lot in his seventy-three years, but he had never seen anything like the Silvering. As the story unfolded, it overtook all other news. There was simply nothing happening anywhere in the world that could compete. But it was the images from space that finally convinced Martin to go there.

Overlaid on the satellite view of Houston was a spectacular silver blemish, like a birthmark on the planet. It had no angles or hard edges, yet it didn't appear to be random. The shape seemed meaningful somehow, like a character in an unknown language. A photo taken from the International Space Station depicted a column of shining particles, filtering directly into the neighborhood.

Astrophysicists were at a loss to explain it. It was as though a leak had sprung in space. The earth's rotation had no effect; the silver did not move like a laser across the surface as it turned. "Interstellar space dust" was the official description offered. Extraterrestrial by definition, but evidence of alien life? No one could say.

Naturally, the internet exploded with its own ideas. There were the usual conspiracy theories about top secret government projects, the most popular being that Houston's Third Ward was a testing ground for some means of exterminating the poor. Others believed it was a silent attack by aliens from a parallel dimension. The Second Coming was another popular notion, although whether it was God or the Devil who had arrived, even religious leaders refused to say.

Martin wasn't sure what he believed. All he knew was that he had to see it for himself. And he was not alone. He picked up two hitchhikers on the drive from New Orleans: a man whose car had broken down and a teenage girl he suspected was a runaway. Their eyes shone with reverence like his own. Like him, they had felt similarly compelled.

When they reached Houston, they had to take a circuitous route to get anywhere near the area. Cars had been piled up on all the freeways for weeks, most of them now abandoned. Martin drove as far as he could and then he and his passengers followed the wandering horde on foot.

Helicopters circled above and the noise of shouting was deafening. Martin pushed his way through the crowd until at last he saw the gleaming silver spires. The images online hadn't done it justice. His heart ached at the sight of it.

He was old, but he wasn't frail. And after several hours, he finally managed to shoulder his way through the crowd. He sighed with contentment as he stood at last on the mirrored street. It shone so brightly it was visible even though the crush of bodies. The people around him had skin of varying hues, but not silver. They were all tourists. Pilgrims.

The shouting voices weren't as loud here, and the noise seemed to have more purpose. Martin felt himself pushed and jostled by the crowd, guided towards one of the gleaming houses. It looked like a temple in an alien landscape. Outside, a small stage had been erected.

Here was where the residents were gathered. They stood out in drastic contrast to the invaders. Martin gaped at the shining silver people around him. Everything about them was silver: their clothes, their skin, their hair. Their eyes. They moved with an eerie grace, reflecting back the brilliance of the light.

"Robot angels!" cried a child's voice.

Someone laughed uneasily at that. From a distance the natives looked as metallic as their altered city, but Martin brushed against a silver girl whose clothes and hair were like spider silk. He gazed at his hand, expecting it to change, to reflect the brief contact his skin had made with hers. But it remained pink and pale. Likewise, the falling silver snow did not adhere to the newcomers. He felt pierced by an odd sense of rejection, even shame. He felt *unloved*.

And then he saw her. Carmen Ayala.

199

She stood on the platform outside the temple. The surging masses began to chant her name.

Carmen raised the arm they had all come to see, revealing the severed end, the cascade of frozen silver. The chorus soared in volume.

Martin's breath caught in his throat and instantly his sorrow melted away. He knew why he had been drawn here. He had never believed in God, but he knew what he was looking at now. There was only one word to describe it: miracle.

It was a long time before the crowd settled down, quieted by a gesture from the tall silver man beside Carmen. He seemed young and their body language suggested intimacy. Her son perhaps. He took his mother's arm, stroking the silver icicles where her hand had been. Then he produced a meat cleaver.

The crowd stood in reverential silence as he handed the blade to Carmen and knelt before her. He laid his arm along a small table and waited.

Carmen looked up, surveying the crowd for a moment with eyes like beacons. Then she raised the cleaver and brought it down. Martin winced at the meaty THUNK as the blade connected with skin. The man screamed, and a terrible shudder ran through his body. But he did not move his arm.

It took six blows for Carmen to sever the hand. Silver liquid spurted from the wound with each chop, pouring in thin rivers over the table and pooling on the stage. The man was still screaming, his voice high and frantic. The pain was impossible to imagine, yet there was something alluring in it.

200

He stumbled to his feet and held his bleeding arm aloft, waving it in an arc over his head, splashing the audience with gleaming droplets. Some held aloft cups while others opened their mouths, like children catching snowflakes on their tongues.

An awed murmur went through the crowd as they watched the wound heal before their eyes. The motion of the waving had sculpted the spurting silver blood, solidifying it into an elegant flourish.

Some in the crowd fell to their knees, bowing their heads as if to a deity. Others wept. Still others pushed violently against one another, trying to get to the front, reaching for the severed hand. Like the wound, it had hardened into a solid object, no longer resembling soft human flesh.

Carmen held it up and the people screamed and cheered, their voices full of hunger. Crazily, Martin thought she might toss the hand into the crowd like a wedding bouquet. But instead she brought it down hard against the table, smashing it. It did not shatter like glass or any other familiar substance. It burst into a cloud of glittering dust. Greedy hands clutched at it, grabbing as it dissipated in the air, lost among the falling silver.

For a moment all was silent, and then a man beside Martin began to shout. "Me! Me! Please – me!"

But Carmen shook her head gravely at the request, and Martin knew why. The man was not one of the Chosen. Only the Silvered could be mutilated and transformed into art. Only the Silvered

201

could be reborn.

The ritual continued. A woman offered her leg and Carmen obliged, leaving her with a curving spray below the knee. Martin had to cover his ears against the screams of agony, but once they faded, the woman's ecstasy was palpable. She raised her arms to the sky, silver tears streaming down her silver face. Then she hobbled away, her transformed leg like the splayed petals of a silver lily.

The crowd had begun to sing, a jarring cacophony of hymns, prayers and discordant wailing. The music of damned souls.

Carmen waved farewell and vanished inside the temple. A few people tried to follow, but four silver men stood guard, forcing the intruders away. The majority of the crowd took the hint and began to disperse, but a few stalwarts remained, like beggars hoping for scraps.

Martin stood in the middle of the gleaming street, trembling. All around him fell the silver flakes, but even if he caught them and pressed them into his skin, they did not stick. Others were trying to do the same, to no avail.

"They call us 'The Lost'."

He looked up at the voice. It was the hitchhiker he'd brought with him, the runaway. The girl had hardly spoken a word on the long drive. She glanced back towards the stage where Carmen had performed her atrocities.

"I thought I was lost before," she continued with a wistful sigh. "Now I feel . . ."

Martin completed her thought. "Forsaken."

"Yeah."

"Why here?" an older woman's voice demanded. "Why this shithole?"

Martin turned to see a well-dressed couple. They were clearly not local and they stood out like blood on snow. Until the Silvering, they'd probably never even set foot in a place like the Third Ward.

The runaway looked them up and down with contempt. "You don't get it," she snarled. "This isn't something you can *buy*. These people were chosen. This *place* was chosen. You can't have it just because you feel entitled."

They both bristled at that and the man opened his mouth to reply. But another voice spoke up first.

"It wasn't chosen. There's a wormhole opened up in space that let the Silver in. It just happened to fall here."

The skeptic was a middle-aged man in a sweatshirt that said "Portland". Whether it was Portland, Oregon or Portland, Maine, he had come a long way.

"Then why are you here?" Martin asked. "If you don't believe, I mean."

He shrugged. "I don't even know. Curiosity I guess. Had to see it for myself."

"Me too," the runaway said. "I saw it on TV. I never saw anything so beautiful in my life before, ever." She looked pointedly at the rich couple as she said it.

They shifted awkwardly. No doubt their lives were filled with countless beautiful luxuries that they took for granted. Martin could feel their discomfort as plainly as he'd felt the agony and rapture of the people on the stage. The woman's hands fluttered to cover the ostentatious rings she wore. Odd that she hadn't thought to leave her jewelry at home. But then, her gold and diamonds might as well be rusty iron when compared to their glittering surroundings.

"So..." Martin ventured, addressing the runaway, "you came to see the beauty. And now that you're here..." He trailed off, leaving the question unspoken.

A sad smile teased the corners of her mouth and she gazed over at Carmen's house. A group of people were sitting outside it on the steely ground. The guards stood watch by the door, a silent warning to the tourists. A Silvered family drew near, and Martin noticed a pronounced limp in the little boy. His foot was twisted at an angle that looked horribly painful. The family were allowed inside, and the tourists scrambled to their feet, trying to push in behind them. But the guards held them back, slamming the gleaming door in their faces.

All was silent, and then the air was rent by the high-pitched screams of a child. The hordes of tourists stood frozen, listening, wishing they could see. At last the door opened and the family emerged. The child still limped, but instead of a crooked foot, now he limped on a shining crescent. It was as though a tiny moon had sprouted from his ankle.

The tourists stood aside as the family

passed, staring with hunger and reverence. Martin felt it too, what had been called "Silver Envy", but that was where it ended. He had been drawn here to see the place, but he had no compulsion to mutilate himself.

"It's a fucking cult," said the man from Portland, his voice heavy with disgust. He jerked his chin at the tourists outside Carmen's house. A group of them were holding hands and rocking back and forth. Others were singing. Some held rosary beads or other religious objects. "An asteroid could have fallen here and wiped out the whole city and people would still come and think it was a miracle."

"What is it if it's not a miracle?" the rich woman asked.

Portland shrugged. "Just one of those random things."

The runaway gaped at him. "Random? No way is this random! How do you explain the transformations? If you chop off a part of one of *us*, we'll bleed out and die. But *them*..."

"I didn't say it wasn't inexplicable," Portland continued, managing to sound both reasonable and patronizing at once. "Just that it isn't some kind of divine intervention. This could all stop at any moment. The wormhole could close. No more dust. It might melt away like snow. Then what? Do all these people go back to normal? What happens to those transformed hands and feet? Do they become rotting stumps once the clock strikes midnight?"

205

The girl was silent, her eyes narrowing. When she finally spoke, her voice was a savage hiss. "Blasphemer."

There was such venom in the accusation, and in her cold glare, that Martin felt as though ice-water had been poured down his back.

The girl found unlikely allies in the rich couple, who turned as one to stare at the skeptic in their midst. "Blasphemer," they echoed.

All around them, heads turned, and the word became a soft chorus, then a chant. A few Silvered were visible, scattered throughout the milling tourists, but they didn't speak. Neither did they intervene as several of people began to move towards Portland, like sharks scenting blood.

Portland shook his head in disbelief as he backed away. "See what I mean?" he spat, pointing at the approaching mob. "It's a cult! You people are out of your fucking minds!"

But as the chanting rose in volume to become a collective scream, his fury gave way to fear.

Martin could only watch in frozen horror as mob rule took over. Portland's own screams were lost to the noise of the crowd and he vanished beneath a forest of clutching arms. The group moved towards Carmen's house, dragging their victim with them.

To his left Martin noticed a young couple, the woman heavily pregnant. He'd seen them earlier, pulling up handfuls of silver grass to eat, presumably to turn the baby inside silver. Now there was raw animal fear in their eyes. But as soon as they noticed Martin watching them, they began to mouth the word "blasphemer", like atheists in a church pretending to sing along with the choir.

Martin knew he should probably do the same, lest the mob turn on him next. But he just couldn't make his lips cooperate. All he could do was watch as Portland was hauled up onto the stage. The Silvered guards made no move to stop them, and Martin supposed they would only act if someone tried to get inside the house.

"Look at yourselves," Portland was shouting, his voice barely audible over the frenzied chanting. "You don't even know what you're doing! You don't know why you came here or what the Silver is! How do you know it's--"

He was silenced with a savage punch to the gut that made him crumple to his knees. The crowd parted, stepping away to give the watching masses a clear view. Portland clutched his stomach as he writhed at their feet, helpless as someone new took the stage.

He was a lanky scarecrow of a man, his bare arms streaming with blood from numerous cuts. Martin had seen others with similar wounds. Even with no Silver visible on their skin, the desperate still cut themselves hoping to find Silvered blood. Their cries were all around them now. They wanted the ecstasy of Carmen Ayala and her acolytes.

The leader of the cultists raised his hands for silence and an expectant hush descended on the crowd. At a nod from him, his followers yanked

Portland to his feet and dragged him forward. Although he desperately wanted to, Martin couldn't look away. From the corner of his eye he saw the pregnant woman and her partner edging away and he wished he could do the same.

"This man does not believe," the leader said. "He only came here to mock those of us who do." His voice was calm, almost soothing.

Heads nodded and there were murmurs of agreement, but the crowd seemed too awestruck and full of anticipation to resume their feverish chanting.

"He will never be one of the Chosen. But we must show him that he is wrong about the Silvering."

Portland's captors forced him to his knees before the leader. The scarecrow man looked down at him like a benevolent father on an errant son.

"I will show you the truest miracle," he said.

"You can show me whatever you want," Portland hissed. "It doesn't change the fact that you're all insane!"

Scarecrow smiled at that. A soft thread of laughter stitched its way through the crowd and Martin felt his own lips forming the shape of a camouflaging smile. He noticed the runaway up on the stage behind Portland, her eyes wild, her grin maniacal.

Scarecrow pulled a small knife from his belt and held it up. It looked rusty to Martin, but perhaps it was only caked with dried blood. Scarecrow pressed it against the skin of his arm and drew it down, adding another long cut to the others already there. Blood streamed from the wound, spilling onto the stage, deep red against the gleaming silver.

"We've all searched," he said, displaying his bleeding arm, "but never found the cherished color. Never felt the cherished agony. Never transformed."

A woman in the crowd gave a despairing wail in agreement.

"But then," he continued, "we have never made an offering to them."

At this, the crowd cheered, screaming and stamping their feet. Panic leapt in Martin's chest, and he raised his arms in concert with those around him, hoping no one could see the terror in his eyes.

Portland was screaming now as well, but he could not escape the iron grip of his captors. The cult leader leaned down, holding the knife up to Portland's face. He didn't keep his followers waiting long before plunging the blade into one of Portland's eyes, twisting and cutting until it popped free. He held it up, a wet red pulpy mass. The clamor intensified, drowning out Portland's harrowing screams. Then he threw it high into the air, into the drifting silver flakes.

People leapt for it as it fell back to earth, and a cry rose among the scrabbling masses as a woman caught it and held it up for all to see.

"Silver!"

A man beside Martin began to sob, falling to his knees and kissing the ground.

"Silver! Silver!"

On the stage, Portland thrashed in torment, but there was a new note to his cries. His voice rose higher and higher until it approached something that sounded like… joy. When his contortions finally stopped, the leader gestured for him to be released.

Portland stood shakily and faced the crowd. The blood streaming from his empty eye socket was still black, but even from a distance, Martin could see the flecks of silver forming in it.

"Now you begin to see, my friend," Scarecrow said. And he handed the knife to his new disciple.

Portland accepted it calmly and the crowd fell silent once more. Martin held his breath. Part of him hoped there was still something of Portland left inside, that he would turn the knife on the scarecrow man and put an end to this delusion. But there was no denying what he had witnessed, what they had *all* witnessed.

The silver dust was falling harder now, and Martin brushed at his bare skin, startled to see that it was finally beginning to stick. Others around him were noticing the same phenomenon, weeping with delight.

Portland raised the front of his shirt, holding it in his teeth as he gripped the knife with both hands, positioning it to one side of his belly. He didn't hesitate for a moment before plunging it in and dragging it across in a jagged horizontal line, disembowelling himself.

He dropped instantly to his knees with an anguished howl as his innards began to spill from the gash, pooling beneath him in a flood of silver gore. In an instant the others pulled him onto his back. A wave of hands gathered up his intestines, raising them above the wound as they solidified, sculpting them into a ghastly, glittering blossom. And all the while Portland was smiling, his face a mask of wonder.

Martin felt his stomach lurch in sympathy with the wound, but not the euphoria. He backed away, wanting only to go home. His eyes sought the crowd for others similarly horrified, but found only zealots. The silver flakes were becoming a blizzard now, and Martin saw a woman covering her children in piles of gleaming dust. They squealed with laughter as she buried them.

He spotted the young couple again, and made to join them. Then he saw the expression on the pregnant woman's face. She had witnessed a miracle, not an atrocity. Martin forced himself to smile and waved his hand in a vague gesture of blessing. She returned his smile and caressed her bulging stomach before turning to her husband, who was taking what looked like an icepick from her handbag.

Screams came from every direction as other believers began to follow Portland's example. With each new horror, the silver only fell harder. Soon it would be too dense to see through. People ignored Martin as he pushed past, lost in their own obscene tributes.

211

The crowd was becoming impenetrable, bodies packed like sardines. Some were in the throes of pain or its ensuing pleasure while others were searching for the means to achieve their own transformations. Martin heard several gunshots as he strained against the mob, and shuddered to imagine their results.

At last he could see the boundary, the place where the Silver stopped falling. Beyond it were waves of people fighting to get in. They could have his place; he wanted no part of it. There must be others, he thought. He couldn't be the only one.

"Hey."

He ignored the voice, but he couldn't ignore the hand that clamped down on his shoulder.

"Where are you going, friend?"

Martin swallowed. Then he arranged his features into something resembling a peaceful smile as he turned towards his detainer. It was a young man with a gaping silver hole in his forehead. Martin could see right through it.

The lie came easily. "I want to get my wife," he said. "She's out there."

The man cocked his head. "You can get her afterwards."

"I don't want to do it without her. We share everything." His heart twisted as he suddenly wished he could have shared her death two years ago.

"You will," the man said. "You'll share it with all of us." He smiled expectantly at Martin, his teeth stained with silver blood. Then he handed over his gun.

Martin's fingers closed over the weapon and he took it, surprised by its weight. He had never held one before. He managed to retain the smile as he raised the gun. "Thank you," he said. He tried to pull away, but the man's grip was like iron.

"No, no, you can do it here."

Martin was breathing hard now. Soon his mounting panic would be obvious and he would become an unwilling convert, like Portland. He had no choice. He lurched backwards, aiming the gun as he brought his knee up into the man's groin. If it hurt at all, the man gave no sign of it, but his smile vanished in an instant and he shouted the word Martin had come to dread.

"Blasphemer!"

The gun fired before Martin even realized he was pulling the trigger. A splash of silver erupted from the man's chest, but he wasn't even slowed. Martin squeezed off two more shots into the crowd before turning and running for the boundary. If he could just get across, he might be safe. They might not follow.

He had played sports in his youth and he felt a flash of youth again as he ran, shouldering aside the glazed-eyed cultists who clutched at him. He wriggled out of his jacket as a woman missing half her head tried to tackle him and he kicked a Silvered child like a football as it tried to trip him up. Almost there, almost there. Twenty yards, ten, five…

It wasn't a person that stopped him, or even

a weapon. It was the Silver. It had drifted against the boundary, as though an invisible wall separated the area from the outside world. Martin stumbled and fell across the bank of silver, sprawling half in and half out.

"Help," he gasped, reaching towards the people on the far side. "Please help me!"

Several of them came to his aid, taking his arms and trying to pull him across. But the mob inside did likewise, and there were far more of them. Martin kicked and struggled, trying to resist. Then he glanced behind and his eyes widened as he saw Portland there. The man no longer resembled anything human. His face was obscured by the gleaming coils and bursts of frozen silver from his abdomen. But Martin could see Portland's arms clearly enough as he raised the chainsaw and brought it down across Martin's back.

Pain consumed his entire being as the churning blade buried itself in his skin, spanning the length of his body. He screamed, but the sound was lost in the roaring buzz of the motor and the deranged cheering of the crowd.

Gouts of red blood and bits of flesh rained down before Martin and he screamed and thrashed, desperate to crawl away from the Silver. At the same time, he felt a bizarre change taking place. His back opened like a mouth to the vicious sawing, but only half of him welcomed the assault. His upper body was in agony – pure, excruciating torment with no hope of relief. But the mangled remains of his lower body tingled with unearthly pleasure. The sensation stopped at the boundary where he had fallen between two worlds. His lower body was a flowing mass of silver, like an eruption from a metal volcano, cementing him where he lay. The people who had tried to help released his arms and backed away, shielding their faces from the sight.

The hellish chorus of voices swelled to a hum of white noise as Martin lingered on the edge of consciousness. He felt the nearness of death, a feathery teasing just out of reach. The Silver would not let him go. And as the ground beneath his lower body began to rumble, and then to crack open, he caught a glimpse of the horrifying beauty at its core. He had just enough sanity left to wonder whether both parts of him would survive being torn in half.

Other Yseut
and Romance Tristan

Adam Golaski

Tristan's corpse and Yseut. And Yseut lies aside
Tristan's corpse. It stinks horribly. What else to do
but die beside her lover? Only while fever eased
and her liquid hallucinations ceased did she wonder why: why die? Instead, live with grief. Bite into
grief ('till blood wells up around white teeth).
Crabs all over her lover's body. His stomach roils
with life. Water laps at a stone ledge, echoes
throughout the cave; light echoes ripples across salt
crystal.

     A statue of Yseut and a statue of Yseut's sis-
ter. Yseut the statue holds between slender middle
finger and thumb a gold ring. Yseut the actual gave
a gold ring to Tristan. "Take this ring for the sake
of my love." Yseut reaches for her lover's left
hand — gross, gangrenous patina, bone; Tristan's

hand is bare. Every color pinwheels in the air. Yseut is frozen. Yseut is a statue. Is ice.

Over Yseut a shadow. Tristan the Dwarf is come to claim Yseut. He steps on a crab. He's tall and strong. He grips Yseut's dress at her breast and lifts her, carries her out of the cave. Snow. The shore. Great green rubber boots. Tristan the Dwarf carries Yseut to his cabin.

He lays her down on wide planks — warm; beneath the floor hay slowly composts and the heat from its decomposition rises. Smells faintly of ammonia. Tristan the Dwarf fills the tub with cold water. Yseut remembers: when he puts her in the water, she will scream. A fire in the fireplace. She follows the pulse of a particular ember. Roughly, Tristan the Dwarf removes Yseut's clothes. And roughly he dumps her in the bath. She screams. His cabin is rustic and modern. Off-the-grid green. Yseut faints.

Yseut wakes. Tristan the Dwarf enjoys her, indulges his desire. He went into her while she was unconscious. When he's aware she's aware he says, "You are my wife, Yseut." Yseut says not a word, sends her mind to the Bay. Tristan the Dwarf ejaculates, embraces Yseut, kisses her mouth, and leaves her on the bed.

She speaks inaudibly. She tells a story, "...charmed by the boy's crush on the maiden, the chaperones made sure the boy and the girl were partnered in the rowboat. The boy and the girl sat side-by-side as Kaherdin rowed the boat and told the boy and the girl about the Bay. The girl spied a sea cucumber, tubules expelled. Entangled, a crab. The boy gazed at the small of her back, her dark, unblemished skin exposed as she leaned over the gunwale."

Tristan the Dwarf stopped Yseut: "Shut up! I know that story! I am that boy! You are that girl!"

Yseut whispers, "You lie, Tristan the Dwarf."

"Tristan the Dwarf! Tristan the Dwarf! I am Tristan, your husband! The Dwarf? The Dwarf is a villain!"

Yseut, from the bed where she was raped replied: "If you are Tristan, what happened next?"

"I saw a harbor seal. I touched your bare shoulder and whispered, 'Look.' You sat up and turned toward me, but looked past me. You asked, 'Where?' I pointed. The seal dove. Kaherdin said, 'You frightened it, Tristan. When you pointed, the seal mistook your arm for a rifle.' Kaherdin tethered the row boat to a ring in a boulder so we would not be wrecked by the whirlpools the incoming tide made. He told us what seaweed we could eat. We let the tide creep over our bare feet. I said, 'My mouth tastes like the ocean'; you said, 'Mine too,' and I thought it was as if we kissed but I didn't dare say so."

Yseut, who has heard the truth, faints.

A small bird flutters at the ceiling. It's a bat. Firelight rushes up the walls. Yseut feels she's in the midst of metamorphosis.

A contraction. The bed is soaked. Tristan offers to change the sheets and turn the mattress, but

Yseut would need to be moved and she doesn't want to move.

"He'll arrive quickly," Tristan promises; this Yseut knows.

While Tristan attends to the sweat on Yseut's brow, she notices no ring on his finger. She's about to ask, Where is the gold ring I gave you? but another contraction takes her breath and the boy in her womb screams. She thinks, "No woman knows what her womb carries."

Her son is born.

Yseut cries out: "Why is he so still?"

At the foot of the bed is a young man, still connected to the placenta. He is dead. Yseut, in pain, sits up. There is blood. Her thighs, her groin, the bed — on the body at the foot of the bed. Her blood. A line of pain zig-zags through her whole self. Her son looks like his father. The ring —

"Tristan," Yseut asks, "did you put this ring on our son's finger? Tristan, why did you put this ring on our son's finger? What did you say, Tristan? Tristan," she asks, "how long have I been in this bed? What kind of birth is this?"

Tristan's grimace his answer; grim he drops the placenta onto the stomach of the newborn man (the umbilical coils itself) and hefts him from the bed. Yseut says, "Yes, hold him, I'm so tired." She lies down — sees sleepily through the haze of her eyelashes Tristan take their son.

Yseut is awake in pain when the statue of her sister appears at the foot of the bed. Daylight creeps in around the blinds. In the hearth, what was a great log is charcoal. A wind in the flue swirls ash. Yseut spoke to the statue of her sister: "Brengain, where is my husband?"

"He is in the cave."

"Brengain, sister, how long have I been in this bed?"

"Since Tristan the Dwarf carried you here."

The bat is curled against the ceiling.

"Brengain, where is Tristan the Dwarf?"

"He is in the cave."

Where Yseut's shoulder touches the edge of the bed is numb so she shifts slightly; pain shocks; she sets her mind on it — "Who suffers sees," says Yseut. Yseut asks, "When was it I began to give birth to my husband?"

The statue is gone. In its wake, Yseut finds strength enough to get out of bed — though it is an agony for her. On a hook hangs a heavy greatcoat. It's oily. Yseut steps into shoes too big.

From the front door to the shore footprints in snow. She follows. Foam rushes around; shoes fill with seawater. She sees the cave-mouth. Wind lifts the sea and Yseut's eye is drawn to what floats at the horizon: a red coffin and a brown coffin. Let them float: Yseut walks to the cave.

Tristan the Dwarf is hunched over the body of Yseut's husband. Now Yseut understands how the Dwarf knows what he knows about her love. In the Dwarf's hand is what's left of Tristan's heart.

Tender is the Tether

Rhys Hughes

The idea was mine but Tess took it and changed it for her own purposes. I could hardly complain about that. We had an understanding. I was honest with her from the start and in return she held back nothing. Tess colludes with my most inspired schemes, however obscure they seem, and opposes only those she judges to be mundane.

I told her how I planned to collect discarded umbilical cords, as many as possible, several thousand or more, and link them together into a cable of immense length. It wouldn't be easy to obtain them but I had friends in hospitals and clinics around the world and they would help, and I felt that after one year I would have enough.

"But what's the point?" Tess wondered.

"The finished cable will stretch through time as well as space. I intend to connect a receiver to both ends."

"What do you mean?"

"A telephone receiver, of course."

She shrugged, evidently deeming me demented.

"Surely you see?" I demanded.

She didn't, lovely Tess with her curly dark hair tipped by the sun with honeyed gold and her bemused lips the colour of coffee, and she blinked her eyes rapidly at me as if fanning my idiocy and her exasperation with stroboscopic lights, and I had to continue:

"The umbilical cord is what links us directly to the past, each cord an attachment to the previous generation, so if I make one cable from several thousand cords I will be able to dip into the distant mists of time, because the generations will accumulate. How many umbilical cords link us to the first human beings? That's the question."

"Probably less than we imagine," answered Tess.

"Well, only three hundred generations separate us from the invention of the wheel. But I want to go back further than the dawn of civilisation. I plan to penetrate the Palaeolithic. I want to unite myself to some unique ancestor. I want an *original* conversation."

"Do umbilicals conduct electricity the way copper wires do? How can this telephone of yours be powered?"

"Sound will travel in vibrations down the line, provided the cords are kept taut, and it will travel in both directions. Each speaker will just

222

need to take it in turns to talk and listen."

"Interesting," said Tess, "but it can't work."

"Why do you say that?"

"Because time travel into the past is impossible."

"I want to try anyway!"

"Sure, why not? If it fails, which it will, you can redefine it as art, as a conceptual project of some kind, but I am curious as to what you'll say if you do manage to get through?"

"To the person who answers my call, I will talk dirty. Why waste any time on another kind of conversation? What else will we have in common apart from our libidos? Nothing! I will engage in sex talk and once it's all over I will sever the cable and put the escapade down to experience. Such a thing should be done once only, but done very perversely, and I tell you all this now because I never hide."

Tess nodded. As I've already said, we understood each other, and our relationship was based on honesty and trust, mainly on those two aspects at least, there were a few lesser ones that also contributed to the domestic glue of our marriage, such as irony, temerity, tenacity, whimsy and zing, but there's no need to go into detail.

So the matter was settled. I would embark on my scheme to erotically harangue an ancient hominid via a telephone line made from many joined umbilical cords, and Tess would do nothing to obstruct my progress. She was free to amuse herself in her own way during this time and I wouldn't

ask unnecessary questions or monitor her movements. We were a modern couple, decadent,
tainted and sweet.

The months passed and my collection of umbilicals grew and in one of the spare rooms of the
house I connected them together into a single long
and strong cable. Eventually I had sufficient for my
scheme. To both ends I fixed a telephone receiver
and then coiled the cable around my arm and went
down into the cellar to perform.

The cellar of our house is a rather unusual
one.

Not because of the shape or atmosphere of
the subterranean space but thanks to the circular pit
in the middle of it, a feature that wasn't exposed
until we pulled up the planks that covered it.

Maybe it's a well but there's no water at the
bottom.

We have dropped small stones in but never
heard a splash. In fact the pit doesn't seem to have
an underside.

It's a fathomless hole and we have tried
many times to measure its full depth, Tess and I,
with a plumbline, but all to no avail. This is why I
now regarded it as perfect for my project.

It was deep in years as well as leagues, of
that I felt sure. And so, with a dim grin on my lips,
I gently lowered one weighted end of the umbilical
line into the geometrically neat abyss.

As it dropped, it really seemed that it was
pushing deeper into time as well as penetrating the
dankness of vertical space. At last the cable pulled

taut and I lifted the receiver at my end to my eager ear. The moment had arrived, as moments nearly always do.

I heard at first only vacant hissing, a primordial static.

Then a sound of heavy breathing took over.

"Hello! Who's there?" I cried.

"Me," came the reply.

"Who is me?" I demanded.

"I am me, you are you," was the logical answer.

"What are you wearing?"

"The bear, the tiger, the big bird."

I was excited by this response, but I wanted clarification. "The fur of a bear, skin of a tiger, feathers of a bird?"

It never occurred to me to ask what language we were conversing in. I guess it was the spaces between our words, not the words themselves, that did most of the work, because those spaces have always been the same, in any tongue anywhere. The voice said:

"No, the souls of the bear, tiger, bird. I wear the souls."

"Take them off now."

"I will not. Without them I am defenceless."

"That's the way I want you. I am your master for tonight. Take off the souls, slowly, one by one. Describe the process. First unbutton the soul of the bear, let it slide to the floor. Have you done that? Speak to me and tell me if you've done that. The bear."

"You are not my wife, you are not my chief."

"I am your god, your totem, which means that I can be your wife and your chief, anything I wish, for I come from the future. I know things that you will never know. Gear ratios, the pasteurisation of milk. If you fail to obey me then your eyes will curdle."

A brief pause and then, "The bear soul is off."

"Tell me how you feel."

"I don't know."

"Abashed perhaps?"

"Yes. Like a club that has bashed a head. Wet."

"Because you are excited?"

"No, it is raining here outside the cave."

"Take off the tiger."

"It is tied on far too tightly."

"Strike the knot with your axe. You do have an axe?"

"What are men without them?"

"Hit that knot, hit it..."

"Argh! Now I am wet from pouring blood!"

"Is the tiger soul off?"

"Yes, it is, and my wound pulses like a drum."

"Keep going, hairy chops."

"What is next?"

"Remove the bird quick."

"The soul of the bird was fused to my spine by a lightning bolt. It will never come off. Not even an axe can free it. Once, long ago, I voyaged to the far end of the valley and climbed the mountain. I touched the snow on the peak. I saw the world in all directions and it was good and it was bad. I knew I would never be the same again. The clouds gathered, they turned dark, perhaps they shut their eyes. Then one blaze of fire cooked the meat of the sky. Another fell on my back."

"Yes! Keep talking!"

"One day the bird will fly and take me with it. I know this because my dreams have told me so. My dreams met me in a dream, another dream, a dream within a dream, deeper than any dream I have known. They jostled each other, crowded the cave of my yearns, jabbed with twisted fingers at me and laughed. When they stopped laughing, the same way a hyena will stop crunching a rib, they told me how the bird already had me in its beak but I didn't know. When I am least expecting it, up it will flap, cooling all the sweat on my body with its wings."

"Enough! I am spent."

"What do you mean by that?"

"I am fulfilled. You have satisfied my craving!"

"But I haven't yet told…"

I yawned theatrically, thanked him curtly and then I took the kitchen knife I had carried with me into the cellar and severed the cord. I wanted nothing more to do with that prehistoric pervert, even though I was the one responsible for making him do what he had done. Yes, the result was exactly what I had wanted, but as always in the aftermath of an encounter I felt dirty and this feeling filled me with an ironic disdain for myself that was perhaps also a little pleasurable.

As I turned to climb the steps out of the cellar, the door opened and it was Tess who stood framed there. She hadn't come to berate or mock, we were beyond such things, but I was eager to understand why she hurried down and brushed past me impatiently.

"My turn now," she said.

"But I've severed the cable," I told her.

"I don't intend to use *your* contraption. I've created one of my own. It is quite different from yours. Look!"

The line coiled around her arm was thicker than mine had been. In the gloom I blinked at it but was none the wiser, so I reached out and touched it. Rubbery with suckers? She had no time to satisfy my curiosity. But as she unwound it, I saw it was made entirely from linked tentacles. Clearly she had gathered them while I was collecting the umbilicals. I wondered from where she had obtained so many.

"Various places," she replied, as if reading my mind, "and all of them strewn with more tentacles than can be counted. Beaches, islands, antique shops, restaurant kitchens, forensic laboratories, school storerooms, baths, pools, private clubs, reefs, slums, the penthouses of glass towers, in boxes and conduits, clinging to the anchors or masts of ships, pressed flat by the pages of enormous atlases in libraries."

"You have wired telephone receivers to both ends?"

"I thank you for the idea."

"You also plan to call the distant past?"

Tess giggled at my naivety.

"What interest have I in that? None at all! I won't be communicating with the past but the future, speaking to the lifeforms that will inherit the planet long after our species has been made extinct. The future! These are tentacles, not umbilicals. The future!"

And now I began trembling and I wasn't certain why. As she lowered the cable into the pit, I asked her:

"What will you say if you manage to get through?"

Of course her answer was the expected one and it was my punishment but I couldn't grumble, not after what I had done, I had to just incline my head and accept it as she told me:

"To the entity that answers, I will open the legs of my soul. What else will we have in common apart from our spirits? Yes, I feel sure the future has more to offer than the past does. But now I think you should leave. I want to be alone with my octopus."

"You will be the dominant one, as I was?"

"Not this time. That's not what I want, the games of the troubled soul. I prefer tentacle tenderness instead."

229

I chewed my lip and maintained a grim silence as I mounted the steps back into the upper world. I truly had only myself to blame. How can one justify an utterly offbeat jealousy? Her lover didn't exist yet, wouldn't be animate for many millennia. Calm down, I told myself, get a grip, but this advice only reminded me of suckers.

With a mighty spasm, I shrugged off the mass of centuries that hadn't happened and went to brew coffee.

Stygian Chambers

Orrin Grey

--When did you first begin having the dreams?

The voice is like a recording. It scratches scratches
scratches

scratches

--When did you first begin having the dreams?
   It was then, which is now. After the house.
After what happened in that house. They said that
the girl had gone missing and we were supposed to
look in that old, abandoned house.

I never even knew that it *was* a house. I always thought it was a warehouse of some sort. *How odd*, I used to think, *there being a warehouse in this neighborhood.*

That's where it is, a neighborhood. Quiet brick streets that let grass grow up, let the rain seep down, into the dirt underneath, and the things underneath the dirt. The bugs and the worms and they crawl and crawl and—

-- The house.

Yes, it was in my neighborhood, the one where I grew up, but there was a wall around it. Tall and sharp, like the wall around a warehouse, which is why I thought that's what it was. The building itself was tall and square, too, the roof flat, like a warehouse. And the windows, tall and thin. Like coffins.

It had been abandoned for as long as I can remember, and when we were little, we used to dare each other to go over the wall. There was a wooden gate, big enough to drive a truck through, and a smaller pedestrian entrance, blocked by iron bars. Both were always locked when we were kids; a rusty chain flaked off little orange bits when we squeezed between the bars, which of course we did.

The ground on the other side wasn't grown up, like you might think. I guess the wall kept the sunlight from shining down, so that the only things that grew there were brittle grasses and little hollow shrubs that rattled in the wind.

One time—the *only* time—I squeezed through those bars myself. It was a sunny day, but it was never sunny on the other side of that wall. It wasn't enough to go *through* the gate, of course. You had to go a little way. Throw a rock through one of the windows, maybe, or at least peek in through the dusty glass.

Would that I had thrown a rock through a window that day. Instead, I went around the corner of the building, so that the gate was lost from sight. It seemed much braver to me than looking in a window. Gone around the corner anything could happen to me, and the kids who waited on the other side, bright-eyed and eager, would never even know.

Standing just around the corner of the building was a man. He was wearing a green raincoat, and his back was to me. He was digging a hole in the ground. Not a very big hole, but big enough. Big enough to put a person in. When I rounded the corner he stopped, his shovel sunk into the gravelly dirt, and started to turn around. The hood of his raincoat was up, but it wasn't raining.

I ran before I saw his face. Ran as hard and as fast as I could, even though it was only about thirty or forty feet to the metal gate. I crashed against the bars and tried to squeeze through but, can you believe it, suddenly I couldn't fit. I was so terrified. My face was red and I thought I was going to pass out. When the other kids saw how scared I was, they ran, too, and so I was alone, puffing and squeezing against the metal bars, willing my bones to bend, my flesh to turn to jelly so that I could ooze through. Every second, I could feel that man in the

233

raincoat behind me, his shadow up against me, and then —

Then I was through the bars and back out on the street and I ran all the way home and didn't look back.

It would make a lot of sense if I said that I never went near that house ever again, but I was a kid, and my curiosity was stronger than my fear. I went by there every day, walking four extra blocks on my way home from school so that I could stare in through the bars of the gate. I never saw that man standing there again. Never saw anything.

When the girl went missing, they rounded up people from the neighborhood to help look for her. I had moved back to care for my father when he took sick, and when the deputy came to my door, I agreed to join the search party. How could I say no? ~~I didn't want him to come into the house~~

At first, we looked in culverts and drain pipes, in the creek where we used to play as kids, in the dark woods along the bike path. I didn't know that we were going to that house, or I would have made up some excuse. They knew that my father had been ill, after all. What if he needed me and I wasn't there to answer his insistent knocking. It would just go on and on and on and on and on and on—

When we got to the metal door the chain was already broken. It lay in two pieces on the ground, one inside the metal gate and one outside. The lock was still stuck to the chain, rusted in place.

"She might have gotten in here," one of the men said, swinging the gate to and fro, as if we couldn't tell, just by looking, that it was open. It made a sound like brakes going out. Tires screeching on wet pavement. Two bright eyes—

I'm getting ahead of things.

We didn't know that she was dead then, you see. We thought we might still find her hiding somewhere, hurt or scared or sleeping. We hadn't yet imagined all the blood.

So we went on into the grounds of that house, around the corner where, as a child, I had seen the man. It was night and we had flashlights and I shined mine at the ground to see if I could tell that the dirt was different where he had been digging, but the night before had been rainy and all the ground looked the same.

The house didn't have normal doors, like a normal house. Nothing about that house is normal. It had double-doors and they were the color of weathered statues and they opened outward so that the dark spilled down the steps. The dark inside the house was *thicker*, somehow, than the dark in other places, and our flashlights just made beams and cones that only showed exactly what they were pointing at and not anything else.

The floor inside was black and white, but not checked. The black tiles made diamond shapes to offset the larger diamond shapes of the white tiles, yet they're what drew the eye, what I mentioned first — why is that, do you think?

The first room of the house was tall, two stories, and it looked like there was a mural or fresco on the ceiling, but time and mold had obscured it and what had perhaps once been a representation of the Last Supper was now just eyes peering out of a seeping blackness.

There were stairs leading up — marble, with gilt bannisters — and doors going off in other directions. Past that first room, the house became an endless series of hallways all alike. They seemed impossibly long, so that we must be walking past the limits of the house, past the dirt and the walls and into the neighborhood surrounding us.

The hallways were lined with doors all alike. Behind some doors were rooms, while others just opened onto more hallways. Most of the rooms were bare, their lack of furnishings serving to render them indistinguishable. It was impossible to tell what had been an office, a bedroom, a den. The rooms were more like cubicles in a high rise — each one a functional square, nothing more.

Only one room was different. It had padded walls, like in a mental institution, and the door locked from the outside. We all looked at one another and we said, "why is there a room like this in a normal house," though we all knew already that the house was far from normal.

We became lost in the rooms all alike, in the halls all alike, with the doors all alike, and to combat our sense of disorientation, our growing fear, we agreed that we needed to split up. We didn't yet have any *reason* to be afraid, you have to understand, and we were ashamed. We were supposed to be the grownups; the big, brave men, trying to find a lost girl, not afraid of some house just because it was spooky and strange.

Which is how I found myself alone at the top of the steps.

I don't know where I was in the house by then. I hadn't realized that the house even had a basement, but then again, why shouldn't it? Many of the houses in the neighborhood had basements — probably most of them did. This house seemed so huge and strange I had completely lost any bearing on where I was in those twisting halls — turn down one, then another, then another, and you should come back to where you started from, shouldn't you?

The stairs went down. They seemed damp and unfinished in comparison to the rest of the house. The smell that came up from down below wasn't one that I could immediately place, but it made me think of metal, moving slowly in the dark.

As I went down the stairs, I called the girl's name, gently, coaxingly, as we had been coached to do before setting off on our mission. At the bottom of the steps, I found another hallway, but this one looked different from the others. When I was in school there was a building on campus that connected to another building across the street through an underground tunnel. This hallway reminded me of that tunnel, complete with a metal pipe that came up from out of the floor and ran along the wall.

The pipe was rusted and damp and smelled like the drain of a shower. The hallway was damp, and water dripped down from above. I thought maybe I was going under the street but, like I said, I had lost track of where I was in the house, so I might have been going anywhere.

--Do you remember how you came here? I ran.

I ran out of that building out of those double doors down those rain-wet steps out that iron gate out into the street. There were eyes in the dark, big and bright, and they were coming right toward me! And then—

--You were hit by a car. They brought you

here.

I don't remember an ambulance ride. I don't remember a hospital. Where did I go?

--They brought you here so we could take care of you.

All I remember is this room.

--You had blood on your hands, on your shirt.

I was hurt in the accident.

--You were, but it wasn't all your blood, was it?

No. No. No. No. No. No.

I don't want to talk about the basement. Please don't make me. I'll tell you anything else. Anything you want, just don't make me talk about that place, about what happened there.

--Tell us about your father, then.

His illness made him seem so strange and thin and small. Like when seed heads burst into downy streamers. He seemed to have burst like that. His hair was just wisps plastered to his head. The dome of his skull was like a lampshade. His lips and gums were pulled back so that his teeth seemed to be bared, always, like he was growling, and his eyes had sunk away until they were just pinpricks in a mask, and then nothing at all.

He didn't even seem to struggle when I

pushed the pillow down over his face. It was hard for me to tell when he was dead, he was already so still. I wore his green raincoat when I went to bury his body by the corner of the house. When I cut the chain and let it rattle to the ground.

I kept the hood up because of the rain that night.

I didn't hurt the girl, though. I didn't want to hurt her. I didn't want to do *that* to her. Put her limbs all backwards-on like that, like doll parts. I didn't want to make her move like that, her one remaining eye peeled back and staring. It was the house that wanted to hurt her. It was the house. I can still see her, in the shadow of that *god-damned statue in the basement of that house she is waiting for me still.*

No, you're right, I'm feeling better. You didn't want to know about that, you wanted to know about the dreams, when they started. I think they started after I came here. I never remember having them before. They started after I left that house.

I fell up the stairs from the basement. I remember the bark of the steps against my shins — funny, that I remember that. Then it was hall after hall, all alike, and at every turn my brain concocting some new horror to lurch out of the shadows, spider-quick, but nothing ahead save more halls.

I ran like I had when I was a child, and every hallway felt like I was trying to squeeze myself through those bars all over again. My flashlight was still in my hand, but I was running so hard that its light bounced everywhere, and the blood just looked like a shadow until I slipped in it.

They were all dead. The men I had come into the house with. No, that's not quite true. Some of them weren't quite dead yet. I saw them in the cone of my flashlight, picked out from the thick dark inside that house. Saw them where they jutted, here and there, out of the walls, the blood-slicked floors. My beam caught the face of one, just his head and one shoulder, his eyes gone, replaced with what looked like fleshy cobwebs, his mouth stuffed with something, his lips gaping open and closed around a soundless noise that he no longer had lungs to make.

The house hadn't finished with them yet, you see, but it has by now. That's why you haven't found them. Why nobody has found them. Why nobody will. I suspect that you think I killed them, but I didn't. They're still in that house somewhere, buried in the walls somewhere, just like her.

I ran outside and there were those burning eyes and I woke up here and it was between those eyes and here that I began having the dreams, I think. In them, I'm standing outside the house and looking up at the window. It seems like it was a long time ago, maybe when I was still a child.

The windows don't look right. They're arched, like the windows of a church, even though

241

the windows in the actual house are tall rectangles, but I know that it's the house, in that way that you know things in dreams.

I'm looking at one particular window. It's lit with a violet glow — flat, it provides no illumination beyond the pane of glass, but creates a perfect silhouette of a familiar figure on the other side. The figure raises a hand to the glass, and I raise mine in response.

I'm drifting up a set of stairs. These stairs are black and gold — they resemble the stairs in the house, but are not identical to them, like the windows — and I am drifting up them and up them and up them.

I am a little boy, sneaking down the hall to listen outside the door of my parents' room. I drift down the hallway until I reach a door that I know opens onto the room of the purple light. There is a brass knob and, beneath it, a keyhole. I bend down to look, press my eye up against the keyhole, and on the other side —

--Do you know where you are?

I can't be sure. Why won't you just tell me? Don't you know where I am?

--We brought you here to take care of you.

Can't you tell me where I am? Tell me the name of this hospital. The name of my doctor. Tell me an address, a street, a telephone number. Let me see your faces. Step out from behind that light and let me see you.

--We brought you home.

I'm sorry. I didn't mean to. I swear I'll never do it again. Don't you hear me say I'm sorry?

--We brought you into our house.

It wasn't me. It was the house. *It was this house!*

In the basement in the attic in every room of the house there is a black statue that sweats beads of darkness. At its wide base it is like nothing at all — a shapeless geological extrusion thrust up by cooling magma or tectonic plates — but what is it that happens near the top? Are those shoulders, the arms in which they terminate still fused to the base? Is that a head, rugose as a dried bouquet of night-blooming flowers, pocked and cragged like the dark side of the moon?

At the foot of the statue something skitters and moves — then many things do.

When did you first begin having the dreams?

Behemoth

Clint Smith

"Lo, she was thus when her clear limbs enticed
All lips that now grow sad with kissing Christ,
    Stained with blood fallen from the feet of God,
The feet and hands whereat our souls were priced.

Alas, Lord, surely thou art great and fair,
But lo her wonderfully woven hair!
    And thou didst heal us with thy piteous kiss;
But see now, Lord; her mouth is lovelier."

        — Algernon Charles Swinburne, "Laus Ven-
eris" (1866)

November, 1987

        Dox Ingram pulled into the auto-repair
shop's lot, immediately registering the presence of

Chancy's car. The other guys — Pete, the shop fore-man, and a few other techs — were standing around the vehicle, perplexed, their breath visible in the early-morning air. Aside from the chill, Dox had woken many a morning to a cluster of men idling over some puzzle. Eighteen years ago, in the jungle, it was different. It typically involved the avoidance of (but always the potential of) impending death.

It was a somewhat amusing irony: how, dur-ing the early stages of his adult life, he'd selected an occupation in which his surname was his central identity; and then, somehow along the way, he'd meandered into his current craft, still bearing his name on his chest, now with the less-formal indica-tion of his first name. Dox's parents had named him after the well-known black painter and printmaker, Dox Thrash; but whereas the early twentieth-cen-tury artist had fostered a legacy in painting (later galvanized by the espousing of W.E.B. Dubois and Alain LeRoy Locke), Dox Ingram — despite his par-ents adamant and often terse encouragements that their son pursue a lasting, expressive craft — had persuaded himself that the gentility of art was not in his nature, and rather sought the fraternal em-brace of the Army, opting for the medium of south-east Asia and decorating its canvas, often heartily, with carnage.

Despite his occasional melancholy that he had made decisions and chosen a path that had profaned not only the name but his parents' dreams, Dox Ingram wore the distinguished appel-lation with a pride rivaled only by the care he took

245

in his craft as a mechanic.

Dox hadn't seen, or heard from Chancy Mays since the previous Friday, when the young mechanic had been coaxed — at the aid of several dancers — deeper into the interior of the Sphinx Club. Going to the "gentlemen's club" had not been Dox's idea; and he'd been gently adamant that it wasn't really his scene. Not anymore, at least.

And now, as he drew closer to the repair shop's lot, a quivering double-exposure overlay the scene before him — like two, zoetic snapshots of distorted Polaroids competing for a coeval reality. Dox's mind recalled the week before: the woman in the lot, talking to Pete. She was tall, almost as tall as the shop foreman; but her height was aided by a pair of knee-high stiletto boots. It was not uncommon for customers to directly discuss repair problems and transactions with the shop foreman, but, with her domineering gestures and confident intonation, it was an unusual occasion in that Pete was being told what to do.

Dox's disinterest in the exchange was steady until he and the woman made eye contact. What was, in actuality, a one-second connective stutter, felt to Dox as though he'd stopped to gormlessly appraise the woman. She wore a cropped leather jacket with a fur-lined collar. Thick-fibered fishnets. Her dark hair was long with color-dyed parts growing out; but it was the eye makeup that triggered his hesitation. Her eyes were ringed with dark smudges, as if raggedly rimmed with soot, and he couldn't tell if a bout of emotion had caused her mascara to smear or if the aesthetic was intentional: a botched tribute to Siouxsie Sioux. *One of the Banshees*. He would later learn that she called herself Isobel.

Dox shook his head, dispelling the recollection. Something wasn't right.

Now, getting out of his own car, Dox approached, addressing the other mechanics. "Chancy finally show up?"

A collective shaking of heads, with Pete putting in, "Son of a bitch just dumped it."

Dox looked over his shoulder at the shop. "You mean he ain't even here?"

"Damn doors are locked," said Pete, lighting a Chesterfield.

Dox approached the kid's car, peering inside. Sure thing, the keys were dangling from the ignition; he didn't bother trying the handle. Not for the first time over the past four days, Dox's concern for the young man took on an altered, tricky-to-define dimension.

"Tell you what," said Pete, "when I find that kid I'm gonna —"

An erratic rustling sounded from the within the trunk, causing the men to distance themselves from the vehicle by a few paces. The sound was like a metallic bristling — something coarse rearranging itself, testing its boundaries.

"To hell with this," said Pete, scissoring the cigarette from his mouth and flinging it aside as he twisted around, retreating into one of the open garage bays. Dox looked over at the service manager,

Danny. "So you still ain't heard from Chancy?"

Danny shook his head. "We called yesterday when he didn't show — phone just rang all day. Pete wouldn't let up — called him just about every fifteen minutes. Then," he gestured at the 82 Cutlass Supreme, "this was just sitting here this morning, parked crooked, keys inside."

Cautiously, Dox moved nearer to the vehicle, but his body went rigid, fight-primed, as the commotion from the trunk momentarily escalated. The sound, paired with Dox's imagination, brought to mind snake-like contortions — a reptile abrading itself against the interior of its shell, the anticipation of birth.

"You smell that?" said one of the other techs.

Dox was still several feet away from the trunk; but yeah, there was something. An aroma. A warning. A few of the other mechanics exchanged loaded gazes. Dox understood this sort of quiet conference: the eyed silence, the assent. There'd been plenty of times when — nearly two decades before, as a much younger man — he'd traded the same knowing glances when it came to the fate of another soldier; but to vocalize something so certain — to annunciate the truth of a grievous injury, of a failed mission — was to preemptively articulate a young man's doom. Leave that up to the officers, Dox thought then and, in a way, thought now. *They should be the ones responsible for uttering the end.*

Pete returned then, his large frame ambling toward them, grasping a long, leather sheath and withdrawing a stainless steel slim jim from within.

It was an accepted fact that folks in their line of work—as opposed to locksmiths and law enforcement officials—maintained a collection of dodgy lockout tools. Mumbling to himself, Pete inserted the metallic blade, and with a few swivels and tugs, popped open the driver's side door. With a grunt, Pete crouched in and yanked the keys from the ignition.

Without slowing, though the men were now stammering for the shop foreman to take it easy (Dox had not been fully aware of it, but his hand had instinctively moved to the interior of his toolbag, gripping the handle of a straight-pein finishing hammer), Pete rounded the rear of the vehicle, mumbling threats about the possibility of this being an elaborate prank; he jammed the key into the trunk and twisted.

The trunk's lid snapped open with an urgent disgorgement as several shapes surged up and out of the cavity. Dox fell back into a defensive position, his initial assessment being that the dark interior of the trunk was a living organism disemboweling itself with chimera flair. What swiftly spilled out was a wave of jittery, mammalian limbs, eyes and ivory canines. Dox recognized the contours of these shapes as a pair of animals, dogs; but they weren't normal: too long in the torso, their foal-like legs criss crossing each other as they struggled to escape. The essence of their structure was highstrung sinew. Something akin to, but exceeding, distorted ferality. But it was their gore-slicked coats that most appalled Dox. He staggered back just as

249

the lead dog lunged out of the trunk, causing Pete to collapse on his ass in a sprawl.

The dogs were matted with a burgundy mucus, their glistening pelts catching the morning sunlight, some of viscous fluid flicking beads into the air as the dogs landed hard on the ground, the sound of their nails clacking on the asphalt as they scrambled away. Simultaneously — and it only recalled itself in the minutes afterward — three or four blood-covered possum slithered out, dropping to the blacktop with slimy splats before skittering away beneath the rows of cars.

Dox was so preoccupied with the animals that it took him a moment to register the other things were slowly spilling from the trunk: several black, bird-shapes had taken flight, careening out and away. Dox ducked as they swirled, looping and diving, graceful and leathered, before corkscrewing with each other into the sky. Reassessing the car, Dox saw that the rear of the vehicle had become furred with spiders, a fine, frantic insectile mesh.

Pete had gotten to his feet, but was clumsily scrambling into the garage, swatting at the arachnidan shapes covering his forearms and legs.

The men all backed off as though the car were diseased. But Dox, wincing his focus, took a few tentative steps nearer, scowled at the car in a manner akin to confronting a long-dismissed adversary; and similar to sizing up that enemy, Dox, his hand clasping the handle of the straight-pein, crept nearer the now-still cavity of the trunk. *The pit.*

Dox bore no illusion that Chancy Mays, the young mechanic, would be alive, but anticipating the appalling state of his corpse would have required Dox to access some gruesome compartment of his imagination. It would have required him to think like a soldier again.

"Yea, for my sin I had great store of bliss:
Rise up, make answer for me, let thy kiss
    Seal my lips hard from speaking of my sin,
Lest one go mad to hear how sweet it is,"

1970

Dox was enduring his second, and what would prove to be his final, tour.

A little over a year before, he, along with his fellow soldiers, lingered on the margins of Chu Lai, and from there, the throng of their numbers grew methodically scattered across southeast Asia, from divisions winnowed down to battalions, carved out still into consolidated companies and finally manageable platoons.

Most of the platoons were led by sergeants

who continued to adhere to Westmoreland's principal strategy of "search and destroy," and during Dox's first tour, he dexterously participated in racking up NVA and VC body count. Mutually, he'd witnessed his fellow soldiers — though admittedly in fewer numbers — dispatched in ghastly fashion.

Dox and the brethren of his Eleven Bravo fellowship pushed farther east and south, until they settled in locales difficult to decipher on most maps. The tethers of snaking trails buoyed to makeshift bases and the occasional airlifts were the only real things maintaining connection to the larger arteries of the Army.

Immediately following his return from a weeklong stint of R&R, Dox's platoon swiftly setup near a remote LZ, and several days after that, he assisted in the installation of a temporary basecamp roughly two klicks to the east. But in those days before splintering off from his larger infantry, he remained at the central LZ.

Dox had finished helping construct a makeshift bunker (wide, semi-circle, corrugated structure which reminded him of the straw barns in the Illinois countryside). He had about an hour to kill before the next project. He was rounding the corner of one of the ad-hoc barracks when he caught sight of a pair of boots, laced too tight, poking out from between a tall stack of wooden pallets.

Dox approached slowly, but Ryerson, seated on a mound of sandbags, spoke before coming into full view. "Heard you and I were hand-picked for something *real* special," said the younger soldier, sitting in the column of shade.

Dox grunted, lighting a cigarette, dismissing the statement and eyeing the slender book resting on Nathan Ryerson's knee. "What's that?" said Dox, tilting his head to indicate the book. Ryerson closed the cover and rose out of the shadow, resting his forearms on tented kneecaps. The younger soldier smirked. "Conrad. Bit of cliché reading this during, well" — Ryerson gestured around them: the disheveled camp, the looming, humid heaps of jungle beyond — "all this; but it's still important."

Dox scowled. "Let me see." Ryerson angled the cover of *Heart of Darkness* toward Dox, who huffed in apparent disgust. "Man," he said as though deflated at the presentation of some disappointing gift. "Some racist shit right there."

Ryerson smiled, nodded. "Yeah," he said, "I think that's an unavoidable component — the social deformations brought on by that shit. But it's sort of too easy, you know? — too much on the surface. Besides, that's not why I dug the damn thing out." Ryerson reached his hand out, silently requesting a drag from Dox's smoke. Dox narrowed his eyelids with brief annoyance, handing over the cigarette to his friend anyway. Ryerson exhaled smoke, returning the tar-coiled cylinder to Dox. "I'm sort of snagged on a subtext here though, what may very well to be centrally intended commentary."

Dox waited. He looked down at Nathan Ryerson, who was squinting, aiming his attention at the hunched, tree-lined hills; he exhaled though his nose. *Fine.* "Which is what?"

Ryerson was, in Dox's estimation, not reckless but heedless. The young man didn't want to die, that was clear; but he operated with a chilling certainty—no hesitation. He wasn't much respected by some of the other soldiers, but it seemed more philosophical: they didn't like his ass because he was both fearless and thoughtful: they didn't like when he talked, and Ryerson certainly had some shit to say—they only liked when he raced headlong into the jungle, cutting down VC.

"There's this whole thing—there are these moments—when the net Conrad has cast gets tugged down toward, I don't know...something *else.*"

Dox swiveled a panoramic examination of the camp. It was quiet, for now. His gut told him to move along, that his friend was in a contemplative mood and that he, Dox, was about to be loquaciously consumed. But he hung tight. Dox appraised his friend. Something had shifted since their return from their most recent infusion of R&R. An aspective depletion. He wondered, then, if this had to do with something that happened a few weeks before, out on the fringes of Bangkok.

Dox had first encountered Nathan Ryerson upon their arrival at Chu Lai; and though, like the unlikeliness of their companionship, they had somehow, over the course of many months, remained in the same companies and platoons; and so it was even more of an unlikely surprise when their R&R windows aligned at the same.

In Bangkok, for most of the soldiers, R&R really meant I&I; and while Dox and Ryerson were certainly interested in the disciplines of Intoxication and Intercourse, they'd grown accustomed to sidestepping the common throngs of young men gravitating toward the body-bustle of districts like Patpong, Nana Plaza, slipping into the shadows past the night markets and into exterior extremities. Dox and Ryerson were marginal men, whether in the unravelling hell of Vietnam or elsewhere.

Because they were swift studies, they listened and learned; and although it was profoundly risky, they came to understand that true exotic depredation existed on the fringes of these tourist-tainted places. After a day or two, Dox and Ryerson secured leads on warehouses that bore more than your typical prostitution rings. The money was no different, as these lascivious venues existed in seedier segments on the verge of the city. Literally, some of the locations were underground, actual dens beneath the earth; the licentious commonality being that they all bordered on the provincially dangerous.

Dox and Ryerson took their chances. And sure there were risks—more lethal, Vietnamese versions of being "Shanghaied"—but, for Dox Ingram, it was like an existential leaching, an atavistic transfusion of animal impulses, one with lure of excessive, depredations, manifested by the paraphernalia of flesh and want. Though they went their separate ways at the opportune time, Ryerson's thing, if his tales could be believed, seemed to be a primary focus on fellatio. The kinkier, the better. Dox was a little more straightforward. He and Ryerson would agree and on a timeframe and rally point. After that, they were on their own. Both men were able to insert themselves into these clandestine bordellos, willingly knotting themselves into a sinuous pit with these venomous, unsubmissive women, indulge in their unusually aggressive, erotic tastes, and slide out unscathed.

Corporeally, that is. Because for Dox, leaching these heretofore unrealized impulses was a fleeting exercise; as it was simultaneously a study in awakening something darker inside — a shadow casting a shadow.

It was all transactional, but the fringe women extracted something else, something more intimate than seminal seed. With the typical prostitute, the transaction was perfunctory — sure, they devised all sorts of interesting tricks, accessorizing their acts with appalling ingenuity; but it was clear there was no real reward beside wads of Baht. With the fringe women, there was a sense that they extracted something else. They were pleased, satiated in their post-copulatory repose in their secluded dens. The transaction seemed to be more reciprocal than the twenty-two-year-old Dox Ingram was privy to or could articulate.

But something hadn't been quite right with Ryerson on this most recent bout of R&R. He returned more sullen, more reflective than usual. Dox goaded him, teased him about having gotten in over his *head*, but his friend made it clear he didn't want to discuss this particular conquest. Dox was fine with that. There were plenty of things he'd encountered that he wouldn't necessarily share with an acquaintance or, for that matter, even a friend.

Now Ryerson, still seated in the shade, tapped the cover of the book with his knuckle and said, "It's like terrorism against a whole host of masochistic, male-orientated pursuits." Dox rolled his eyes but continued to listen. "There's no denying the essence of Conrad's portrayal of race; but, even further than that, most everyone gets distracted by it."

Dox exhaled smoke, dropped the butt and dug the papered nub into the dirt with his heel; he grunted. "So people get too distracted by race, huh?"

Ryerson glared at him, let it smolder for a moment. "You know that's not what I mean, man."

Dox did, but still enjoyed fucking with his too-sensitive teammate. Ryerson blinked finally, evidently understanding Dox's silence as encouragement to proceed. "What I mean is that there is something more universally insatiate beneath these man-made, reified ideas—it's like they've ignored the underlying issue." Ryerson slid the book between his palms, as though seeking warmth from it. "There is something being contemplated about our own universal, carnal vice and temptations."

Dox frowned. "So you think it's about sex?"

Ryerson laughed. "In a way." He now stood, stretching. "There's this whole business at the end with Marlow confronting Kurtz's 'intended'; but I just can't shake that image of his woman across the river: there's some sort of, I don't know, manipulation or echo of Kurtz's, like, moral flimsiness — the gravity of his depravity."

"*Ooh*," said Dox, grinning at that, not missing an opportunity to break his buddy's balls. "I like *that*" — he snapped his fingers, mockingly intoning a generic blues melody — "*The gravity…of his depravity…the gravity…*"

Ryerson smirked, shook his head. "It's like Kurtz's river woman is some sexual emissary, raising her arms as an invitation back."

They walked for several paces before Dox indulgently said, "Back to what?"

Ryerson's expression was pained for a moment, clearly giving this some consideration. "I don't know, man…some sort of monster." They were closing in on the camp's central bunker. Ryerson said, "A mother monster, maybe."

But Dox ignored Ryerson's continued explanation, and simply mumbled a repeated reprisal of the impromptu blues tune. "*The gravity…of his depravity…*

"Yet I waxed faint with fume of barren bowers,
And murmuring of the heavy-headed hours;
     And let the dove's beak fret and peck within

258

My lips in vain, and Love shed fruitless flowers."

1987

Police officers were now languidly weaving through the repair shop itself, examining papers, filing cabinets, training their flashlights into the rear stalls and work areas.

Dox was astonished at how low-key the officers were about confronting the scene: a young man, his body severed in asymmetrical pieces, the evidence of animals fleeing. The pair of detectives appeared to be less interested in all this, and more interested in Dox.

After a time, a man who seemed to be the lead man on this, who introduced himself as Detective Hood, closed in on Dox, jutted his chin and introducing himself. "Listen, I'm sorry about this, that you had to see that."

The "that" to which Detective Hood was referring was Chancy Mays's nude and dismembered corpse lying in an unceremonious heap in the trunk of his own car. The young man had, quite literally, been evidently torn limb from limb (Dox — in a glimpse, followed by a palm-to-mouth revulsion — had been visually singed by the blasphemous basinet of the trunk: the head that had been raggedly removed from the torso, the limbless carriage, the pale extremities avulsed into smaller pieces. In

259

their compartmentalized panic, the animals, or something else, appeared to have indulged in the remains.)

Dox nodded but did not look directly at the man. "Ain't the worst I've seen."

Hood appraised Dox, nodded softly, the aspect of a man with enough tact to accommodate time for grieving. With good-cop flourish, Detective Hood closed in on Dox, jutted his chin and said, "Was wanting to know if we could talk for a few minutes in private. Of course I want you to know — "

"I know, I know — I know how it works" said Dox, waving off the rehearsed speech. Dox had been questioned by cops before. More often in his younger years before the war, when some small town sheriff would all-too-eagerly give him shit about what he was doing after sundown. "I'll talk to you."

A minute later they were in Pete's office, Dox sitting in the shop foreman's swivel chair which he'd rolled out to the middle of the room; Hood, after sliding aside a black ashtray, rested a haunch on the corner of Pete's desk, notepad and pen at the ready.

Dox didn't wait for some preamble, but rather gave a thoughtful exhale as a dedication and licked his lips as an epigram.

He began: "The last time I saw Chancy was last Friday night; but there wouldn't even have even been a Friday night if we'd not noticed the keychain."

"Keychain," said Hood, not a question, just a monotone echo.

Though paraphrasing, Dox proceeded to explain that, one morning the previous week, a woman had dropped off an 86 Lincoln Town Car, and it wasn't until they rolled the vehicle into the garage that the techs noticed the bullet holes in the hood and the grill.

Hood said, "Bullet holes?"

"Yeah," said Dox. "The mechanics don't ask a lot of questions, you know? Try to be considerate of peoples' property. And Pete said that it was just some body job."

"Peter Croke, correct?" Hood lolled his head to the side, presumably at the big man talking to the other officers in the parking lot. "This shop's foreman?"; he swirled the pencil like a tornado, indicating the facility.

"Yes, sir."

Hood scratched something on his pad; his eyes ticked toward Dox. "Right." Dox gave a concise account about how the woman had been picked up by friends, and that Pete had assigned the body project to Chancy. Around lunch time, the young tech had approached Dox, who was already behind on other jobs around the shop.

Chancy was dangling the keys in front of Dox. "Check it out," Chancy said, sort of giddy. "I knew it, man."

Barely glancing at the kid, Dox said, "Knew what?"

261

Chancy indicated the key chain: on it, a silver, sinuous shape of an *S*, what was uncommonly recognized as the logo for a local exotic show club, The Sphinx. "Told you she was a stripper."

Dox said, "Man, you didn't need to tell *me* that."

Now, Dox—mentally shifting back to the present, sitting here in front of a police officer—had difficulty describing to Detective Hood how the essence of the woman's presence had lingered among the men, particularly Chancy. Dox said, "The boy was just, I don't know, sort of preoccupied. He just seemed"—he stalled, for he was no one to disparage the concept—"susceptible."

Hood said, "Susceptible how?"

"You know. Just." Dox exhaled. "Innocent."

Hood nodded. *Proceed.*

Dox explained that, as the day began to close, the men—as was typical for a Friday—began to disperse, heading their separate ways for the weekend; but Chancy lingered, conversationally tethered to Dox. Chancy had said to Dox, "Pete said that the lady paid for the Lincoln job in cash…said he thinks she's one of the featured acts at The Sphinx."

Located on the dilapidated frays of a metropolitan sprawl, The Sphinx was a particularly notorious show club. The massive, three-story brick building had originally been an opulent residence, home to former tavern owner Emile "Pop" Shapiro, who had, in the early 1920s, converted the first floor into a delicatessen; but during the mid-40s, not long after the War, Pop had been forced to sell not only the deli, but the house itself. After sitting vacant for a number of years, it had been purchased by a monied party who'd transitioned the first floor of former house into cocktail bar called the Turf Club. At some point in the late fifties, the establishment — responding to the community's declining economy, which mirrored a much larger, more macro deterioration — simply acquiesced to the needs of a stagnant void, yielding to the way of all opportunistic enterprises — yielding to (appropriating a cliché for expediency) the way of all flesh. The windows were bricked over, the carport removed, and the old hulk of a house became the gentlemen's club known as The Sphinx.

The neighborhood's proximity to the interstate affected the district's identity, as though the busy thoroughfare were a hearty artery, with much smaller capillaries of poorly paved roads existing in a sort of symbiotic exchange in the name of transit.

The community in which the strip club was situated bore typical, late-70s hallmarks affluent retreat, but also contained those strangely wooded stretches which provided a delicate gray plexus between wide swaths of warehouse districts and industrial parks. The weak trees appeared to have been petrified: a rickety, organic symbol of economic emaciation.

"Oh yeah?" Dox chuckled, more at the kid's eager naivety than at the distractive novelty of what a strip club had to offer. "You don't say."

After a few beats, Chancy said, "We should

go."

Dox hefted his work bag and looked at the young man; he smiled. "Not tonight, man."

"Come on," said Chancy. "Besides, Pete said Friday's are the best at that place."

"Pete said that, huh?" Dox had never witnessed their shop foreman provide any genuine advice. "Well, that place is a pit down on the low end of town, so Pete might just be a connoisseur." Dox hefted his gear, veering around Chancy. "Besides," said Dox, smirking, "smiley whiteboy like you? Man, those girls'd eat you alive."

The young man followed. "Come on, Dox," was Chancy's final whine-tinged entreaty. "Working on that car all week has driven me crazy. I mean, what sort of woman causes a person to put a bunch of bullet holes into her car?"

Dox had slowed, stopped, and sag-spun on Chancy, appraising the boy. There was an innocence there, sure, but it contrasted with something else more foolish—something subtle yet somewhat tangible. Something dangerous, subterranean. Dox had witnessed a spectrum of depravity in his stint in Asia that would make most men lightheaded. Around here, though, it was a mild form of distraction—a paltry rite of passage for a culture consumed with obtaining its identity—a sort of sport which groomed one for further acceptance among their male counterparts.

Dox exhaled, wearily inspecting his watch. "Grab your gear, man," Dox said. "And don't forget your coat."

Dox Ingram proceeded to tell Detective Hood that — after having reached an agreement that Dox would only stay for precisely a single round of drinks — they'd agreed to drive separate cars to The Sphinx. Once carded, covered, and inside, Dox appraised the interior to the accompaniment of some blaring Def Leppard track. It had been perhaps a decade since he'd last stepped foot inside the place, and the years had not treated her well. Much of the luster had been lost and cosmetic updates had been neglected. It appeared that the only thing that had been updated was the music.

What was certainly (at one interval in the home's early days) a living room or parlor, had been essentially gutted and renovated into a mirror-walled showroom, with the typical elevated, catwalk-style stage dominating the central space; a long, oak-topped bar occupied a length of wall in the shadows beyond. They ordered drinks, all the while Chancy clearly engrossed in finding the "bullet-hole" woman.

Despite Dox's insistence that he was only staying for one drink, several hours and drinks passed; and despite what Dox had unfairly assumed about Chancy's bucolic innocence, the young man fared quite well at navigating the night's nuances, receiving attention from several women in the bar.

"It was getting late," Dox was telling Detective Hood, "and I sort of, well, interrupted a conversation he was having with a couple young women."

265

Hood said, "Either one of them the woman you'd mentioned before? This" — he checked his pad" — 'bullet-hole' woman?"

Dox shook his head. "No. I hadn't even seen these women before I saw Chancy talking to them." Hood stared at Dox. *Go on.* "I tried to get him to call it a night, but the kid had found a rhythm, was sort of a natural, in fact — said the girls had 'plans' for him. I thought I knew what that meant, thought they might be, I don't know…"

Hood provided an assist: "Fucking him?"

Dox shrugged, unable to look at the detective any longer. "I tried a few more times, tried to convince him to come with me, but the girls started getting physical, one of them shoved me…I didn't want to cause a scene."

Hood frowned, his pencil slashed notepad's surface. "So that's when you left the establishment?" Dox nodded. "And that's the last time you saw the young man?"

Dox nodded, stifling the morbid urge to gesture toward the parking lot and say, *Well…until this morning.*

Hood opened his mouth to speak but a young, uniformed police officer leaned into the small office, wrapping his knuckles on the paint-flecked jamb. "Excuse me, sir?" he said. Dox glanced at him, and for a fleeting, flickering second mused that the rookie-looking cop could be Chancy's polished twin brother. Hood ticked his chin up and furrowed his brow, clearly an irritated signal for the initiated to speak freely. The young, interrupting officer hesitated then cleared his throat. "We just received a run on a home-invasion and homicide — they're radioing units from — "

Reinforcing the officer's announcement, another uniformed officer passed the door, speaking into a walkie, which reciprocated with the laconic, static-lashed communique from the disembodied female dispatcher. "*Back-up respond to 4700 block of Tuxedo Avenue...*"

Hood scowled, as though trying to better overhear details from the handheld in the hallway. The detective nodded and tipped his head, releasing the young officer, who then simply said, "Yes, sir," before hustling out of sight.

Hood shook his head. "It's been getting worse lately." With his face still honed on the now empty hallway. "Last month, got a call in the middle of the night, you probably saw it on the news...found that dad in his car up on the northside...toddler still strapped in her carseat...father had" — Hood was still staring through the doorway; as words failed him, he brought his fingers, evidently unconsciously, up to his eyes, as if lazily removing gauze; but then, as though stung by a flimsy current, he blinked and looked over at Dox. "Sorry," said Hood, his smile earnest and unapologetic. "Sometimes I feel like the world lost its goddamn mind a long time ago, and we're just hustling to catch up." He looked down at his notebook, clearly trying to find his place.

Hood asked several other questions to which Dox responded with laconic guilt. But then

Hood circled back around. "Can you tell me any-thing else about this woman with the shot-up car?" he said. "The lady that Chancy was so...let's say...enamored with?"

Dox then looked directly at the detective, pausing. He had to make a decision.

The first thing he could supply is a name: Isobel — *She calls herself Isobel.*

But the truth — the entire truth of what hap-pened the previous Friday night...the part which he was contemplating omitting — stung him with menacing immediacy: *The scene is illuminated in a lightning-strike distinction, but simultaneously recalled with reluctant torpidity: Dox tries, one last time, to pull Chancy away from the cluster of women, but one shoves at Dox, snarling at him to get lost. Chancy — clearly in-toxicated more now by the promiscuous prospects of these women — chuckles, says he can take care of him-self. The girls are becoming more aggressive, more phys-ical, shouting that he, Dox, doesn't belong here. Dox can interpret that several ways but chooses to let it go. And then Chancy is being happily hauled away, pulled into the curtain-shadowed rear of the showroom.*

Dox murmurs a curse, turns, and softly collides with the Her. Dox begins to apologize but then stops short when recognition seizes him. Nearly nose to nose, she is as tall as Dox, and between the hanging panels of her dark hair, her expression is completely composed. Silken expectation. She is dressed nearly identical as she had been the morning Dox saw her in the parking lot earlier in the week: cropped, fur-collared leather coat, the fishnets, the knee-high boots with the heels. Her eye makeup is different, though her sockets are still ringed black smudges — a Goth-generous application in the vein of Nina Hagen, Dox thinks — to accentuate her eyes, the irises of which, Dox realizes, are so black that instead of possessing the trick of absorption they exist to penetrate. Without evident reservation, she swiftly leans in on Dox, her lips working near his ear as she raises her voice above the music. "Your buddy," she says, her voice husky, "seems to be enjoying himself."

Dox blinks, pulls away slightly, she does the same, her features taunting Dox to mimic the move of leaning in, cheek-to-cheek in order to speak; he hesitates, finally arcing his upper body nearer to her. "He's a big boy...I'll keep an eye on him."

Still smirking, she appears to consider this before, with no visible inhibition, pulling Dox closer to her. "Do you want some company while you wait?"

Her name is Isobel.

There is a booth-lined lounge in a secluded side-wing of the club (Isobel smoothly strides between a heavy curtain and past a bouncer without comment, Dox follows, apparently vouchsafed in her presence), and though the walls still rattle with the thump of music, the relative calm here is insulated by irregular shadows on the fringed halos of neon.

The two of them are beyond casual conversation, and the spartan simplicity of animal honesty sobers Dox a bit. She says, "People have a charge to them," the booth's cushion beneath them squelches as she slides closer to Dox. "I could tell that morning, even from across the parking lot...you have a kindred radiation."

Dox has been told a lot of things by prostitutes, but he senses this to be more than a seductive preamble;

he listens cogently, as if being provided the parameters of a lethal mission. Though he gives no indication, he understands precisely what she is describing, for Isobel herself is veritably vibrating a violet-tinged penumbra of blackness. Dox says, "You don't know a single thing about me."

"You've seen things," she says quickly, "that's unmistakable. You've been scorched by...something," she says. "I cannot say precisely what you've seen, Dox. Only that you've encountered something." A stretch of music-sutured silence between them. Then: "But I can show you things too, Dox...I can help you the rest of the way through."

Dox hasn't fallen for one of these tricks in many years, and now has a strange, submissive quiver to do so — to give in. Gently, literally by the hand, Isobel coaxes Dox from the booth and guides him deeper into the interior of the former house. Wordlessly, Isobel leads him down a darkened corridor, to a paint-flecked door. Open now, the passage reveals a stairwell leading up to the second floor. Tethered to an invisible leash, Dox follows the belly-dancer sway of Isobel's gait as she pulls him to the landing, draws him to the end of the hallway, and steers him into a small, candle-lit room.

Stuttering shadows leap and heave, altering the light against the walls from sepia, to umber, to pitch.

While Dox, despite turning his back on what his parents had intended for him, he has always adhered to some form of art, of intrinsic elevation. And though perhaps too pompous a description in the bays of an auto repair shop, the sex — though not necessarily reciprocal — is viciously transcendent and superior to any encounter in his forty years of existence.

To answer the police officer's question: yes: Dox can tell Detective Hood anything he wants to know about this woman — about the how the shadows play on her pale skin with living, tribal stripes, about how the central, indentation of her spine flexes and snakes as she instructs him to enter her, about how — though lying supine — he embraces the sensation of being blindly dragged headlong through riptides of primordial respiration, about how she allocates her torso as a vase for depravity, about how Isobel seldom grants windows for that warm, amniotic repose before summoning his arousal again and again and again...and about how the penetration is multiform, particularly in the aspect of Dox Ingram's copular capitulation.

At some point before dawn, Dox finds himself clothed again, back in the corridor again, watching the door to Isobel's room not unkindly close on his face; he's teetering down the stairwell. The music in the club has been extinguished, but the house maintains the static of unseen energy. Through a nondescript sidedoor, Dox slips out into the cold, waning-night, expelling a spill of visible breath. He'd parked on the street, and clumsily makes his way to his vehicle. He has the presence of mind to appraise the location of Chancy's car, which, now, is gone.

Dox had recalled all this in several seconds-worth of eye-contact avoidance. In stalling, he found he preferred looking not at the detective, but rather the darkened garage where he and Chancy Mays had worked as comrades and craftsmen.

Dox can tell Detective Hood anything he wants to know, but — in a shift meant to salvage his

271

own culpability — said, "No. She never showed up that night."

"Ah, with blind lips I felt for you, and found
About my neck your hands and hair enwound,
    The hands that stifle and the hair that stings,
I felt them fasten sharply without sound."

1970

Dox, Ryerson, and several other soldiers from the platoon were called into the central bunker. A meeting, was the chatter, delineating the shrewd parameters of a hush-hush mission.

Indeed, a short time later Dox and Ryerson were seated in a stifling briefing room, the darkened space infused with cigarette smoke and astringent light from a projector. A number of ranking officers — their lieutenant, an E7 he didn't recognize — remained sentinel and silent in the periphery.

The slides and presentation detailed aerial photos and maps of the outer edge of a dense, river-fringed region roughly six-and-a-half klicks west. There'd been erratic and unexpected activity in the area which had the viability of eliciting high-value intelligence.

This night mission—observation and recon only—would be brief but, like all their activities here in country, potentially lethal. A team of seven would be escorted into the region, before individually dispersing and obtaining a single vantage point.

The coordinators would provide the mission-men additional ammunition for both their sidearm and M16, and with the only specialized piece of equipment being utilized were starlight scopes.

Those planning this night mission made great efforts to form a distraction of sorts in the north, essentially freeing up the small band of soldiers, Dox and Ryerson among them, to set out to the west.

It started off as seven men, and as they traveled farther into the jungle, one or two would be peeled off by the ranking officers and guide them to their set up. Dox and Ryerson were the last, presumably the ones traveling to the most remote location. And so, quite literally at a fork in an overgrown path, the men paused, assessing their surroundings, listening to the directions of their sergeant. Before splitting up on their overnight assignment, Ryerson murmured to Dox, "Want to meet me for breakfast in the morning."

Dox, not smiling, gave his friend a narrow look and hefted his backpack.

The coordinating unit finished setting up Dox's "blind" shortly before dusk, but sky light was quickly extinguished. They'd positioned Dox about midway up a ropy, tight-trunked hill, offering a vantage point to a curving yet overgrown path near a spacious, sinkhole ravine which stretched across about fifty yards.

Dox gave affirmative responses to his understanding of the repeated guidelines: *strictly a reconnaissance mission…no engagement unless forced…active VC artery…utilization of starlight scopes to collect intel on times, activity…retrieval unit dispatched at six-hundred hours tomorrow…*

There was a peaceful period at twilight where the clinging colors of the darkening sky's magenta was set in contrast with the green fecundity of the jungle — the overhead netting of verdant lushness set against a panoramic lavender dome.

When it swept up, the dark itself — merely an insulation of pitch between the darker shapes of wide leaves and overarching, creeper-corded limbs — had the effect of suppressing sound. Regular jungle noises inevitably emerged and but continually receded.

Hours passed. Dox, several times over the small-hour span, caught himself dozing off. He chomped on a tumble of caffeine pills.

Snapping. Shuffling. Distant. Dox bristled. It

had been so quiet, so still, that (despite the stimulants) he must have nodded off. He remained seated, hunched forward, his .45 and machine gun at his boots. He first scanned, naked-eyed, along the rim of the ravine; then he brought up the starlight scope.

The landscape within the scope was identical to the dark one of his natural vision, but with the greenish, phosphorescence touching the contours of the jungle. Overnight light was meager anyway, but there was a brilliant moon in the cloudless sky, which clearly coincided with the night scopes and the timely intentions of those who'd coordinated the deadhour mission.

And then, a wavering figure emerged along the narrow, overgrown path. Dox momentarily bristled before ceasing to budge—a frigid fear seized him: not at the mere emergence of this figure, and certainly not at the possibility of violence; but rather the identifiable gait of the silhouette. The shape staggered, wavered as though unconcerned with its clumsy approach. Dox had in mind the intoxicated sway of his friends back in the small town where he grew up, shuffling, drunk, hobbling home across the darkened countryside as they reluctantly retreated for the night from a summer bonfire.

Dox slid his hand over the handgun's grip, pulled it up to his lap. Through the starlight scope: tinges of moonglow accentuated the figure's lineaments, powdering him just enough to provide a delicate green frosting along the vegetations' fleshy

275

exterior.

Dox's hand was shaking a bit, rattling the cylinder of magnification; he steadied it, clenching his teeth, breathing steadily through his nose, he squinted, and with corkscrew scrutiny strained his ocular focus.

Ryerson was moving gracelessly — a disturbing cadence that, while almost brusque, created little noise; he toted the machine gun at waist level.

Dox's first impulse was to call out, to somehow stop his friend, but the scene and its implicating narrative was so alarming that he was petrified. Dox watched Ryerson stride along the trail and disappear through the unruly verdure curtain.

Dox sat still, his eyes darting, mentally figuring the court-martial calculus for an unforeseen scenario. The mission directors had briefed all participants in the placement of motion detectors at intermittent locations, increasing the likelihood that they'd be aware of Ryerson's abdication.

It took Dox a few minutes to quietly disconnect himself from the blind and steadily stalk down to the trail.

After several minutes at a stalking pace, Dox arrived at what felt like a frond-walled cul-de-sac. Even with no starlight scope, generous moonlight slanted through the jungle's canopy at haphazard angles — like reckless light glowing between overhead train trestles: enough illumination for Dox to detect the pale shapes on the far side of a diminutive clearing. Sound, too, was discernible. The notion that Ryerson was being used as bait was a possibility that, for Dox, came regrettably late. Bracing himself, Dox lifted both his handgun and his anglehead flashlight; he steadied himself and thumbed on the beam.

Roughly fifteen yards away was a pulsing mass of skin and limbs — a miniature orgy of sinuous, rhythmic thrusts and gentle heaving. What Dox at first took as his friend being slowly enveloped by albino constrictors slowly gained identifiable dimension.

Ryerson was in the middle of a three- to four-woman tangle, on his knees, his fatigues dropped around his ankles, the nude women slowly sliding all over Ryerson, their flesh pale milky in the harsh light of the anglehead — all that skin set in contrast with the pitch of the jungle. They ran their fingers through his hair, stroked his face, fanned their splayed hand over his body, massaged each other's bodies. With the contours of their breasts and hips, they could have been any one of a thousand girls in Bangkok or any of the forgettable villages in which they encountered. They could have been replications of the *same* girl.

But there was one woman directly in front of Ryerson — in a casual, push-up position — her lower body obscured in a low divot in the ground. Indeed it did appear as though she had simply slithered up from a pit. She had Ryerson in her mouth, and while she supported herself on slender, extended arms, she was tugging at his shaft with a ragged, siphon-like exertion; her breasts dangle-swayed

277

with a pendulous pulse as she pulled at Ryerson, whose hips passively responded with each suction-tug of his rigid member. As improbable as the tableau was before him, there was something equally unnatural about the quality of her mouth, how it affixed itself to Ryerson's penis with a fleshy, funnel-like flexibility, as though she had merged the skin of her lips with the skin of his sex.

Not a single member of this copular endeavor glanced in Dox's direction, but rather continued their act with a sort discretionary compact: quiet sighs, murmur-moans. Despite himself, Dox felt himself beginning to grow stimulated merely by the sibilant sound of erogenous undulation.

Only once did the woman (the one leaning out of the pit, who Dox would have sensed as, owing nothing more than her aggressive movements, as "the star" or central emissary) lewdly flick her eyes in Dox's direction: nocturnal-animal pricks of mercury in the beam of the flashlight.

Uncountable options and consequences presented themselves to Dox—not the least of which being that the mission coordinators would certainly discover that Ryerson had abandoned his post; but one of the overwhelming realizations was that he was not where he belonged—that he had blundered into a margin for which he was conceptually unprepared. He had the sense that, even stepping another foot toward the scene to retrieve his friend would result in the inability to retrieve *himself* from—from what? He was still uncertain of what he was seeing. Where these girls from a nearby village? What would happen if they were *all* found here? His thoughts rapidly untangled into the insane possibility that they were all somehow the *same* woman — that the woman from the pit was just different reflections unclothing Ryerson with her supple echoes of flesh.

His hand rattling, Dox lowered the handgun and, biting his lip, thumbed-off the anglehead. He pulled away, retracing his steps back to his assigned blind; his vision was cast back into the dark of the jungle, and though the shapes of pale skin were evident in the distance, the majority of the world was dark, and all that remained were the noisy respirations of arousal, and the wet sound of seething, overlapping kisses.

Dox did sleep, but rather remained rigidly sentinel in his blind during the slim sequence of night. As a morning blush suffused the sky, Dox — quaking slightly at the nadir chill of the passing night — remained fixated on the path from which, he hoped, Ryerson would emerge. For the hours until the extraction team was scheduled to arrive and retrieve him, Dox occupied his mind less with the narrative of how Ryerson had come to that rendezvous, and what would happen in the wake of his discovery. Since Ryerson had not returned along the observation path, he assumed he'd found an alternate route; but the real possibility of other consequences loomed.

It was nearly noon when Dox heard and then saw the slow approach of the extraction team moving in from the north; but they operated in a less covert manner from the previous day — brusque, less cautious. A portion of them moved in on Dox, while the remainder pushed ahead, off in the direction the trail took to the south. Dox slowly, stiffly, removed himself from the blind, casting *I'm-fine* nods at his fellow soldiers. His sergeant immediately began questioning Dox, appraising him with heated intent.

After a minute or so, the sergeant closed in on Dox at a nearly nose-to-nose distance; he lowered his voice: "Are you aware of the current location of Nathan Ryerson?" Dox unintentionally hesitated, pinching a slight frown as he opened his mouth, which produced no sound. He started again to speak, almost gesturing toward the trail, when a radio, cradled by a nearby soldier, squelched a message, which hissed in tandem with several others in the distance. One solder down by the path waved, summoning the extraction team to proceed south. The sergeant again appraised Dox with a silent, sour assessment, which Dox absorbed with neither pride or defiance. The sergeant said nothing as the team, Dox included, threaded their way, business-like and gun-ready, to the south.

Dox's pulse quickened as they closed in on the cul-de-sac. A small team of soldiers was already stationed in a loose ring, M16s raised as they studied the jungle. The soldiers stepped aside as the sergeant moved in. Dox did not follow too closely. But near enough.

Near enough to see the ragged lip of the pit. Near enough to see Ryerson's corpse impaled on the punji sticks — his shredded fatigues clung to his crooked body, supported on the sharpened stakes, the position of his body something ridiculous: his zigzag limbs hanging at unnaturally contorted angles in a sort of harlequin tranquility.

He heard the buzz of insects, saw the murky curtain of black flies hovering over the hole. The birds had been at work on his sockets and the softer parts of his face, though a single, intact eye remained in its ocular cradle. The state of his friend's mouth was a deformed, imbecilic rictus.

His eyes were open. One of the slender stakes had penetrated Ryerson's throat, just above his clavicle, just below the Adam's apple. Blood had saturated and dried into his fatigues, lending his clothing a purplish aspect. One of the soldiers swiveled at the hips and discreetly vomited.

Dox shivered and toggled his attention to the sergeant, who stared directly at Dox. Dox had fucked up, but not as badly, he thought, as the mission's coordinators. *Had they misjudged the mission's vague anatomy? Or had they simply misjudged Ryerson's constitution — his mental condition?*

"Did you observe Ryerson at any time last night?" said the sergeant.

Dox swallowed hard, surprising himself at

281

how fast he lied by shaking his head. "No, sir."

The sergeant's gaze held for a moment before he exhaled a series of expletives.

Dox would later discover that the overall mission was a success, whatever that meant — likely a piece of intelligence was collected which had resulted in a minor victory. Ryerson was a hapless casualty. But for now Dox, with the back of his hand against his mouth, mentally digested the scene before him, absorbing the terrible tableau with a gravity of guilt — ingurgitating the images with a similarity to how, surely, his friend's blood had been absorbed by the thirsty earth.

"I see the marvellous mouth whereby there fell
Cities and people whom the gods loved well,
    Yet for her sake on them the fire gat hold,
And for their sakes on her the fire of hell."

1987

The Sphinx Club was one of those structures with a few elements to bear in mind: it was not far from the interstate, which acted as a lure to an all-purpose variety of transience; it skirted the city, which lent it an urban feel; but it was also a former residence on the residential fray of the city.

Up ahead, Dox saw dark shapes sprinting across the street, scrambling down the sidewalk and disappearing into the night. It called to mind packed parties in his younger days when people fled with the approach of the police. It had all the hallmarks of a raid. He gave the chaos a wide berth, drove a half circle and parked along a sidewalk about a block from the Sphinx.

It had been a week since both Chancy's body had been dumped at the shop and Dox's subsequent interview with Detective Hood. But only hours earlier, Dox had received a grainy message on his answering machine: for the better part of a minute, it was simply static—the raspy air seeking purchase on a sneaky frequency; and then her voice dovetailed in: *We know your men are coming, Dox, as they always do.* Isobel says something unintelligible before her final line: *Time to run, my love.*

He'd stood there in the dimness of his kitchen, contemplating the ownership of his "men," and contemplating who was going to do the running. Eventually, he was moving—he retrieved a few items from the bedroom—sliding his keys into his pocket, tucking a heavier item into his waistband—before exiting the house and firing up the engine of his car, a crowbar resting on the passenger seat.

If he'd pegged Hood correctly, the detective—having followed-up Dox's uneasy interrogation—would have already visited the Sphinx and questioned (or had attempted to question) any of the women working the night of Chancy Mays's disappearance; and if Dox used the more dependable part of his imagination, Hood and his law enforcement associates would have continued to thoroughly pursue answers.

Dox, of course, was too late.

Within minutes of parking his car at a safe distance, Dox was approaching the building. He darted out of the way as a vehicle, its lights off, tore out of the Sphinx's parking lot and raced down the street.

Whatever had happened, had happened recently — within minutes. The entire scene was raw.

Here in lot, two black-and-white police cruisers were present; one of them, a Caprice with its engine idling, bore a K9 emblem on the back quarter panel. As confirmation, as he cautiously approached Dox noted the metal grate separating the front portion from rear where the animals were secured during transportation. The back door hung open, and in the frigid December air, steam rolled out, visible beneath the lamplight above. Though he stayed clear, Dox then noticed a heaped shape in the back seat — a mound which glistened slightly in the scant light.

With disciplined swiftness, he moved along, nearer to the front door, hustle-hunching his way inside.

No bouncer. Hard rock chugged along, with Dox's pace in sync with the lippy melody of "My Michelle" as he swept into the central lounge.

Empty — the stage, the tables, the booths.

The mirrored walls reflected swirling, lunatic light. Here and there, in irregular segments slicking the gray-tile floor, were designless mop-smears of glistening crimson. Dox ignored this, weaving across the space quickly, leaping on stage and pushing through the curtain. Backstage was next. Almost empty, though there were signs of chaos: overturned chairs, debris on the floor, as though its inhabitants had suddenly fled.

Dox recalled the winding layout: the hand-clasped course he'd taken with Isobel little less than a week before — presently finding himself in the narrow hallway which led back to the private quarters.

Back here, Dox reminded himself that a successful immigrant family had once lived here, and this area served as a confluence for all manner of mundane, domestic commerce. *How many times had a mother toted laundry across the floors of this passage? How many times had a father carried a sleeping child up to bed?* Now Dox crossed the dim arteries of thresholds and conduits, jamming the tapered end of the crowbar into the jamb near the handle. With a few competent jerks, wood splintered, then the lock and its apparatus tore free of the housing, clattering to the floor.

Flinging the door open, he mounted the unlit ascendance of the stairwell, crowbar crossed in front of his chest as he swept onto the second floor. Down below and behind him, Dox heard disparate shouting — indecipherable orders.

As before, all the doors were closed on either

side along the corridor. But tonight, toward the end of the hall, the door to Isobel's room was open, throwing a casket of lambent light on the hard-wood floor.

Dox's footfalls were paired with creaks as he crossed closer. Doesn't matter, he thought. *She knew I was coming.*

Dox stepped into the light, aligning himself with the threshold.

She stood with her back to him, covered in some sort of dark robe. As before, candles lined the walls, tinting the space with a drowsy glow. With no indication of being startled, she turned around; and with no flourish but still possessing some air of regality, she simply raised her blood-smeared fore-arms, and her entire aspect was transformed into the vaulted arches of an apse: a blood-daubed dio-rama.

What Dox had mistook as a robe, he now recognized was a mass of fur, a collection of hides. The police cruiser, the K9 unit, he calculated. *The glistening shapes in the rear.*

"What took you so long?" she said, her voice husky, serene.

Nude beneath the torn and gore-spattered pelts (some of the blood had brush-stroked her torso), she stared at Dox with those familiar, black-iris eyes; but — in an optical trick at Dox's dis-tance — her sclera had shifted, gone brilliant orange like owl's eyes — an abhorrent tint of tangerine. The color itself seemed to hum in the space between them.

"I *knew*," she said, "the instant I saw you — before our encounter...before you and I, well, *tasted* each other — that you had witnessed my sisters...that you'd been a spectator of our nadir."

He didn't have to ask some insipid questions like, *Why Chancy?*, or, *Why'd you'd have to do that to the kid?*, but Dox's expression of grief and anger was suited to do just that.

She said with no discernable pleasure, "Your friend was not special, Dox. Quite ordinary, actually."

The sound of approaching sirens compelled Dox to speak. "That kid didn't shouldn't have been one of your *men*."

She laughed then and sighed with sympathy. "All men, particularly the takers, are *our* men." She paused as though imparting a heart-breaking sentiment. "The man you daily deem your foreman — Pete, is it? This Peter Croke person? — he is the most susceptible of all of you." As the narrative threads intertwined, Dox inadvertently began lowering the crowbar. "Pete has visited this house on many occasions, and we have adopted that pathetic man as — oh, I don't know: a particularly pliable drone of sorts." Dox clamped his molars, crowbar hanging at his side. "Progression requires elaboration — ornamentation, ostentation."

Now it was Dox's turn to laugh. "So you fucking tear a kid to pieces for what? *A lesson*? Progress?" She tilted her head then, her chin lifted as if hearing a hymn of exultation. Dox heard the sirens, the shouts, the throb of rock music. "Is this the kind

287

of progress you're talking about?"

She said, "It is the *only* form of progress."

Dox began backing away, ready to retreat. "Wait," she said, the first flash of — *What?* — desperation in her voice. "Stay with me."

Dox hesitated, curling his upper lip. When his voice failed, he simply shook his head.

"I can protect you — I can show you what's next: I can peel back the skin of this century's season and show you what's next...the *fin de siècle* that ends all. Your brothers will continue their wars, their mitotic masochism...they will continue to lawlessly penetrate parts of this world where they are not wanted...you will see them drag people into the streets...in time, your brothers' violence will be broadcast as voyeuristic beatings and casual homicides...the men — the law and the outlaws — in their panic, will eventually turn on one another..."

As the scroll of her tongue unrolled a narrative, causing Dox to look through her now as he was inadvertently paralyzed by the images of riots...fires foresting urban stretches of major cities...each ornate window of a luxury hotel hemorrhaging brilliant, billowing flames...a limp, bullet-torn child. He thought about Chancy. He thought about Detective Hood and his detectives — *It's been getting worse lately...the world lost its goddamn mind a long time ago*; he thought this house itself: that it had once been built by an immigrant family, had thrived in its nuclear wholesomeness before becoming a casualty of a deteriorating economy...the once dignified, family-owned enterprise giving way to abandonment...entrepreneurs insinuating themselves...the business-venture failures in between...and this, a hive of deprivation...

"You can be my *consort*," she said, again raising her arms—her furs—with priestess regality. "You can be my *slav*—"

Dox swept his arm behind him, to his lower back, his free hand clutching the grip of the .45 he'd retrieved from his nightstand and, with ingrained ease, nimbly brought the weapon level with the woman's face.

He'd been so preoccupied by the mesmeric images that he'd not noticed the women who'd crept up behind him. They fell on Dox, pulling at his waist and upper arms, dozens of fingernails scratching him, scrabbling for the gun. He heaved and shrugged but lost his balance, falling back into the hallway. The women—Dox caught a wincing glimpse of hanging hair, feral eyes—slid over him expertly, tearing the gun away. Dox howled as one of them bit his forearm.

A shout tore down the corridor. "*Drop the weapon!*" Though still struggling, Dox could feel a slight alleviation as a few of his assailants pivoted, training their attention on the voice's owner.

"*I said drop the goddamn weapon!*" In the open spaces between the jumble of limbs, Dox saw the uniformed police officer, his flashlight and handgun aimed at the pile.

Collectively, the women, saying nothing, appeared to catch their breath before the slow swell of their growls filled the narrow passage. In snarling unison, they sprang away from Dox and scrambled down the hallway. Dox saw the police officer take one shot before the doors on both sides of the corridor swung open in unison as more women spilled, overtaking the man. His screams lasted merely moments before devolving into something mangled, pulpy, and then the screams ceased, replaced by sounds of rending fabric and flesh.

Dox, grimacing, lurched up, first sweeping up the .45, taking inventory, and sliding into Isobel's room and locking the door behind him.

She was gone, of course, the window which gave onto the unusual stair step of roofing. She had slid out of her furs, the canine hides crumpled in a gory heap in the center of the candle-lit room.

In achy strides, Dox progressed to the shattered window. Sirens and shouts dopplered the neighborhood; he slid through the mouth of shards and steadied himself on the roof, skidding down the way he imagined Isobel had done moments before, onto the low rise which hung over a small backyard awning, dropping to the ground in an ungainly spill.

Dox kept moving though, seeing the erratic flashlight beams drawing up on either side of the house. Limping, he accelerated to the anemic labyrinth of trees which acted as pathetic, insulative fencing to the adjacent properties; and he kept moving despite the shouts and overture of gunshots from within the Sphinx.

He kept his head down and, as he'd been groomed to do decades before, he kept his legs moving. Yet this time there was no chopper wait-ing, no brothers to watch his back. He fumbled for his keys. He'd have to drive himself to safety.

Dox once again considered the grotesque concept of sanctuary.

Monday morning, Dox was unusually late for work. Also unusual was Dox's appearance when he'd arrived at the shop: absent were his customary coveralls, instead he wore a fade flannel and jeans. He ignored the perfunctory greetings of his co-workers, gliding purposefully past them and be-tween bays; one of the mechanics said, "Hey, Dox — where's your uniform, man?"

Conversely predictable this morning: the requisite reverberation of the radio filling the cold shop. Something new by Whitesnake. Dox fucking hated Whitesnake.

But least out of the ordinary this morning: Dox, toting the sidekick of his worn, fabric tool bag.

The shop foreman's office was in the rear, at the end of the hallway.

Sitting at his desk, Pete's meaty, cigarette-fisted hand hovered over an ashtray. Without glancing up from the splayed pages of a *High Soci-ety*, he said, "Shit, Doxy…was wondering when you were going to show — "

As he crossed the threshold, Dox slid his

hand into his toolbag and, in one skilled sequence, withdrew the straight-pein hammer and, in an unfaltering gavel-swing, came down squarely on Pete's hand. The ashtray shattered and the cigarette exploded, momentarily creating a blown-dandelion flurry of ember filaments.

Pete's peal was agonized as he rocked away from his desk, spilling out of his swivel-chair and roll-collapsing to the filthy floor.

Dox already had the hammer raised for secondary blow when Pete raised his functioning hand. His jowls quaked. *"Wait!"* he gasped, his breathing phlegmy. The two men stared at each other for a stretch; and as Pete evidently put the pieces together, his face went hard, his expression defiant. "You weren't even supposed to be there," Pete tried to unsuccessfully catch his breath. "When I saw...the news—the cops and their fucking botched shakedown—I knew you'd said *something* to that fucking detective." Dox didn't budge, his features deadened. Pete said, "I didn't have a choice, you son of a bitch." The foreman licked his lips. "She said they'd spill all sorts of shit to my wife, find my fucking kids—I didn't know they were going to *kill* Chancy."

Dox—sensing the other men standing in the hallway behind him—slowly lowered the hammer; after a time, he dropped it back into the toolbag. On the way out, he shoved past a cluster of shocked mechanics. Goddamned Whitesnake was still droning in the shop.

It was the middle of the night, a few days from the first of January. Dox lay on his bed; and though a wide rhomboid of warm, orange street-lamp light swathed the ceiling, the house was frigid. Dox figured he was being deprived of an appreciable amount of sleep with each day that passed without confrontational consequence. They'd find him, he figured, once he poked his head out of his domicile foxhole.

Either the police were having trouble finding Dox, or Pete was too much of a coward to notify them about being assaulted. It had been over two weeks. If they were going to come — whoever *they* were — they would have been here by now.

There was another possibility: the police had their hands full.

Lately, he'd been hearing more sirens at night. Longer successions of gunshots. More prolonged echoes of agonized screams.

Even now, with the outer layer of Midwest winter growing dull and inhospitable, indistinct winged things had become unusually active, coursing past his second-story window, the leathery spasms of their shadows appeared in streaking snatches. This anomaly would compel Dox from the bed to the window during the hush of deadhours; he would shuffle to the pane and appraise the city street below; and if he waited long enough, was vigilant enough, the peculiar snippets would increase, grow more aberrant.

In addition to the muscular bats — and they were some sort of bat, Dox was certain — he'd seen the black, crawling particles of movement in the dark bumpers of gutters, uneasy shifting along the dendrite contours of starved trees. He'd grown wide-eyed, his breath foggy the glass, as a team of three massive bucks galloped, in single file, down the center of the pothole-pocked street, the forks of their glistening antlers catching the orange lamplight. A few nights later, he'd caught sight of a cluster of seven or eight possum emerge from a ripped-open wedge of chain-link fence in an adjacent property. The tightly-grouped gang of possum dropped off the sidewalk and skulked into the street, their thick, rat-like tails snake-trailing behind them. Then, near a sewer grate near the curb, they slowed and paused; at the grate, their movement implied some sort of mutual, clumsy feeding. Dox took a moment to pass a palm over his face, and when returned his attention to the possum, their bodies had coalesced into a disjointed shape. The shape — arms and legs, draped now in loose-fitting tatters — twitched, uncoordinatedly struggled to its feet. Though it existed in featureless silhouette, Dox noted a beard, a bottle dangling from a long arm; and then the shuffling figure weaved back the way it'd came, crouching down to crawl through the uneven aperture of the damaged, chain-link fence.

Tonight, though, had been merciful. Tonight, lying on his bed, unsuccessfully seeking some form of peace, had been quiet.

And then, Dox ticked his eyes from the ceiling to the black wedge if shadow on the other side of the room. She was there. Here. Dox lifted his head off the pillow, to better fix his sightline on her.

Dox, not having realized he'd been holding his breath, exhaled; and at that precise moment — as though the sudden expelling of air had actually breathed life into her taxidermy-like form — she demonstrated mobility by walking soundlessly toward the foot of the bed, into the orange phosphorescence cast from the window. The ragged, sooty residue ringing her eyes gave them a disembodied aspect — lidless, glistening eyes levitating in ash-smeared sockets. She was smiling.

Her nude torso was a strip of pale flesh flanked by the bulky, black fur coat — not the shredded hides of dogs that she'd adorned weeks before, but an enormous and elegant fur coat, which shone silky in the scant light. He had a flashing image from childhood: the cover of some old magazine — *Puck*, he thought, of a woman looming just above the shoulder of an open-mouthed bear.

She carried with her the gossamer aroma of rot.

Dox came up on his elbows and attempted to slide off the bed, but she pressed him back; Dox eased onto his elbows. Slowly, she allowed the fur coat to slide off her milky shoulders and fall to the floor.

Dox slid off the bed, rose slowly, and took several tentative paces to align himself with her.

And though he felt his legs — muscle, groaning connective tissue, bone — weaken, he did not lower himself to his knees. He would not appease her, in that way, tonight.

She did something with her chin as she flowed toward him, rolling the boa-constrictor curvature of her haunches. Dox, despite his thrumming pulse, felt himself growing stiff.

"*Say...my...name...*"

His lips wrapped around the sinuous syllables — *Is* — his jaw yawned to enunciate — *o* — and his tongue uncleaved from his palate in the consummating cadence — *el* —

They slid into each other in a union both corporeal and ineffable, as Dox was willingly consumed by the mother monster that incorporates us all.

Dox breathed a comply, wanting to say the name "Isobel," but his lips wrapped around something else, his tongue contorting to slip over another moniker; and with its articulation came a spatial shift, and the undulations of purring arousal blossomed into the moan of a behemoth. It was never her true name, but the only moniker which held the strained, membranous integrity that now served as Dox Ingram's faculty.

Dox would not die tonight, nor scores of winters hereafter. Perhaps, if he could incrementally appease her — perhaps some variety of prevarication might interrupt the inevitable and quell her ovulation of violence. He understood that this ceaseless negotiation didn't require his life — or even his blood, for that matter — simply the static, reciprocal transaction of eviscerating submission.

Made in the
USA
Middletown, DE